]

AUTH

★★★★★ "...heart-pounding excitement."

★★★★★ "Suspenseful from beginning to end."

★★★★★ "...twists leading to a bittersweet climax."

★★★★★ "I was hooked from page one."

★★★★★ "Right up there with Baldacci and Thor."

★★★★★ "Another great Blake Jordan adventure."

★★★★★ "A totally unexpected ending!"

★★★★★ "The ending was great."

★★★★★ "...the action is nonstop."

★★★★★ "An excellent addition to the series."

—Amazon reviews

WANT THE NEXT BLAKE JORDAN STORY FOR $1 ON RELEASE DAY?*

*KINDLE EDITION ONLY

I'm currently writing the next book in the Blake Jordan series with a release planned soon. New subscribers get the Kindle version for $1 on release day.

Join my newsletter to reserve your copy and I'll let you know when it's ready to download to your Kindle.

kenfite.com/books

THE BLAKE JORDAN SERIES

IN ORDER

The Senator
Credible Threat
In Plain Sight
Rules of Engagement
The Homeland
The Shield
Thin Blue Line
Person of Interest
Abuse of Power

This is a work of fiction. The characters, incidents, and dialogues are products of the author's imagination and are not to be construed as real. Any resemblance to events or persons, living or dead, is coincidental.

November 2017

For NJ, my youngest,
who has inherited the creative gene.

RULES OF ENGAGEMENT

A BLAKE JORDAN THRILLER

KEN FITE

1

Yuri Kanatova shielded his face from the torrential downpour as he cautiously walked away from the idling vehicle parked at the edge of Sunset Marina. The overnight storm was supposed to miss the quiet town of Ocean City on Maryland's east coast, but pushed west unexpectedly and stalled over the city.

Using a high-powered tactical flashlight he had brought on the three-hour trip, Kanatova illuminated the path in front of him, taking slow, careful steps on the slippery wooden walkway that led to pier eleven.

As he approached, a bright flash of lightning struck close by, causing him to close his eyes and shudder. The immediate sound of the accompanying thunder added to the man's apprehension as he slowly opened his eyes and shined the light on his watch to check how much time he had left. After confirming that he was slightly ahead of schedule, the man continued along the walkway until he reached the edge of the pier.

Keeping one hand to his forehead to continue shielding his eyes from the rain, Yuri used the other to illuminate the side of the indigo blue NauticStar powerboat and shined the light on the mooring line, following it from the vessel to the metal bollard attached to the dock to keep the boat in place. Bending down to set the flashlight on top of the pier, Kanatova began untying the knot as lightning struck again, followed by a strong gust of wind. It pushed the man, causing him to loosen his grip on the mooring line as he stretched his hand out to steady himself. That was the moment he realized he had made a mistake.

Yuri watched helplessly as the wind knocked his flashlight over. It rolled, disappeared over the edge of the wooden walkway, and sank into the murky water below. Undeterred, the man cursed under his breath, turned back to finish loosening the rest of the line, and climbed inside the vessel as it started to drift away.

Once inside, Kanatova started the engine and let it warm for a minute as he slid his fingers over the small rectangular touch screen on the onboard Garmin GPS system and entered the coordinates he'd been instructed to memorize—latitude 38.344270, longitude -74.579354. After locking the location into the GPS, Kanatova began to steer the drifting vessel to correct its trajectory and slowly began to head out of the marina and into the open sea. He knew visibility would be low at four in the morning, and the storm had made it even more difficult to negotiate the choppy waters as he headed east out into the Atlantic.

At a top speed of just over fifty miles per hour, Kanatova had planned to travel for under half an hour to reach his destination. But with the strong, unrelenting wind making the water more difficult to navigate—in addition to the rain now traveling sideways and hitting him square in the face—it would take longer.

Still, he pressed forward and decided that the strong wind coming from the east might actually help him.

Forty minutes into the trip, the rain let up and the sky cleared as Kanatova finally passed through the outer edge of the storm. Slowing the vessel, he used a sleeve to wipe water away from his face and blinked several times to clear his eyes. He hadn't yet reached the coordinates he'd been given, but experience told him he needed to scan the horizon in case the target had drifted farther due to the strong winds.

After looking south, Kanatova turned his gaze to the north. His eyes scanned everywhere and everything.

There should have been a bright, pulsating strobe marking the location in case there were complications, but he couldn't see anything but choppy water surrounding him in shades of dark blue along a gray sky.

"Where are you?" Kanatova said to himself, feeling his heart starting to beat harder than it had all night and knowing he had no room for error on this mission. His eyes continued to scan the dark water. He turned west, back toward the coastline. "Could I have missed it?" he asked himself as his eyes flicked back and forth, becoming more desperate by the second and realizing that the stakes of failing would be death.

Then something on his right caught his eye. A bright flash streaked high into the dark sky momentarily and then disappeared. Kanatova turned in the direction of the flash and scanned the area carefully.

Hoping it wasn't just a flash of lightning from the storm now moving to the west of him, the man held his breath and kept his eyes fixed on the location. Five seconds later, Kanatova had his answer. A red orb, brilliant in appearance, lit up the night sky. The color streaked across the Atlantic as the bright object began to fall toward the ocean, and Kanatova realized what he was seeing: the descent of a distress flare.

Quickly, he turned the vessel toward the direction of the flare and accelerated before he lost sight of it.

The glowing orb fell slowly, taking approximately thirty seconds to complete its journey from high above. Kanatova watched it become brighter as it neared the water, causing its red hue to reflect more brilliantly off the top of the ocean waves before it finally hit the water, quenching the flame, and sank into the sea.

The man thought about the flashlight he had brought with him. He could have used it to help him locate what he was sent out into the open water of the Atlantic to find. Kanatova slowed as he approached the area where he thought the distress flare had come from, stopped the vessel, and took a step back to scan the area in every direction, hearing nothing but cold water slapping up against the sides of the NauticStar.

"Dimitri!" he yelled and waited for a response as the wind picked up again. "Dimitri, can you hear me?"

Squinting his eyes and shielding his face from a spray of water hitting his boat, Kanatova saw what looked like a light from three hundred meters away. It disappeared for several seconds, then came back into view.

Keeping his eyes fixed in the direction of where he'd seen the light come from, he felt around for the controls, repositioned his watercraft once more, and headed straight toward the location. A relieved smile fell upon Yuri's face as he realized that the light he was seeing was, in fact, coming from the strobe, which was only disappearing every few seconds because of the rise and fall of the tall waves. When the pulsating light remained steady long enough to lock in on the location, he made one final push and raced toward it.

Squinting, he could see the outline of a small raft drifting at the mercy of the ocean's current. He continued to approach and, with each glow of the strobe, could see the face of the man as he held it tight.

"You're late," the man waiting inside the raft yelled over the sound of the engine as it approached.

A confused expression spread across Kanatova's face, hidden from the man in the raft. The voice was not one he'd been expecting, one of a grizzled warrior ready to lead a group of aimless men. It was not the gruff voice of an experienced, battle-worn man hell-bent on inflicting harm on American innocents.

It was the voice of a younger man. Yuri stared at him, unsure how to respond.

"I said you're late," the man repeated, his voice intentionally deeper this time as he stared at Kanatova.

"Dimitri," he said, remembering the plan and finding a weight underneath one of the benches. Stretching out an arm, he handed the weight to the young man. "Please understand, there were complications."

"Which one are you?" he asked, taking the weight and tethering it to a steel loop on the side of the raft.

"Yuri," he replied as he grabbed a railing and offered his hand to help the young man climb aboard.

Dimitri stared at the man, reached inside his jacket, and found a knife. He grabbed Yuri's hand, extended the blade, and punctured the raft. He stepped onto the boat as the raft deflated and sank into the ocean, pulled down by the weight he had attached. Dimitri turned to Yuri. "We're behind schedule. Let's move."

2

As Kanatova approached the harbor, Dimitri sat atop the slim bench located directly behind him. The majority of the storm was now far west of them, though a light sprinkle remained over the harbor as the vessel slowed and the men made their final approach into the marina, with Yuri docking at pier eleven.

After placing the mooring line back on the bollard, Yuri signaled to the man he'd rescued that he could exit.

Dimitri stepped onto the slippery wood and steadied himself. He heard the rumble of thunder in the distance as he noticed two men approach from a parked vehicle and stop at the edge of the pier.

Yuri finished securing the vessel and walked with Dimitri to meet the two men who were waiting for them. Seeing the dissatisfied expression on one of the men's faces, Yuri stepped behind Dimitri to get out of his way. The men formed a circle around Dimitri, who stood silently and stared at the two men in front of him.

"This is Makar," said Yuri, gesturing to the expressionless man to his left. "And Andrei," he added as he looked to the tall man next to Makar, who seemed disturbed. "The others are waiting at the safe house."

"How many?" asked Dimitri after pausing for a brief moment to look over each of the men before him.

"Seven," replied Yuri. "The two specialists you requested and five others, men loyal to the homeland as well as to our cause." Kanatova waited for the other men to speak up and add to his words, but neither said a word. Instead, they just stared at Dimitri, assessing the young man and deciding if he was someone capable of leading them and carrying out the intricate plan he had proposed from half a world away.

Dimitri motioned for Yuri to join the other men. Then he palmed a hand across his head to dry his wet hair and flung the water to the ground. He crossed his arms and looked up at the three men, slowly moving his gaze left to right, from Yuri to Makar, and finally setting his eyes on Andrei. "Tell me, Andrei," said Dimitri, sensing that the man was deeply bothered by something, "why are you so troubled?"

There was no response at first. Then Andrei turned to his right to look at Makar, who maintained his expressionless gaze. He then looked briefly at Yuri before shifting his eyes back to the man in front of him.

"I'll ask you again," said Dimitri with an annoyed tone to his voice. "What is bothering you, my brother?"

"Brother?" asked Andrei as he stepped forward and lowered his gaze to Dimitri's feet before slowly looking up as he assessed the man. "I could be your father." He laughed and turned to look at the others.

Nodding to himself, Dimitri said, "So that is the problem." Dimitri stepped outside the circle and kept his eyes on Andrei as he put his arms behind his back and started pacing around the three men slowly. "Andrei, you knew my father, did you not?"

Andrei straightened up and nodded. "You know very well that I did."

"Then you know he was not an old man himself. Did you expect him to have an old son?" He paused for a moment, waiting for Andrei to respond, but he didn't say a word. "What is the true concern here?"

Andrei looked behind him to see if his sentiment was shared by his associates before responding. "Dimitri, we need a warrior with experience who can help us. Someone who understands how to fight. Someone who understands how the Americans operate, to help us bring this cowardly nation to its knees." He paused a beat before continuing. "We were loyal to your father, and the prospect of continuing where he left off was appealing to us. But we need someone experienced to lead us. Someone we can respect."

Dimitri continued to pace slowly, keeping his hands behind his back and thinking about the words being spoken by Andrei. He stopped once he got to the front of the men and stared at the three of them now lined up side by side. Looking to the other two, he said, "Yuri, Makar, do you agree with your colleague?"

There was no reply at first. Then the expressionless Makar asked, "How do you plan on fighting and *winning* a war against a nation that you have never lived in or even visited? You are young, Dimitri. Convince me that I am wrong. Show me that you are capable of leading us, and you will have my support."

Crossing his arms, Dimitri nodded again. "And you, Yuri?" he asked, noticing that the man who had rescued him was now staring down at the ground. When he did not respond, Dimitri stepped closer. "Tell me," he said softly while standing before the nervous man, "do you agree with their assessment of me?"

Yuri looked up. "I do not agree," he said with a nervous voice and furrowed brow. "You have my support."

Dimitri tilted his head to one side and stared at Yuri. The man did not look him in the eye and instead turned his gaze back to the ground. Stepping back out in front of the men, Dimitri stared at each of them.

"Andrei and Makar," he began, searching for the right words, "you make valid points. I am young. And I do not have the experience of a seasoned warrior. But make no mistake about it, I have one thought that occupies my mind day and night—my father's legacy. And despite your concerns, I can assure you that—"

"I knew your father for many years," interrupted Andrei. "Before you were even born, Dimitri. He spoke highly of you, his one and only son. He did not want you involved in these kinds of things." Andrei paused before adding, "You contacted us and provided a plan much different than your father's. His desire was to destroy the infrastructure of American intelligence gathering. Yours is centered on working alongside it."

"As I was saying," replied Dimitri as he stared at Andrei, not pleased with being interrupted by the man, "what happened to my father and protecting his legacy consumes me. His defeat will not go uncontested."

The men looked at each other as Dimitri continued. "What my father failed to understand was that you can fight a war against America, but you cannot *win* a war against her. No, you can only win small battles. What I have proposed is a new way of thinking, my brothers. If you did not agree, you would not be here."

"But it does not follow the rules of engagement, Dimitri," said Andrei. "You cannot work with the enemy."

"That is exactly why it will work. We will strike at the heart of those responsible for my father's defeat. We will work with the enemy only as long as we need to." Sensing that there was still hesitation amongst the group, Dimitri continued. "We will hit the American people hard, using their own government against them. I will finish what my father started and will not hesitate to remove any obstacle that stands in my path." He looked back at the men, one by one. "If you believe that I can and will lead you as I say I will, if you believe that my inexperience will help me to think differently so that we may succeed, step forward."

After waiting several seconds, Makar stepped forward. Dimitri turned to Yuri, who hesitated until, out of what Dimitri believed to be fear, the man finally took a step forward to join Makar. Andrei defiantly took a step backwards and fell out of line as he stood behind the others. Dimitri smiled. He unfolded his arms, reached into his jacket, and found his weapon. He looked it over, admiring it, and then looked up at the men.

"I hate insubordination," said Dimitri as his eyes passed Makar and settled on Andrei, who stared boldly and defiantly at the young man. "But I must admit," he continued as he gripped his gun tighter, "I respect a difference of opinion, as it only makes a team stronger. What I *cannot* respect, however, is indecision."

With that, Dimitri raised his arm and pulled the trigger, sending a bullet into the forehead of Yuri Kanatova. The other two men flinched in response as the sound of the weapon firing echoed around them. "Quick. Put his body in the back of the vehicle," he said and looked at his watch. "We need to leave now."

3

I WAITED FOR JAMES KELLER IN THE PRESIDENT'S DINING room, located down the hall from the Oval Office, just past the president's private study. Gregory, the president's personal chef, had already taken my order and placed two steaming cups of black coffee on the small table that Keller, and the others who had held the office before him, dined at when having casual meals alone or with staff members. Chef, as Keller liked to call the man, already knew what Keller wanted: three eggs with wheat toast and strong black coffee. I told Chef I'd take the same, and I sat alone, sipping the steaming coffee as I waited for my friend to arrive.

The president entered with a newspaper tucked under his arm, and I stood to shake his hand. Taking a seat across from me, Keller set the paper down on the table to his right. I read the upside-down headline.

"Russian spy ship patrolling off America's east coast," I said. "Guess the *Times* got tipped off somehow."

"The leaks are all over the place, Blake. Hard to tell where they come from. Could be from within the intelligence community or inside the damn White House." Keller took a sip of coffee before continuing. "This one's not too bad. They send one of these ships up from Cuba about once a year, it seems. They're harmless. You and I both know that the Russians like to play two cards: intimidation and misinformation." Keller grabbed the paper, turned it over, and smiled. "Enough about that. How are you doing, son?"

I took a sip of the hot coffee and set the cup down. "I'm fine, Mr. President," I said and forced a smile.

Keller looked me over as Chef returned and set two identical plates of food down in front of us. We thanked the man, and the president lowered his head, briefly closed his eyes, and began eating. "Blake," he said after what felt like an eternity of silence between us, "have I ever told you about how I met my wife?"

I smiled and shook my head. "No, sir. I've heard a lot of your stories over the years, but not that one."

Keller nodded and looked down again as he gathered his thoughts. "I was just a kid, really. About twenty years old, tail end of the Vietnam War right before the Fall of Saigon. My parents knew how much I loved to read and would send me care packages from time to time. Mostly letters. But they also sent me novels. Used paperbacks. All they could afford, really." Keller looked past me as he reflected on his younger years.

Wondering where the president was going with his story, I set my fork down and leaned back in my chair.

His smile broadened. He shook his head as a flood of memories from many years ago rushed over him. "My parents," he continued, "they knew I liked reading spy fiction, adventure-type novels back then." Keller turned his gaze back to me. "But sometimes they'd send over these coming-of-age-type books. My last Christmas over there, I got a package from them. They sent me a used copy of *To Kill a Mockingbird*. Harper Lee."

I nodded to let him know I wasn't *that* young to not know the author or the book.

"So I read the thing when I could. Wasn't my kind of book, but it started to grow on me. And all over the pages were markings and notes from the previous owner, which I didn't appreciate at first. Who writes in books like that?" he asked, furrowing his brow and taking a sip of his coffee. "A lot of people, it turns out."

Keller's personal chef entered the room and walked over to the table and warmed up our cups of coffee. We thanked him, and I pushed my plate aside as I started to get pulled deeper into the president's story.

"Son, the handwriting was just beautiful. The notes the previous owner made in the margins, they were just so insightful. Said the theme of the book wasn't about prejudice but, rather, about the coexistence of good and evil. It made me appreciate the book even more. And I have to tell you," said Keller, his face brightening as he paused to think about that time in his life, "when I finished the thing, I almost put it away, but I decided to read it again. This time, instead of skipping right to the first chapter, I carefully flipped through the first few pages, thinking I'd be intentional about it and go through it slowly this time."

The president looked at me, inviting me to ask the next logical question. So I did. "What'd you find?"

"The previous owner's name and address. Right there on the inside cover, just in case the book got lost."

"Margaret?"

Keller nodded. "Margaret Nelson. She lived in New York City at the time. Her parents donated the book."

Shaking my head in disbelief, I asked, "So what did you do?"

"I wrote to her, son," Keller said with a chuckle. "Told her I had her book. We exchanged letters for about six months or so. We wrote about the novel. Then I wrote about the war, and she told me about everything happening back at home. Nixon. Watergate. Ford's pardoning of the man. After a while, our letters became more personal. Blake, I was falling in love with a woman I had never met. When the war came to an end and I was sent home, they told me I'd pass through Grand Central Station. I told her that I wanted to meet her. She wrote back and agreed on the condition of only wanting to get her book back," said Keller with quiet laughter. "Said she'd be wearing a pink rose on her lapel so I'd know who she was."

"What happened?"

"Well, I got there and found the spot she had told me to go to, and the most beautiful woman I had ever seen approached. She smiled at me and I smiled back. Then she kept walking past me and disappeared."

"It wasn't her?" I asked.

"She didn't have the rose. I stopped and looked all around and finally spotted a woman in the crowd standing alone up against a large column. Blake, I was just devastated. She was an older woman, must have been in her early sixties, I guess around my age now. I just stared at her from across the large room."

Confused, I asked, "So what did you do?"

"I walked up to her, son. I saluted, presented her the novel, and told her how excited I was to meet her. And I asked if I could take her to dinner as a way of saying thanks for lending me her book for so long." I shook my head, but Keller held up a hand so he could continue. "She said, 'Son,

I don't know what this is all about, but that woman I saw walk by you gave me twenty dollars and asked me to wear this rose and wait here for fifteen minutes. Said if a soldier approached, to tell him she'd be waiting in that restaurant over there for him to return her book to her.' So I thanked the woman and left to go find Margaret."

I put my elbows on the table and leaned in, resting my chin on my folded hands. "Do you still have it?"

"The book?" asked Keller as his smile started to fade. "We lost it in the move from Chicago to the White House." I noticed that Keller's eyes started to tear, and he blinked repeatedly to try to hide it from me. "Looked everywhere for it. Both of us did. That book represented the special bond that Margaret and I had together. And it's gone." Keller took a long sip of coffee as we sat in silence. "I miss her," he finally said as he looked down and twisted the wedding band he refused to stop wearing. "But the good Lord doesn't take us down a straight path, does he?" Keller paused again. "When's the last time you saw her, Blake?"

"Jami?" I asked and looked away as I shook my head. "At the funeral, I guess. So about three months."

"You should call her," he said, twisting his wedding band. "You only live once, son. Try to make it count."

4

MEG TAYLOR SAT IN THE APPROPRIATE SEAT RESERVED FOR the *New York Times*, second row back from the podium, right behind the Reuters guy and directly in front of a reporter from the *Chicago Tribune*. Flanked by journalists from the *Washington Post* and AP Radio, both yelling over each other the moment Press Secretary Jeff Brewer finished answering a question, Taylor struggled to keep up and get a word in.

"I can assure you, Mike," said Brewer, gesturing to the NBC News representative all the way to his right, "that the United States Navy is closely tracking the Russian vessel as it heads north along the east coast."

Brewer paused to take a breath as Meg spoke up, along with forty-eight of her peers, trying to get a follow-up question in front of the press secretary. Brewer turned to his left, his eyes connecting with Meg's before shifting to the reporter seated behind her. "Yeah, Bob," he said to the *Tribune* man. "Go ahead."

"This is the second time in a month that the *Viktor Leonov* has been spotted near the US coastline. Both times, the ship made a port call in Cuba. This is becoming a common occurrence. What are we doing to—"

"The vessel remained in international waters," replied the press secretary tersely.

"Now wait a minute, Jeff," interrupted the *Tribune* man. "Thirty miles out isn't international waters."

"Bob, as I said," continued Brewer, "the Navy is keeping a careful eye on the vessel. It poses no imminent threat to us. In fact, it already turned east and is heading out to sea. It's just an intimidation ploy by the—"

"But that's not the point, Jeff. Three weeks ago, the ship was spotted thirty miles off the coast of Connecticut, the farthest north a Russian vessel has ever traveled along our coast. Now I'm sure I'm not the only one here to have done his or her homework," said the reporter, looking at Meg, who turned around to look at him. "It's a Vishnya-class spy ship built by the Soviet Navy in the eighties, specifically for intelligence gathering. The thing's outfitted with high-tech equipment designed specifically to intercept communications. The fact that this ship is coasting along the coast, gathering who the hell knows what kind of information, poses a very serious threat to our country. What is the president doing about this?"

As Jeff Brewer fielded the question, Meg felt a vibration in her pocket and reached inside to grab her cell. It was a text message from her boss at the *Times*, Robert King. "Do it now," the message read.

Sliding the phone back into her pocket, Taylor focused on the press secretary as he droned on about the aging *Viktor Leonov* ship and its potential communications-interception abilities. Meg wasn't focusing on the words the man was saying, but instead focused on the question she knew she had to ask. When Brewer finished the last few words of his response to the *Tribune* guy, Meg saw her opening and took it.

"There are reports," she said loudly along with half of the other journalists sitting in attendance who also began speaking, and Meg held her hand up and smiled at the press secretary and caught his eye again.

"Yes," he said, gesturing to Meg. "Sorry, I'm not sure I know who you are," he added, furrowing his brow.

"Meg Taylor, *New York Times*, filling in for David O'Malley."

Brewer nodded and smiled. "That's right," he said. "Hope Dave's resting up so he can come back and beat me up some more." A handful of journalists laughed to themselves. "Please, your question, Meg."

Taylor took a quick, deep breath. She had rehearsed the question for what felt like a thousand times since last night. "There are reports claiming that the *Viktor Leonov* is involved in something more threatening."

Brewer raised an eyebrow and lowered his head. "More *threatening*, Miss Taylor? Care to elaborate?"

Meg brought a closed fist to her mouth and cleared her throat as the rest of the press corps turned to her. "A newspaper in the United Kingdom published a story suggesting that..." Meg paused for a moment, not used to so many people staring at her. She took another breath. "Suggesting that Russia has been using the ship, not for intelligence gathering, but for seeding the US coastline with each pass the ship takes."

Brewer stood behind the podium, looking confused. He narrowed his eyes and looked at Taylor. "Seeding the coastline? I'm sorry," the press secretary said, shaking his head slowly. "What does that even mean?"

"The report says that a Russian military expert claimed

that Moscow has been quietly seeding the east coast of the United States with nuclear bombs for some time now," said Taylor and cleared her throat again. "It said that they dig themselves into the ground and sleep until given the command to detonate."

Brewer looked down at his notes and nodded again as the rest of the journalists turned around to watch the press secretary field the question from the young blonde woman in her early to mid-twenties.

"Miss Taylor," he began, still staring at his notes resting on the podium and stacking them with his hands before looking up at her, "what newspaper did you say this was reported in? Was it a British paper?"

"The *Independent*," replied Meg.

"Okay, an online newspaper," said Brewer, looking at Taylor sideways. "The *Independent*. Sold to and now controlled by a wealthy *Russian* businessman just a few years ago, I believe. *That* newspaper, right?"

Feeling her face turning a shade of red, Meg interrupted the man as he began to wrap up the meeting. "Jeff, I have it on good authority that the *Independent* was leaked this information from President Keller's administration, just like every other leak Keller's been dealing with since he took office."

Brewer's expression shifted from amused to a state between annoyed and concerned.

"They verified the claim," continued Meg, "with a former colonel and defense ministry spokesman for the Kremlin. Any response?"

"That's all for today. We'll pick back up on Monday," said Brewer, closing his notebook. "Thank you."

The other White House correspondents surrounding Meg stood as Jeff Brewer turned and disappeared through a door. The reporters all walked together into the press corps offices as Meg thought about the conversation she had just had and felt her phone vibrating again inside a pocket and answered the call.

"Taylor, you missed your chance," a voice boomed, coming from Robert King, the Washington bureau chief for the *Times* and Meg Taylor's boss. "You had him up against the ropes and let him off easy."

"Mr. King, the press secretary wasn't budging. I had nothing else to throw at the guy and he knew it."

"I brought you on, Taylor, because you showed promise. But what I just saw was an embarrassment."

"Mr. King, please—"

"Taylor," boomed King, prompting Meg to hold her cell an inch farther away from her ear, "listen carefully because I'm only going to say this once. You have twenty-four hours to find some serious dirt on President Keller, and none of this Russia nonsense. Find something substantial and I'll keep you on until O'Malley returns. And if you can't do that, I'll find someone who can, and you'll be back home watching *them* on the TV. Got it?" Meg tried to speak, but King interrupted her. "Twenty-four hours," he repeated and hung up.

After standing alone for several minutes, Meg finally placed a call. "It's me," she said. "I need your help."

5

AFTER LEAVING THE WHITE HOUSE FOLLOWING MY LATE breakfast with the president, I took a cab back to my apartment down in Alexandria. Traffic wasn't bad for a late Friday morning in DC before a holiday weekend. Normally, I'd head over to the Eisenhower Executive Office Building, where I had a small office, but I decided to take the day off since the rest of Keller's team had left Washington early to enjoy the long weekend with their families. I didn't have a family to go home to. I was one of the few who stayed behind.

Listening to the drone of the car engine, I rested my head against the backseat window as my thoughts drifted back to Keller and our conversation over breakfast about his late wife, Margaret. I stared out the window, watching the city streets pass by in a blur as memories of Mrs. Keller from the last twenty years began to wash over me. I thought about how alone the president must have felt returning to the White House after the funeral. I felt bad for my longtime friend as I remembered how alone I had felt returning to an empty home when my wife, Maria, had been murdered years ago on the cold city streets of Chicago.

"Which one's yours, buddy?" the cabbie asked, and I lifted my head and became fully present again.

"This is good," I said when we approached the intersection of Madison and Washington. "I'll get out here."

The driver looked over his shoulder and tapped his brakes, letting me out in front of a small building close to where I lived. A habit I had, never liking to be dropped too close to my building. I handed the man some cash and stepped out of the cab and onto the sidewalk. As the driver pulled away, I waited a second before I started heading east toward the Kingsley, where I had called home for the last few months.

Seeing a familiar face up ahead, I smiled and turned to my right, where I noticed a bookstore I didn't remember seeing before. Knowing that the man down the street wasn't going anywhere, I stepped inside.

I walked past the display area near the entrance, circled around the rows of nonfiction books, and stopped when I got to the section I was looking for. I ran my finger across the books on the shelf until I got to the one I was searching for. I thumbed through it for a few minutes before I closed it and headed to the back of the bookstore, found the café, and purchased a sandwich, two cups of coffee, and the novel.

I left, headed in the same direction as before my quick detour, and stopped a block farther down the street. "Sammy, how've you been, man?" I asked the older man I stopped to visit with whenever I saw him.

"Frank," he said, referring to me by the name I had decided to give him once, "I appreciate it, man." He stretched out his weathered hands and accepted the coffee and set it down before realizing that the sandwich in the bag was for him, too. Keeping the novel tucked under my arm, I stood in front of Sam and turned to look back west as I heard a car approaching from behind as it sped up and passed us.

"How've you been?" I asked again as Sammy took a cautious sip of his coffee and shrugged.

"Could be better, I guess," he replied, and I took a sip of my coffee, becoming concerned with his response.

I took a step closer and saw that his lip looked a little swollen. "What happened?"

Sammy looked down the street past me, then looked over his left shoulder for a moment before he replied, "Couple of nights ago, these two punks came at me in the middle of the night, man. Thought they were going to try to take my stuff. Instead, they just stood here about ten minutes asking me questions. Wouldn't leave me alone, man. Said they'd give me money, but gave me a whole mess of trouble instead."

"What kind of questions did they ask you, Sam?"

The man got quiet as I took a seat on the sidewalk and joined him underneath the awning in front of the entrance to some business that had closed down months ago. "Sammy?" I said, trying to get him to talk.

"I don't know who these guys are, but they were asking me a lot of questions about some fellow named Blake Jordan," he said and paused to look at me. "Said they needed to find the guy, that it was important." My heart started to beat faster as he continued the story. "Told them I didn't know who they were talking about. So they described him. Five feet eleven. Short brown hair. Hazel eyes. Said I didn't know the guy."

Sammy got quiet.

"Then what happened?" I asked, although I already had an idea where this was going.

"They said, 'Sure you do.' One of the guys picked me up and slammed me against this wall right here. Grabbed my neck and started to squeeze. They said they had seen me talking to him a few times and wanted to know where the guy lived. I told them that I didn't know anyone by the name of Blake." He paused again before adding, "Told them I live on the street. I talk to a lot of people out here, you know."

I turned and looked over my shoulder as another car passed us. "They leave you alone after that?"

Sammy shrugged again. "The guy let go of me and smiled real big. Then he busted me in the gut, man." He looked down to his right. "Fell on top of my shopping cart, got the wind knocked right out of me. The guys said they'd be back, and the next time they came to visit me, I had better have some answers for them."

I felt the hair on the back of my neck stand on end as I wondered if we were being watched right now. "Sammy," I said, "do you know where Carpenter's Shelter is? Five blocks west of here?"

He nodded.

"Good. I need you to get your stuff together and head over there right now. Can you do that for me?"

He furrowed his brow, not happy with my request. "Don't like that place. Besides, this is my spot, Frank."

"I know, but this is important," I said, thinking about the Russian men and the warning I had been given six months ago. "I don't think it's safe out here."

The man shook his head.

"Come on. I'll walk with you."

After a few seconds, he started nodding. "Alright, man. But only until I can think of a new place. And you gotta find me wherever I end up and keep bringing me that coffee," he said as he crouched down and started to transfer some of his things into the shopping cart. I set my book down and helped him. "Deal?"

I smiled as we set the last of his things into the cart and I picked my book up from the sidewalk. "Deal."

We walked the five blocks, and I asked Sammy to describe the men. He said they were foreign and spoke with heavy accents. He wasn't sure where they were from, but knew for sure that English wasn't their first language. I kept looking over my shoulder and scanning the streets until we finally arrived at Carpenter's Shelter. I knocked on the door and spoke with a woman who told me they were full, and I explained Sammy's situation. Finally, she agreed to let him stay for a few days.

The woman gestured for him to enter, and he popped his cart up over the threshold and smiled at me.

"Okay, Sammy," I said as I took a few steps back and started to leave. "I'll find you in a couple of days."

I turned and walked back toward the sidewalk. "Okay, Blake," I heard the man say behind me.

Realizing what he had said, I turned around, only to see him walk farther inside the shelter as the woman smiled at me and closed the door behind them. I smiled to myself and looked north on Henry Street, scanning the area before heading south, back toward the Kingsley, and deciding to take a circuitous path to get back home. As I did, I wondered who the two men were who had roughed Sammy up a few days ago. Someone was looking for me. I didn't know who they were or what they wanted. But I needed to find out.

6

Fifteen minutes later, I arrived back at the Kingsley. Taking the stairs to my third-floor apartment, I unlocked the door and opened it carefully, wishing that I had my weapon on me before I entered. Gently closing the door behind me, I stepped into the kitchen, opened one of the drawers, and grabbed the Glock 22 I had hidden there, before I proceeded to walk through the rest of the apartment.

Rays of sunlight broke through the blinds in my bedroom and illuminated the area, helping me navigate the otherwise dark space since I had decided to keep the lights off after entering my apartment. I was relieved when I cleared all of the rooms and decided that the two guys that Sammy had warned me about hadn't figured out where I lived. Not yet, at least. Setting my Glock down on top of my dresser, I took a deep breath and let it out slowly as I emptied my pockets while trying to figure out who the men could be.

The last thing I pulled from my pockets was a diamond ring, something I had been carrying with me every day for the last six months. It was a reminder of the decision I had made one cold December night in New York. A decision to break the curse of losing everyone I ever cared about by walking away from Jami.

I loved her more than anything, and on New Year's Eve, I had planned on proving that to her. And in a way, I did. Walking away from Jami was the hardest thing I had ever done. But what I needed even more was for Jami to be safe and that meant loving her from a distance. Holding the ring up to my eyes, I stared at it for a moment, thinking about what could have been, and finally set it down and changed out of my dress shirt and slacks and put on a shirt and jeans. I stared at myself in the mirror, then went to the window and looked out through the closed blinds to scan the busy street below my apartment.

I had noticed that there was a CCTV camera across the street from where Sammy had been staying. I figured I could make a few phone calls and get access to the footage from that camera, but Sam had said that the incident happened a couple of days ago. I knew that with every passing day, getting access to that footage would become more difficult. I walked to the dresser and grabbed my cell phone to call in a favor.

But my phone was completely drained and wouldn't turn on, which I thought was strange. It had been at least an hour since I had checked it, just before I left the White House after breakfast with Keller. I found my charger, plugged it in, and set my cell on the dresser and stared at it, wondering if I was being tracked.

A loud knock at the door startled me. My first thought was about the men that were looking for me.

I grabbed my weapon and quickly approached the front door to my apartment.

I moved quickly, aiming my weapon at the floor as I

went. There was another knock, louder this time. I crept closer, looked through the peephole, and saw a man on the other side with his back turned away.

Taking a deep breath, I gripped my Glock tighter in my right hand, grabbed the door handle with my left, and opened it. I reached out, grabbed the man's shirt, and was about to push him against the wall when I realized that I knew him. I loosened my grip, lowered my weapon, and looked past him down the hallway.

"Blake, take it easy," said the familiar voice.

"What are you doing here?" I asked my friend and partner over at the FBI, Chris Reed.

Reed looked me over, straightened his shirt, and nodded to the door. "Well, if you promise not to kill me, maybe we can go inside and talk about it."

I looked down the hallway again.

"You okay?" he asked.

I gestured for him to enter as I tucked the gun into the small of my back and followed him inside.

Closing the door behind me, I locked it and turned the kitchen light on. "A couple of guys are looking for me," I said as I walked around to the other side of the small island in the middle of the kitchen, placed my hands on top of the counter, and leaned against it. "I just found out about it a little while ago. Heard the knock on the door and thought for a second I might be in trouble," I said and looked up at my friend.

"Who are they? And why are they looking for you?" asked Reed.

I thought about it. "Don't know yet," I replied and looked back down. "They were giving some homeless guy a hard time. They described what I looked like to him." I shook my head slowly before adding, "I think they've been following me. Maybe watching me."

Reed crossed his arms and looked at me sideways. "Aren't you tired of this?"

"Tired of what?"

"Living like this. Always looking over your shoulder. Sleeping with one eye open. Blake, I've known you for a long time now," he said and paused briefly, looking me over, choosing his words carefully. "First as my boss, now as my partner and friend. I'm worried about you, man. Mark, Morgan, Jami—we're all worried."

"I'm fine, Chris."

"You don't look fine. You look tired, like you haven't had a good night's sleep in weeks, maybe months."

I stood up straight, removing my hands from the counter I was leaning on, and started to rub my eyes. "Chris, is there a reason why you stopped by?" I asked. "Or did you just want to give me a hard time? Because I could really use your help with trying to figure out who these two guys are and what they want."

Reed stared at me briefly before explaining the reason for his visit. "Been trying to call for half an hour."

"Phone died," I said. "Not sure why, it had a full charge a few hours ago." I stepped into my bedroom, grabbed my phone, and yanked the charger from the wall. I went back into the kitchen and plugged the charger into a closer outlet and turned on my cell to check on the charge. "Tell me what's going on, Chris?"

"Let me call Morgan," said Reed as he reached into his pocket, found his cell, and called Department of Domestic Counterterrorism analyst Morgan Lennox. A man, like Chris Reed, who had worked for me back in Chicago when I ran the first DDC field office as special agent in charge. Reed had been my assistant SAIC before we were both fired for the actions we took while trying to save then-Senator Keller's life.

Chris put the call on speakerphone and set his cell phone down on the counter in between us. It rang once.

"Morgan Lennox," the Australian-born analyst answered.

"Morgan, it's Chris Reed. I have Blake here with me."

"Been trying to reach you for a while, mate," said the data-analytics guy from the DDC office in Chicago.

"Go ahead, Morgan," I said. "Bring me up to speed."

"Hang on," said Lennox as I stared at Chris, hearing Morgan typing frantically in the background. Finally, the typing stopped. I heard him pull the receiver away from his face and answer a question before coming back on the line. "Okay. There's a cyberattack in progress, and I'm trying to help stop it." Before I could ask how bad the attack was, Morgan answered my question. "It's ransomware, Blake. It's spreading across the country at a very rapid rate. And it looks like it was introduced into the network right here in Chicago."

7

I CROSSED MY ARMS AND STARED AT REED'S CELL PHONE ON the counter, processing what Morgan had said. "What do you mean introduced into the network in Chicago? Are you saying that DDC was hit by this?"

"No," replied Morgan as Chris and I heard him start typing again in the background, multitasking while trying to also bring us up to speed. "I'm working with Simon Harris at the Washington DDC field office over by you guys, and based on what we're seeing, the virus is spreading at an exponential rate, and the highest concentration of impacted machines is in the Chicago area. This thing is just out of control, mate."

"Tell me more," I said. "Is this a repeat of the attack we had six months ago?"

"Nothing like that, Blake," replied Chris. "That was a DDoS attack against the network. This is malware."

"Ransomware, to be precise," said Morgan.

"Explain," I said.

"A particularly nasty type of malware," said Morgan as Chris raised the volume on his cell. "It blocks access to a computer or, more specifically, its data and demands money to release it. It moves from computer to computer and hides itself inside documents and other files. It's programmed so that if you don't pay the ransom within a few hours, the price doubles. You enter a credit card number and pay the ransom, it's supposed to give you access to your data—but that's not how this particular strain is working."

"What do you mean?" I asked.

Morgan cleared his throat. "With this one, you pay the ransom, and nothing happens. Actually, it doesn't even look like the payment is going through. We've tested it, and the charge isn't hitting credit cards at all."

I shook my head. "So then what are we dealing with here? Some high school hacker having some fun?"

"I don't think so," replied Morgan. "I've seen something like this before, after the NSA breach where the Shadow Agents hacking group broke in and accessed government cyberwarfare programs. Simon and I are looking at the code, and it looks similar to what was stolen and went up for auction online at that time. I'm not saying it's the same group that's responsible, but the base code that I'm seeing looks very similar."

"So they don't want money," I said. "They want to see how much damage they can do. Could be worse."

"It *is* a lot worse, Blake. And, Chris, this is an update I haven't even given you yet."

I looked up at Reed and waited for Morgan to continue.

"The hackers aren't targeting everyday citizens. I told you that the highest concentration of this is in the Chicago area. Well, from what Simon and I can tell, it's inside every hospital located within a hundred-mile radius. And since so many hospitals are owned by a handful of companies now, they're all on the same network, which is just helping the malware spread even faster. We still need to pinpoint the exact location of where the attack started, but for now, we're just trying to stop this thing."

"Why would they be targeting hospitals?" I asked. Chris and I stared at each other as I started to realize what was going on. "Oh my God," I said in a low voice. "These people want to cripple the hospital system. Doctors, healthcare workers—they're relying on those systems being up and running." Chris nodded and dropped his gaze as I thought about the broader implications. "Have we heard from any of the hospitals?"

"Not directly," replied Lennox. "I can only imagine that hospital staff are in a bit of a panic right now. There are others besides Simon and me trying to stop this. Chris, you want to fill Blake in on that piece?"

Reed looked up at me again. "Blake, you know that the Bureau is the lead federal agency for investigating cyberattacks," he said, and I nodded. "The Cyber Division at the Hoover Building is taking a look at this."

I thought about Roger Shapiro at DDC Chicago and Chris's boss at the Bureau, Bill Landry. The two had created a strong partnership between the two agencies lately, so it wasn't a surprise that they were working together on this.

"Okay, Morgan," Reed continued, "what do you need from us? How can we help?"

"Can you head over to the DDC field office over by you guys? Simon and I are heads down on this thing. Jami's assisting where she can while she waits on Lynne May to arrive, but she could use some help."

I knew of May, the new special agent in charge at DDC Washington. I thought about what Morgan was asking us to do. It wouldn't be unusual, given the relationship between DDC and the Bureau, for Chris Reed to help them out. And given my unique position within President Keller's administration, I had clearance to work with any federal agency on matters of domestic terrorism. I remained quiet, thinking about seeing Jami again.

"Guys?" Morgan said as I became fully present again and looked over at Chris.

"We're on our way," replied Reed.

"Thanks, mate," said Morgan, and the line was disconnected.

Chris grabbed his cell, dropped it in his pocket, and headed for the door. "Let's roll," he said as he walked.

Opening my front door, he turned around and saw me still standing in the same spot. "What's wrong?"

I slowly shook my head. "I'm not going, Chris."

"Why not? Because of Jami?"

"No, because I don't think I'm needed on this one," I lied. "I'll give you a call later and check in, okay?"

"Blake, you know that—"

"Chris," I said, interrupting my friend, "Morgan is more than capable of finding the source of the ransomware and stopping it. And it sounds like this guy Simon is all over it, too. Not to mention all of your guys," I said, referring to the Bureau's Cyber Division. "There's nothing I can do. I'll just be in the way."

Reed stood at the door. "So what are you gonna do, Blake? Stay here and do nothing? Morgan said that Jami could use some help over there. Don't turn your back on her —again," he added after pausing a beat.

I walked over to my cell and picked it up, confirming that it was charging quickly, and showed it to Chris. "You should be able to get a hold of me now if you really need me," I said, setting my phone back down.

Reed stared at me coldly. "What the hell happened to you, man?" he asked and waited for my response.

But I didn't say a word—I just stared at him from across the room.

"The president asked you to form an off-the-books black ops team. We're not operating like a team, Blake. We've been through a hell of a lot together. But for the last six months, you've disconnected from the group. We're supposed to be a team."

"We *are* a team," I said.

"You *sure* about that?" he asked and then shook his head slowly. "I'm not going to give up on you, man."

"Keep me updated," I said as Chris shook his head again, slammed the door shut, and left.

8

Meg Taylor was alone in the press corps office inside the basement of the West Wing. At one in the afternoon, all of her colleagues had already left, some going out for a long lunch, others not planning on returning to the White House until Jeff Brewer's next regularly scheduled briefing on Monday morning.

Even though she was alone, Meg felt uneasy. Rows of desks lined the space like an old schoolroom in the cramped, windowless downstairs office. She leaned back in her chair and looked around the historic space that had been used in various ways over the years, from a flower shop to a presidential gym in the forties.

She turned to look at her laptop, thinking about the ultimatum she'd been given by Robert King. Meg leaned back in her chair, took a deep breath, and let it out. Reaching up to grab a lock of her dirty-blonde hair, Taylor twirled it slowly as she kept her eyes glued to the laptop until they glossed over. Racking her mind, she turned over every rock imaginable, but still came up empty on the assignment.

That was the problem with President Keller. A man

known for having high moral standards. A man who had had every intention of stepping down from his position as Commander in Chief and allowing VP Mike Billings to take the reins after the first lady had taken a turn for the worse. And a man who had stayed in office to honor his wife when she insisted that he remain unwavering in his pursuit to lead his country.

Taylor, like most in the press, didn't exactly agree with Keller's politics.

But, looking over her shoulder and realizing that she was sitting inside the White House, Meg knew one thing: she was lucky to have the opportunity to fill in for O'Malley and couldn't blow the opportunity.

This was her dream job. Sure, Meg was just a fill-in until O'Malley's doctor cleared the newsman to return to his job at the *Times* following his heart attack. But if she could come up with something—anything—she'd make her boss happy and just might secure her spot as O'Malley's regular backup whenever he traveled outside Washington or needed a few days away from the twenty-four-seven pressure of his job.

Growing tired of waiting for the man she had called to get back to her, Meg decided to stretch her legs. She bumped into the chair of the AP guy who had sat directly behind O'Malley, and steadied herself as she removed her heels. Meg began to pace up and down the rows, thinking about King's words. She felt her stomach growl and lowered her hand, resting it on her stomach, as she remembered that she hadn't had anything to eat since breakfast. Knowing that the press corps kitchen was just down the hall from O'Malley's desk, she went back to the desk and grabbed her cell phone before leaving to exit the room.

But as she neared the exit to the old basement office, a

messy desk to the left of Meg caught her attention. She slowed, then stopped as she looked over the reporter's workspace overflowing with stacks of papers.

Meg hesitated and briefly looked all around the room, checking for security cameras. She didn't see any. She took a cautious step to her right and looked around the corner to make sure nobody was returning from lunch. It was all clear, so Meg walked to the cluttered desk and began sifting through the papers.

She pushed aside a white mug with the red CNN logo on it that was halfway full of cold, stale coffee. Meg picked up another stack. It consisted of articles that the journalist had printed from a few different websites, with the related stories paper clipped together based on topic. She found handwritten notes the guy had made to himself across some of the papers. They were in shorthand. Meg used a finger to pull back page after page and furrowed her brow as she tried to decipher the man's awful handwriting.

As she continued to sift through the stack, she noticed something fall out and land on the floor. Meg looked down and saw what appeared to be a five-by-seven photo turned upside down on the gray carpet.

She bent down, picked it up, and noticed the same handwriting on the back of the photograph in blue ink. It had the words "who was in the room for the Syria briefing" written on it along with a dash and the date.

"April seventh," Meg whispered to herself as she turned the picture over. She remembered that during that same time frame earlier in the year, President Keller had ordered the controversial airstrike in Syria, which had drilled fifty-nine Tomahawk missiles into the Syrian government-controlled Shayrat air base. The picture had captured one of the administration's key decision-making moments in Keller's presidency.

Meg stepped to the hallway and checked to make sure nobody was coming. When she was sure that she had a little more time, Meg thought back to that night in April when she'd been called to an urgent meeting at her old paper back home to discuss the Syrian attack. She remembered how Press Secretary Brewer had explained that the surprise attack was retaliation for the Syrian president's supposed involvement in a chemical attack that had killed over seventy innocent people during the Syrian civil war.

Shifting her attention back to the photo, Meg looked at the people huddled together in the situation room. Bringing the image closer to her eyes, she began to study the faces of those who were there that night.

She counted fifteen government officials in the picture—fourteen men and one woman. Eight of the men were seated at a long table with President Keller in the center. The rest stood against the back wall. The president was looking straight ahead at what Meg decided must have been video footage of the airstrike, just outside the frame of the picture. Most of Keller's team were present and watching with him.

Meg started from the left of the photograph and began working her way slowly to the right of the image. She looked at the people standing against the wall, one by one, followed by those seated around the table, whispering to herself the names of anyone that she recognized from Keller's inner team as she went along.

There was the deputy chief of staff almost out of the frame of the image, standing in the direction of where everyone else in the situation room was looking, the senior advisor to the president next to him, followed by the secretary of the treasury along one side of the table. At the corner, next to Keller, was the secretary of commerce, and sitting off in the corner was Press Secretary Jeff Brewer. Directly behind the president, leaning against the door, was a man in a suit with what looked like a wired earpiece coming up through the back of his shirt and into his ear. "Secret Service," Meg said in a soft voice as she kept scanning the image.

To Keller's left was the secretary of state, the national security advisor, and Chief of Staff Emma Ross.

Meg's eyes shifted to the right as she studied the faces of Keller's chief strategist, two members of the National Security Council, the deputy national security advisor, and finally, a man she did not recognize.

She noticed that the man had a name written above his face on the photograph. She brought it closer to her eyes and bent it for the light to catch the writing. Meg read the name and looked up, deciding if she recognized it. She studied the man and realized that he looked much different than everyone else at the table. He looked more like a Secret Service agent than a presidential aide. She found a pen and made a mark.

Taylor checked her pockets, trying to locate her cell phone, but came up empty. She found it on the CNN correspondent's desk. Positioning the picture at an angle to reduce the glare from the overhead lighting, she used her phone to snap an image of what she was looking at and typed the recipient's name as she sent it via text message. When she was done, Meg redialed a number and walked back to O'Malley's desk.

"I told you already, I don't have any more information on the White House leaks that you called about," said the voice on the other end of the line. "And if that changes, I'll be sure to give you a call. Okay?"

"Forget the leaks," said Taylor after sitting back down at the desk and holding the picture up to her face. "Check your phone." She waited until her informant confirmed he had received what she'd texted him. "I need to know more about the man I've circled in the image." She paused. "His name is Blake Jordan."

9

DIMITRI PACED AROUND THE LONG STEEL TABLE WHERE MAKAR and Andrei were sitting, each with a laptop. Five sentries moved about the large long-abandoned building, keeping a close watch outside as the occasional car passed by. Two generators had been brought up on the roof, giving enough power to get the lights and electrical outlets working. Air cards connected the laptops to the internet, and if it weren't for the doors taken off their hinges, the pictures removed from the walls, and the stench of mildew, it might have been a more ideal location to operate from. But Dimitri needed a place to hide in plain sight.

And the location fit that requirement perfectly.

The table had been removed from an adjacent area and centered in the middle of what had been called the Persian Room more than half a century earlier. A large Persian rug, twenty feet wide and fifty feet long, covered the floor of the enormous chamber the men were working from. A high-domed, vaulted ceiling stretched over forty feet into the air, causing their voices to echo whenever they became raised.

Dimitri continued to pace. "Andrei," he said to the more

aggressive of the two men, "when will we get an update from our two specialists on the road? As you know, they are both critical to our plan succeeding."

"Soon," replied the man, leaning back in his chair, his eyes moving to the man circling him slowly. "As I've explained, we must keep contact to a minimum. The Americans are good at tracing communications. The last thing we want to do is open the door for them to stop us before we set everything in motion, correct?"

"Fine. Tell me what is being reported with the ransomware attack you initiated. How is the progress?"

Andrei went to work, going to the usual news websites, and provided Dimitri an update as Makar sat quietly at the other end of the table, listening. "The Americans are working on a fix," he said. "They've got their best people on it to come up with a solution." Andrei paused for several seconds before adding, "The FBI released a statement saying that they're working closely with Silicon Valley to create a patch for it."

"Any attribution?"

Andrei looked across the table and saw that Makar looked like he wanted to speak, so he nodded to him.

"Dimitri, they're now blaming a hacking group."

"The Shadow Agents?"

"Yes, Dimitri," replied Makar, turning his gaze back to his screen as he continued to scroll through the news report in front of him. "They're hesitant to blame any specific country for this yet. It's too soon."

Dimitri nodded. "Excellent. How many casualties?"

There was no reply.

"Do we know anything yet?"

Makar shot a look at Andrei as Dimitri walked around him. "There is no information on that as of yet," answered

Makar. "But as you have instructed, the malware was introduced into the specific hospital that you requested and has quickly intensified, growing at an exponential rate over the past three hours." Makar paused and turned to Dimitri, who had stopped next to his chair and stood next to him. "The Americans are reporting that it has been distributed to virtually every state in the nation. It will continue to intensify. It will be pushed to government networks, then businesses. The Americans will not recognize any kind of pattern. By the time they realize what we're really doing, it will be too late to do anything."

A devilish smile grew on Dimitri's face. He set a hand on Makar's shoulder, patted it once, and squeezed.

"Good," said Dimitri, keeping a hand on his shoulder. "They will be distracted when we hit them again."

On the table next to Andrei, a disposable burner phone began to ring. Dimitri glanced down at Makar, then to his right as Andrei grabbed the phone, held it up to his face, and moved his dark eyes to Dimitri.

"Is it our man on the inside?" asked Dimitri as the phone rang a third time.

"No," replied Andrei as he answered the call. "Go ahead."

Dimitri asked Andrei to put the call on speakerphone. Andrei shook his head, knowing that he couldn't with the cheap prepaid phone he had purchased over a year ago and a thousand miles away from their current location. Andrei listened intently as Dimitri stared, listening to one side of the conversation.

"Very well," said Andrei. "We will contact you when we are ready." The man stared across the large empty room as the sentries securing it came in and out of view while they moved about, changing their locations and vantage points to keep the other three men at the table safe. "Let me know if anything changes," added Andrei. He disconnected the call, set the cell phone down in front of him, and turned his eyes up.

"That was one of the two?" asked Dimitri, now standing over Andrei and folding his arms across his chest.

"It was."

"And?" demanded the young man at least half the age of the one seated in front of him. "What did he say?"

Andrei continued to glare up at Dimitri, his dark eyes set firmly on him. "He said he is in position."

"So he is within range and ready to begin the next phase of the plan as soon as we give the order?"

"Yes."

"How will we know when to act? Have we confirmed if there are cameras so we can hit our target?"

"There are, but we do not have access to them. We confirmed that before you arrived," answered Andrei.

"Then I will ask you again—how will we know the precise moment that our man should act?"

Andrei looked across the table at Makar, who was staring down at his screen, not wanting to have anything to do with the conversation taking place in front of him. Losing his patience, Dimitri reached behind his back and grabbed his weapon, bringing it in front of him and turning it slowly from one side to the other.

"Think about it, Dimitri. The timing does not matter. We strike when we are ready. Our primary goal is to displace the agency, is it not? And with that goal in mind, we will succeed regardless of when we strike."

"And that is the best you can do!" yelled Dimitri, his voice echoing throughout the large empty building. "The woman must die, Andrei. That is part of the agreement that I made with our man on the inside."

Makar looked up and watched as the two men stared at each other. "Perhaps we *should* get the timing wrong," said Makar, pulling down the lid to his laptop a few inches before he continued. The men turned to Makar, prompting him to explain his comment. "Why should we be so quick, Dimitri? Why not have some fun with our target?" He paused. "Have our man trigger the device early. We can still get the girl."

Dimitri smiled once more. "You are right, Makar." He turned to Andrei. "Call your man back. Make it so."

10

After Chris Reed left, I approached the front door to my apartment, locked it, and turned around. Leaning my back against the door, I thought about my next steps, knowing that if these guys Sammy warned me about were looking for me, I didn't have much time. And I hoped they hadn't followed Chris.

I walked into the kitchen, unplugged my phone, and yanked the charger out of the outlet. I dialed a number and held the phone to my ear with a shoulder as I wrapped the long charger cord around its base and stepped into my room. Charlie answered right as I opened my closet door and grabbed my messenger bag.

"It's Blake," I said as I set the bag on my bed, opened it, and looked around the room. "I need your help."

There was a pause on the other end of the line. "What's wrong?" the man twenty years my senior asked.

"Need a place to stay for a few days," I replied as I placed the charger on the bed and went through my drawers and grabbed enough clothes to last me seventy-two hours and tossed them onto the bed, followed by extra magazines and extra ammo for my Glock. I found my tactical flashlight and tossed it onto my bed along with my knife. I looked around the room, thinking of what else I might need to take with me.

"How far out are you?"

"Twenty minutes."

"I'll be ready for you."

"Charlie," I said before he could disconnect the line, "I could use your help with something else."

After another pause, shorter this time, Charlie said, "Sure—go ahead."

"Do you still know anyone you used to work with who can get access to local CCTV footage?"

"I do," he replied. "Just need to know where and when, and the guy can pull the archive in an hour or two."

Walking to my bedroom window, I separated the blinds and looked outside to check the street again. I scanned the area and didn't see anything that looked out of the ordinary.

"You still there?" asked Charlie.

"Yeah. Have your guy pull anything he can get from Madison here in Alexandria. Street view between Washington and Saint Asaph. There's an awning in front of a business that closed down a while back. Directly next to that, I saw a camera. Not sure if it's active or not, but see if your guy can pull anything."

"What's he looking for?"

"African American man, older, homeless. He was assaulted by two men. I need to know who they are."

"When?" asked Charlie.

I shook my head, thinking about it. "Not sure. Happened a couple of nights ago. If he can get access to the feed, see if he can check seventy-two hours back. You have what we need to review anything he finds over there?" I asked as I strapped the messenger bag over my shoulder and looked over my room one last time.

"Of course."

"Good," I said, nodding to myself. "See you in twenty minutes."

I disconnected the line and was about to head out when my cell rang. Still holding onto my phone, I looked down and saw that it was the president's chief of staff calling. I hesitated before answering the call.

"This is Jordan," I said as I moved back to the window and lifted the blinds once again.

"Blake, it's Emma," she said urgently. "Are you aware of what's going on with this ransomware attack?"

"Yes, I just met with Chris Reed. He said that the Bureau's Cyber Division is all over it, Emma. So is DDC. Their Chicago field office is working closely with people at the Washington location to try to stop it."

"Blake, the president is in a meeting about the threat right now and asked me to get with you to make sure you were aware and staying on top of the situation. Are you at DDC now?"

"No," I replied. "But Chris Reed is on his way. I'll get an update from him shortly, and I'll relay that back to you as soon as I know more about it. Right now, they're just trying to figure out how to slow it down."

Ross didn't respond immediately. I pulled my cell away from my ear and held it to my face for a moment to make sure we were still connected. When I brought the phone back, she said, "Blake, I don't want to tell you what to do, but I think you need to get over there. Keller's going to expect you to be on-site."

"I'm dealing with something right now, Emma."

"And I can appreciate that, but—" She pulled the phone away to talk to someone before coming back on. "Blake, I need to go. I'll call you back in half an hour unless I hear from you first. Get over to DDC. Okay?"

"Fine," I replied. "But, Emma—"

Before I could continue, the line was disconnected. I looked at my phone briefly before dropping it in my back pocket. I rested my hands on my dresser and leaned on it, closing my eyes, and shook my head. When I opened them, I saw two items on top of it: the novel I had purchased less than an hour ago and the ring.

I opened the top of the messenger bag still strapped over my shoulder and dropped the book inside and closed it back up. Then I picked up the ring, looked at it briefly, and placed it inside my front pocket.

When I got to the front door, I turned and looked all around, trying to think of anything else I might need.

Deciding that I had what I needed for a few days, I exited, walked down the long hallway that led to my apartment, and descended the stairs. I stepped out onto Madison and walked a block west and then went south on Pitt Street, where my car was parked two blocks farther south at the corner of Pitt and Pendleton.

While I preferred to take a taxi when traveling around Washington, I didn't want to leave my vehicle at home. I climbed into my black government-issued SUV and set my messenger bag on the passenger seat.

Starting the engine, I looked behind my vehicle through the rearview mirror and checked the other mirrors. I didn't see anyone besides an older woman walking north on Pitt. I put it into gear and left.

But I didn't head to the Washington DDC field office. I decided to drive to Charlie's, like I had planned.

Sometimes, you have to decide what you're willing to get in trouble for not doing. Chris and Jami would have to handle the ransomware cyberattack with Morgan and find a way to stop it without my help.

11

THE DRIVE TO CHARLIE'S WAS IN THE SAME DIRECTION AS THE new Department of Domestic Counterterrorism field office. From the Kingsley, I began heading north toward Washington, where I'd pass Reagan National and take George Washington Memorial Parkway the rest of the way. Only I wouldn't exit at I-395 to go into DC. I'd stay on the parkway and loop around Arlington to meet my friend at his home in Rosslyn.

As I passed the Potomac Yard neighborhood, I thought about the new DDC field office.

In the three months since it had opened, I hadn't visited it yet. I avoided it, actually. The office was across the street from the Hoover Building, which Chris Reed and Mark Reynolds, another Bureau agent I partnered closely with, worked from. Back in Chicago when I ran the first DDC office, the Bureau moved from their downtown location to a new building practically across the street from us. We joked that they were keeping an eye on us, only to confirm later that they actually were monitoring DDC, a subgroup of the Central Intelligence Agency formed to fight and prevent domestic terrorism within the United States.

Soon after I was fired as the SAIC, my boss, DDC Director Roger Shapiro, became friends with the FBI's Bill Landry. When Landry got transferred from Chicago to Washington to run the Bureau's DC field office, Shapiro made it a point to keep that friendship going and began collaborating more closely with the FBI. Since then, Landry had been promoted to deputy director, second only to FBI Director Peter Mulvaney.

When it came time to build a second DDC office, Shapiro chose Washington and had it intentionally located as close as possible to the Bureau's Hoover Building, in the spirit of collaboration and partnership. That was how Jami had explained it last Christmas when I visited her in Chicago before we left for New York.

As I approached Reagan National, my mind began to wander, and I started to think about Jami again and the way I had walked away from her six months ago on that cold New Year's Eve night in New York.

Jami and the rest of my team had just helped me take down the terrorists responsible for coordinating a cyberattack against the government along with trying to dismantle a surveillance program that was operating out of a secret NSA building in the heart of Manhattan called TITANPOINTE. With her help, I had killed both of the men involved: a guy named Jeff Clayton and a Russian man named Nikolai Ivanov.

And the last thing Ivanov had said to me, moments before I sent him racing toward his death, was that while I might be stopping *him*, he had already relayed to his people who I was and who I worked for.

And that scared the hell out of me. Not for my own

safety, but for Jami's. If it hadn't been for those words spoken to me, Jami and I might still be together. And that ring would be on her finger, not in my pocket.

A more than competent field agent, Jami Davis had proved many times that she could hold her own in any kind of situation. I had hired her back at DDC in Chicago, and what really bonded us together was the kidnapping of then-Senator Keller and everything she did to help me find the man and get him back alive.

But I had lost my father in the process. Having already lost my wife to the same people responsible for Keller's kidnapping, the only way I could keep Jami safe was by making the hard choice of walking away.

Shortly after Margaret Keller's funeral, I learned that Jami had gone ahead with the transfer to the Washington field office that I had tried to persuade her not to go through with. But she was just as determined about going after what she wanted as she was beautiful—and that was what I loved about her.

I had felt cursed. Like anyone that got close to me, anyone I cared about, either ended up hurt or dead. That was a hard burden to carry. It made me feel broken, and she didn't understand when I walked away.

After I ended things, I came back to Washington and was debriefed on my actions from that night by Bill Landry at the Bureau. I tried to move on with my life and focused on my job working for the president. Jami never called me after that night. I never called her, either. I got occasional updates from Chris Reed and Morgan Lennox, but I avoided Jami and the new DDC field office. I had spent the last six months looking over my shoulder every day, waiting for the Russians to come after me like Ivanov said they would. Based on what Sammy told me about the men that roughed him up, my past had finally caught up to me.

Just as I passed the airport, I heard the muffled sound of my cell phone ringing. Keeping my eyes on the road, I reached inside my messenger bag and felt around for it. I found the phone and held it up to my face.

It was Morgan Lennox. I knew why he was calling, and I didn't want to have that conversation right now.

Dropping the phone, I turned on the radio and heard a woman's voice giving a report on the ransomware attack. She said that Chicago-area hospitals were in crisis mode and turning away new patients. Seven people had died already, and their deaths were being directly attributed to nonfunctioning machines as a result of the ransomware attacks that had made those machines, critical to hospital workers, inoperable.

Then she began to give an update on Washington-area impacts. I raised the volume and held my breath.

"DC hospitals are now preparing for the worst as they struggle with the ransomware attack, with the only two facilities reporting major impacts being Walter Reed Army Medical Center and Children's National Medical Center," the reporter said. She went on, and I lowered the volume as I realized in that moment that, while the malware was spreading virally, the creators also seemed to be targeting specific groups.

In this case, veterans and children.

The woman ended the broadcast, saying they would return with more on the ransomware attack after the commercial break. I turned the radio off and drove in silence for several minutes, hearing nothing but the drone of road noise on my way to Charlie's. I thought about the veterans and children impacted by the attack. I held the steering wheel with one hand and wiped sweat from my brow as I started to feel anxious.

The situation at the hospitals started to weigh heavily on my heart as I looked up and noticed a sign up ahead, farther down the road, directing travelers to take the next exit for I-395 if driving into Washington.

I felt my heart begin to race again. It beat hard and fast in my chest as I started to think about my father and the days and nights that Jami had spent with me by his side in the Palos Community Hospital close to Chicago. I remembered the sounds of the equipment and the frenzy of doctors and nurses who would enter and leave, checking the readouts on the machines and monitoring my father's health, making adjustments when needed. And I thought about the innocent children who were also now in harm's way. Gripping my steering wheel tighter and becoming more upset about the situation with the ransomware the more I thought about it, I heard my cell ring. I reached for it and saw that it was Morgan calling again.

"Morgan, I'm five minutes out," I said as I answered the call.

"Thanks, mate," he replied. "Talk to you in a bit."

He disconnected the call, and I dropped my phone back into the messenger bag on the passenger seat. Looking over my right shoulder, I veered into the exit lane on my right, cutting a car off in the process as I took the exit for I-395 and got on the bridge that would take me across the Potomac and into Washington.

In the distance, I could see the Washington Monument. I accelerated and drove my vehicle hard and fast.

I was headed to DDC.

12

Meg Taylor was seated at O'Malley's desk, waiting for her call to be returned and wondering if she was onto something by looking into the man who she didn't recognize. She hoped she wasn't wasting her time.

Taylor held the picture she'd taken from the CNN guy and stared intensely at the face of one man.

Dropping the photograph onto the desk, Meg moved her mouse to wake up her laptop and reentered her credentials so she could access her system at the *Times*. She opened a web browser and did an online search for President Keller's aides. She found a White House web page and scrolled down the page slowly.

On the "Executive Office of the President" page, Taylor found a listing of Keller's closest advisors, overseen by Chief of Staff Emma Ross. Meg scrolled through names, titles, and stared at the corresponding headshots, which included some of the people shown in the photograph resting on the desk next to her.

Past the long listing of deputy chief of staff for legislative affairs, the press secretary, the director of strategic communications and countless other roles, Meg found a link at the very bottom of the web page indicating that there was a separate listing for Keller's senior advisors. She clicked on it and waited.

A few seconds later, she received a 404 error. The link was broken.

Meg leaned in and furrowed her brow. Scratching her head, she studied the URL at the top of the page and noticed a misspelling. Wondering if that was the problem, she moved her mouse to place the cursor on the misspelled word, corrected it, and hit enter. Immediately, she was taken to the correct location.

Taylor scrolled through quickly, looking only at the headshots of the president's closest aides and ignoring the accompanying titles, long biographies, and details of their current responsibilities. She only wanted information on the one man she didn't recognize in the picture. At the very bottom, the last senior advisory position listed within the national security advisory staff, Meg found what she was looking for.

Picking up the photograph from the desk, she held it next to the laptop's screen and compared the images.

It was the same man. Mid-thirties, same boyish look to him, and the same Secret Service-like appearance about him. And the website listed the same name that was on the photo, handwritten by the CNN guy.

Dropping the picture, Meg whispered to herself, "Senior advisor on issues of domestic counterterrorism," She scrolled down to read through the official bio, which was noticeably shorter than everyone else's.

"Blake Jordan serves as a senior advisor to the president and has held roles in the intelligence community," she said aloud and scrolled down, confirming that there was no other information listed.

Meg scratched her head, feeling annoyed and wondering if there might be anything on a non-White House website about the man. In the past, she'd seen plenty of hit pieces written about incoming presidents, on both sides of the aisle, listing their newly appointed advisors with their background and experience.

She accessed a search engine and performed a search on "Blake Jordan" in quotes. There were no results.

"What?" Taylor whispered to herself as she leaned in to look at the screen on her laptop. She tried the search again, this time removing the quotes, and was presented with a couple of hundred results. Reading through the first page of results, none of them referred to the presidential aide that she wanted to know more about. But that gave her an idea based on something one of her former colleagues had shown her once. Accessing a website known as the "internet archive," she once again tried her search.

This time, Taylor was given search results that did include the man who she was trying to learn more about. She found a twenty-year-old news article from the *Chicago Tribune* showing a younger James Keller standing next to another man with an arm around his shoulder. A teenage boy stood between the two men, holding a sign that read KELLER FOR SENATE with two hands. All three were smiling for the picture as they stood in front of several rows of tables and chairs filled with smiling campaign volunteers.

The caption under the photograph explained that Ben and his son, Blake Jordan, were helping Keller, a family friend, the day he was elected to the senate. Meg read the accompanying story, but there was no further mention of Jordan. She picked up the photo again and held it next to her monitor and stared at the two images—one of a boy; the other, a man—curious about the twenty years between the two photos.

She looked through the rest of the online results, but there wasn't much more on the man who didn't seem to exist or, at the very least, didn't believe in having any kind of online footprint. As Meg went back to the picture of the young Jordan and studied his warm smile, her cell rang, and she fumbled to answer the call.

Turning back to the entrance to the press corps offices, Meg said, "Hello?" and waited for a response.

"It's me," the caller finally replied after a long pause. "I got the information you asked me for."

Meg moved her gaze back to the image on her screen. "I figured it out on my own. Jordan's known Keller for a long time," she said. "Looks like his dad was friends with the man while he ran for senate about twenty years back. Jordan probably went into the service, based on his physical appearance. Keller got elected and hired the guy. It wouldn't be the first time a sitting president appointed a family member or friend as one of their aides. It actually happens a lot." Taylor paused and added, "There's nothing here."

Another long pause. "That's where you're wrong. There's a lot more to it than that, Megan," said the voice.

A confused look fell upon Taylor's face. "Then why don't you tell me what I'm missing?"

"I'll tell you," the man continued. "But I want to see you again." He paused once more. "Tonight."

Taylor thought about it for a few seconds, holding her cell up to her ear with one hand and chewing on a fingernail with the other. Then her thoughts drifted back to the ultimatum her boss had given her earlier. "Fine," she finally replied after weighing the options in her mind and realizing that she didn't have any.

"Blake Jordan," the man said, speaking immediately, "grew up in Oklahoma City. At seventeen, moved to Chicago with his parents shortly after Timothy McVeigh bombed the Murrah Federal Building. His father, Ben Jordan, worked with the ATF out of that building. Requested a transfer. My guess is the whole experience was traumatic for his son; the guy probably wanted a new start in a new city. So they moved."

"Go on," said Meg as she rummaged through her desk, found a pencil, and started writing on a yellow pad.

"Ben Jordan worked with another ATF man, a guy with high hopes of doing more than a desk job. The Chicago ATF office is where Ben Jordan met James Keller shortly before Keller retired to run for senate."

"I found a picture," said Meg, looking up from her yellow pad. "Ben and Blake helped with the campaign."

"That was part of the deal," said the caller. "My sources tell me that Ben Jordan agreed to help Keller if Keller—a former SEAL himself—would help train Ben's son, who wanted to join the Navy after his senior year. Keller trained the boy. After graduation, he got in. Spent time at Camp Rhino in Afghanistan as part of SEAL Team Three during Operation Enduring Freedom before leaving the service to head up the CIA's newly formed Department of Domestic Counterterrorism back in Chicago." The man paused before continuing. "And, Megan, that's just the beginning. You're not going to believe what I'm about to tell you."

13

DIMITRI WAS SEATED NEXT TO MAKAR, READING THE NEWS reports on the man's laptop, when he leaned back in his chair and stared across the room, thinking. "I am reconsidering your plan, Makar."

Andrei looked up over his screen and glared at Dimitri. He did not speak immediately and instead looked back to his screen, deciding on the best course of action that should be taken given their current situation.

"Andrei," continued the young man, "I agree that we strike early, but how will we know when to begin?"

"If you are not comfortable with striking now, then we can coordinate with our man on the inside. But he would prefer that we did not call," he answered with a hint of irritation in his voice. "But if you take the advice of my friend here—" he gestured to Makar "—then we move forward. But understand, Dimitri, that this could create complications for us, as it deviates from the plan we have all agreed to follow already."

Andrei's reply was both sharp and calculated, a way to answer the question while pointing out the obvious flaw with the new plan that had been suggested. Looking to his right, Andrei locked eyes with Makar, who had made a logical suggestion to get the men out of their predicament and get things back on track. Deep down, Andrei knew that the new plan Makar had suggested might work, but he didn't want things to get back on track. He wanted the plan to fail to show Dimitri that he was incapable of leading the operation.

"Then tell me," said Dimitri as he leaned forward and rested his arms on the table, "how do we proceed? If we want to initiate this phase of the plan earlier than originally intended, as Makar has suggested," he said, turning briefly to his left before continuing, "should we begin now, or should we continue to wait?"

Sitting up straight, Andrei replied, "We wait."

The young man pushed his chair away from the table with his legs and stood. He rested his hands on the back of his chair and glanced down at Makar. "I would also like to hear your thoughts on this."

Makar looked across the table and saw the expression on Andrei's face, urging Makar to agree with him. Turning to his right, Makar became nervous. "There are pros and cons to both approaches, Dimitri."

"Explain."

"If we proceed now, it will create chaos within the organization. They will refocus their efforts. Other agencies will pick up the slack. It will create a temporary distraction, which will be dealt with. But—" he paused and looked up at Dimitri, who was still hovering over him "—it could also help draw out our target."

"And if we wait?"

Makar checked his watch briefly before answering. "If we wait, then we can play this out a little longer. Maybe

Andrei is right, Dimitri. There is no need to rush anything. We wait as long as we need to. Why play a card if we do not have to?" Makar lowered his gaze and made eye contact with Andrei, who nodded his appreciation. "I agree with Andrei. We should continue to wait until an opportunity can present—"

Before Makar could finish, Andrei's cell rang again. "Tell him we will wait," ordered Dimitri, agreeing with the two men and making the decision to continue to delay the next phase of the coordinated attack.

But Andrei held the phone up to his face and quickly glanced back at Dimitri. "That is not who is calling." Answering his cell, Andrei listened carefully, keeping his eyes fixed on the other two men as he listened. Andrei smiled and told the caller to give him a moment to relay the information. "It is our other man, Dimitri. After three days of waiting, our other target has retrieved his vehicle. He is on the move now."

A smile grew over Dimitri's face. He walked around the table, closer to Andrei. "Is he following him?"

"Yes."

Dimitri looked down and nodded to himself, realizing that he was being presented with a new option. "Where is he going?" he asked as he leaned on the table in front of Andrei and stared down at the man.

Bringing the burner phone back to his face, Andrei asked the person on the other end of the line for their location and where he thought their target was headed. "He just crossed the river and is passing the Southwest Waterfront. He appears to be heading to the Hoover Building. Do you want him intercepted?"

Dimitri thought about it and then answered, "No. Tell him to follow from a distance and not be seen."

Andrei relayed the order and kept the burner phone pressed hard against his ear, providing Dimitri and Makar with the play-by-play as their man followed the target throughout the streets of Washington.

"He's slowing down," said Andrei a minute later before a surprised expression appeared on his face. "Dimitri, he did not stop at the Hoover Building. He appears to be going to DDC across the street."

"Quick," ordered Dimitri. "Have him back off and call our other man. Try to get a visual confirmation."

Andrei did as he was told and immediately contacted his other man in the field, waiting on a motorcycle on D Street with a view of both DDC Washington and the FBI's Hoover Building directly in front of him.

"It's me," said Andrei. "There should be a black SUV approaching the building. Do you see it yet?" After a moment, Andrei looked at Dimitri and shook his head, prompting the young man to stretch out his hand.

Taking the phone out of Andrei's hand, Dimitri said, "Listen to me very carefully. I need you to make a visual confirmation on the man who is approaching the building. He should be passing you any moment now." Andrei and Makar watched the young man as he began to pace around the large Persian Room.

Ten seconds passed before a smile appeared across Dimitri's face. "Excellent," he said. "I want you to wait five minutes, then proceed as planned. I will have Andrei contact you when we are ready to begin the next phase. Do you understand?" Dimitri paused to hear the man's confirmation before disconnecting the call.

Handing the phone back to Andrei, Dimitri went to his chair and remained standing. "He has a visual on our target.

He's entering the building now. We will execute the next phase of the plan in five minutes."

"If you want to take him out, then we should do it now," urged Andrei. "Proceed within the next minute. Five minutes is too long to wait, Dimitri. By then it will be too late."

Dimitri smiled again and placed a hand on Makar's shoulder. "And what do you think will happen?"

Makar shook his head, not following where the young man was going with this. "There will be chaos," he finally replied. "Panic. The entire building will go on lockdown. If we miss, our target will be safe inside."

"Trapped inside," replied Dimitri, squeezing Makar's shoulder. "The Bureau is across the street. They will send in a team to secure the facility. Until that happens, Jordan will be trapped inside with no way out." Dimitri smiled and patted Makar's shoulder. "My brother is right—let us have some fun with our target."

Letting go of Makar's shoulder, Dimitri ran a palm over his scalp as he turned around and started to think through the possibilities of what he could do to the man. "Let him feel as helpless as I felt when I learned the news of my father," he said softly as his smile broadened. "Now we're really going to have some fun."

14

Entering the underground parking garage of the new Washington DDC field office, I stopped at the guardhouse and showed my credentials to the woman inside and watched as she looked them over. "Executive Office of the President," she said, holding my badge up as her eyes darted back and forth, comparing the picture to my profile. "What's your business?" she asked in a matter-of-fact tone of voice.

"I work for the president of the United States," I replied. "There's an ongoing investigation on the cyberattack from today. I'm here to assist the Bureau and represent President Keller on the matter."

"Just a moment," the woman said and closed a small sliding window and picked up a phone.

Glancing at my rearview mirror, I saw a man on a motorcycle drive by slowly, looking in my direction. The guy saw me notice him. Suddenly, he turned, looked over his shoulder, and sped off down the street. The sound of his engine was loud and echoed throughout the first level of the garage as the woman slid open the window and stretched out her hand. I reached out and accepted my credentials back from her.

"You know where you're going?" she asked.

"No, ma'am."

She stuck her thumb out and jerked it behind her. "Only two levels, you're on the first. I suggest you go up to two and park there. Not a lot of staff here yet, there should be plenty of parking near the entrance still."

I smiled and thanked the woman as she pressed a button to raise the bar to let me enter. As I passed through, I heard the engine from the bike again. Turning my SUV to the right to drive the vehicle up to the second level, I saw the biker pass by slowly. This time, he wasn't looking in my direction, but he did slow as he passed the entrance to the garage and disappeared a few feet ahead, just out of my line of sight.

Deciding it wasn't anything to worry about, I continued to drive my SUV up the steep turn and around the curve, where I found three rows of vehicles. One to my right next to the field office entrance and the other two rows on my left. I noticed an empty spot in the far corner, so I pulled into the space and parked.

Going through my messenger bag, I grabbed my phone but left everything else on the passenger seat. I didn't feel like dealing with security if it was anything like the Chicago field office. I just wanted to get in, help support the team to figure out how to stop the ransomware attack, and then head over to Charlie's.

I walked quickly to the entrance, passing the line of vehicles next to the door, and slowed as I approached. Two guards were seated behind a desk. Both looked me over as I opened the door and stepped inside.

I reached for my credentials again and handed them to the man on the right. "I'm here to see Chris Reed."

He accepted my badge and looked it over as the guard on my left stared blankly at me. "Agent Reed with the Bureau?" the man on the right asked as he looked up at me and slowly handed my badge back to me.

"Yes," I said. "He's here, working with DDC on today's cyberattack. He wanted me to meet him here."

The man nodded. "I know Reed, but haven't seen him yet. You sure he's not over at the Hoover Building?"

My eyes narrowed as I slowly shook my head. Looking past the men into the secure facility, I saw a frenzy of agents and analysts inside. "There must be some kind of mistake," I said and dug into my back pocket.

Finding my cell, I started to call Chris before realizing that I didn't have a signal from where I was standing. Maybe if I was a little farther inside the field office, I'd be able to get a strong enough signal, but right now I had no way of calling my friend. "He said he was headed here to work with someone."

"And who was he going to work with, Mr. Jordan?" asked the guard on my left, speaking for the first time. The way he said it told me that he was suspicious of me. I didn't blame him and had hired men at the Chicago office just like him to keep the team I led safe. "Have a name?" he added, looking me over.

I hesitated and glanced up again to look through the glass doors and took a deep breath. "Jami Davis."

Looking down to the guard on my left, he nodded his approval. "Alright, have a seat. We'll make a call to let Agent Davis know you're here. In the meantime, my friend here already scanned your badge, so go ahead and sign in for me," he said, looking at the registry on top of the counter. "If Davis is expecting you," the man added, his eyes making sure we understood each other, "she'll come out and get you."

"Fine," I said as I grabbed the pen from the clipboard and signed the next blank space on the registry.

Setting the pen down, I decided to remain standing as the guard on my left dropped his gaze and ran a finger down what I guessed to be a listing of employees at the small field office. He picked up the phone, looked back at the listing, and punched four digits into the phone as I felt my heart starting to race again.

After several moments, the guard finally got a hold of Jami and told her that she had someone waiting for her in the lobby. He said my name, paused, and repeated it again before adding, "Yes, I'm sure, ma'am."

Dropping the phone back into its cradle, the guy looked back at me with approval. "She'll be right out."

I crossed my arms and looked back through the glass doorway and started thinking about Jami. We hadn't said much to each other at Margaret Keller's funeral. It didn't seem appropriate, so we had kept the conversation light, focusing on the memories of the first lady instead of the unresolved issues between us.

The glass in the doors and the entire wall separating the interior of the field office to the small lobby where I stood was textured. While I could see movement inside as employees passed by, I couldn't make out faces. Waiting for Jami to arrive, I watched the occasional passerby, wondering if it was her as an employee walked past me every few seconds. Then in front of me, I noticed someone headed straight for the door.

It opened slowly as I caught myself holding my breath.

Jami was stunning. She wore a white blouse underneath

a black jacket with black pants. She tucked a lock of her shoulder-length brown hair behind an ear and squinted as she stared at me. "Blake?" she said to me.

"Chris asked me to meet him here to help with the ransomware attack." I looked at the guards to my right. "They're saying he hasn't been here today." I looked back and shrugged. "Maybe he's on his way."

"He's not coming," she said and gestured for me to follow her in. "Come on, I'll bring you up to speed."

I nodded and walked past the two guards. Jami held the glass door open. I grabbed it and followed her in. Once inside, I let go of the heavy glass door and just stood there, looking around the new field office as Jami crossed her arms and stared at me taking everything in. "Looks just like the one in Chicago," I said as I continued to look all around. Jami narrowed her eyes and glared at me before turning to leave.

As I started to follow her back, there was an explosion behind me. The force of the blast pushed me forward, and I landed on top of Jami, knocking her down. I put my arm over her as I heard a high-pitched sound. When I opened my eyes, Jami and I turned back and saw black smoke billowing into the building.

15

A FEW SECONDS LATER, ORANGE FLAMES APPEARED FROM THE lobby with the dark smoke continuing to billow into the building. A small team of guards ran past us as Jami and I sat up and DDC went on lockdown.

"Are you okay?" I asked, looking over to Jami, and she nodded.

An alarm was triggered, and I heard a clicking sound from all of the doors inside the building locking at the same time. I got to my feet and helped Jami up. We looked out into the gaping hole that had just been created at the entranceway now being manned by four guards as they looked over the bodies of the two men I had spoken with when I arrived a few minutes earlier, and I realized that both of them were dead.

Keeping an arm around Jami, we continued to slowly walk backwards while the rest of the field office workers gathered around us, staring at the growing flames and realizing that DDC had just been bombed.

"Get Bill Landry on the phone!" yelled a woman approaching from behind, referring to the Bureau man in charge across the street. I turned and saw the middle-aged woman working her way through the group of agents as Jami stepped away to distance herself from me, and I realized that I still had my arm around her.

The special agent in charge moved past us and, when she got to the entrance, looked over the bodies of the two guards before staring out into the garage, taking in the damage that had been done. I heard the warble of sirens in the distance growing louder as the woman turned and started to walk back toward us.

"Are we still operational?" the woman yelled to one of her analysts.

"Still going, ma'am, no issues. Systems are up and running," a voice somewhere behind me yelled back.

"Are we missing anyone?" she asked, scanning the faces of her team, and then her eyes locked onto mine.

"Landry's on for you, ma'am," another voice shouted from a deck of cubicles behind me, and I noticed that the special agent in charge was wearing a wireless earpiece, which she pressed. She brought Bill Landry up to speed on the situation, warned him to get his people to lock down the Hoover Building in case a second attack was imminent, and asked for his assistance to bring a Bureau team in to secure the DDC facility.

As she continued to speak with the Bureau man, she kept her eyes fixed on mine. I understood why.

I looked away, trying to think through the last several minutes before the bombing and replaying what had happened in my mind. I had pulled into an open spot and parked. No other vehicles were driving through the garage, as far as I could tell, when the bomb had detonated. I remembered looking out into the garage briefly as I waited on Jami to come get me from the lobby, and I hadn't seen anything unusual.

That was when I remembered the man on the motorcycle at the entrance to the parking garage.

The alarm turned off, but all the doors within the building remained locked. I checked my cell and confirmed that I still had no coverage. I realized that I needed to get closer to the window on the other side of the room so I could try to get in touch with Chris Reed or Morgan Lennox. Then I had a better idea. Turning to Jami, I said, "Morgan told me he was working with you and a man here named Simon Harris." Looking across the large room, I added, "I need to talk with Simon right away. Can you take me to him?"

Looking back, I noticed the SAIC still staring at me as she finished her phone conversation with Landry. Jami started to scan the crowd, looking for Harris. When she couldn't find him, she pointed to the last cubicle at the end of a long row of workstations near the windows and said, "Simon's desk is at the end."

"Walk with me," I said as I put my hand on her back and ushered her through the crowd, turning back again to see the SAIC following me slowly while keeping a hand to her ear as she wrapped up with Landry.

Harris had the same type of wireless earpiece as the SAIC. It hooked over his ear, and I saw that he was talking with someone on the line. "Simon," I said when we reached the man's cubicle. I looked at Jami briefly as she crossed her arms, stood back, and glared at me again. "Are you on with Morgan Lennox?"

Simon didn't respond. He just leaned back in his chair, pushed his glasses up onto his nose, and stared.

"Let me talk to him," I said and held my hand out.

Harris looked at Jami, then back to me before removing his earpiece and handing it over to me.

I hooked it over my ear as I heard Lennox on the other end of the line say, "Hello? Simon, did I lose you?"

"Morgan, it's Blake," I said. "Five minutes before the explosion, there was a man on a motorcycle just outside the parking garage entrance. He made two passes before driving off. There was no other activity inside the garage." I watched Jami take another step away from me and sensed that something was wrong. "There was a CCTV camera right across the street that I noticed as I pulled in. See if you can identify—"

"Don't move," a woman said sharply, and I turned to see the SAIC standing behind me with two guards. The rest of the DDC agents and analysts were behind her, all staring at me as Jami stepped farther away.

"You there, mate?" Morgan asked in my earpiece, but I didn't answer him.

"Who are you, how did you enter this building, and what exactly is your business here?" asked the woman.

I looked to my right and watched as Jami fell in line and stood with the rest of her DDC counterparts and stared at me blankly. Realizing that I didn't have her support, and understanding why, I turned my gaze back to the SAIC. "My name is Blake Jordan," I said. "I work for the president on matters of domestic counterterrorism. Agent Reed asked me to meet him here to work with the Bureau on the cyberattack."

At the other end of the room, near the entrance, I heard the warble of police sirens growing louder as Bureau agents started to approach. I heard the sound of men on foot heading toward us from the garage.

"Arrest him and place him in holding room A," she ordered the two guards standing on both sides of her.

"Please," I said and backed up against the window as they approached. "I have information that can help."

"As far as I can tell," the woman said sharply, "you were our only visitor today. No one else has been to this office all day." She pointed to the lobby. "I have two men dead, and all of this happened after you arrived." Then she pointed at me. "Mr. Jordan, you will be detained until we know what happened here."

I held my hands up and stared at the woman as one of the guards took the earpiece off and handed it back to Simon while the other walked me forward and put my hands behind my back before cuffing my wrists.

I looked to my right and stared at Jami as she glared back at me. The guard snapped the cuffs tight and pushed me through the agency employees, who stared at me with contempt, while the second guard followed close behind. I looked over my shoulder and saw the SAIC walk quickly toward the lobby and meet the Bureau agents as they entered the field office. Her voice trailed off as I was moved farther away.

The guards directed me down a long corridor, stopped in front of an unmarked room, and pushed me inside. I leaned against the wall and closed my eyes. All I could see was Jami walking away from me.

16

FORTY-FIVE MINUTES LATER, I WAS STILL WAITING INSIDE THE holding room. I could hear men shouting from down the hallway, and I imagined the Bureau agents working to secure the facility. Twice they passed the room I waited in and looked inside, making eye contact with me before shifting their eyes around the rest of the room, as if to confirm that there wasn't anything inside that they should be double-checking.

After the second time they passed by, I heard an entry code being punched in outside the holding room.

The guard who had handcuffed me entered, told me to stand up from the table I was sitting at, and spun me around. I expected him to push me up against the wall and pat me down, something they had forgotten to do during the frenzy of the first few minutes after the attack when they brought me inside.

Instead, I heard the rattling of keys being fished out of a pocket behind me and, looking over my shoulder, I watched as the guard grabbed my wrists and started to take the handcuffs off.

"What are you doing?" I asked, but the guy didn't acknowledge my question.

Instead, he just tucked the cuffs into a compartment on his belt and placed a hand on my back. Gesturing toward the door, I noticed the other guard from earlier standing out in the hallway. "Go ahead and exit the room for me, Mr. Jordan," he said with a nod of his head toward the empty corridor and the open door.

"Where are we going?" I asked, but the guard refused to respond. Instead, he kept a hand outstretched and—after pausing a moment to think it through—I stepped out of the holding room and into the corridor.

The other guard took over, and the two of us walked back down the long, dark hallway I had traveled earlier as we turned to get back out onto the main floor where the DDC workstations were located. Looking to my right, I saw a mass of Bureau agents in the lobby area. I decided that they were still checking for additional explosive devices and making sure the building was secure and still operational.

I kept moving, assuming that the guard would escort me over to the Hoover Building across the street. Instead, he pointed to the far side of the room, where I saw an identical set of corridors on the opposite side. "This way," he grunted as I stepped back in line and walked with the man past the cubicle where Simon had been working and where I last saw Jami. Looking over the room, I saw that most of the staff had left.

Through the next corridor, we slowed as we approached a closed door, and the guard gave two hard knocks before pushing it open and gesturing for me to enter. I took a long look at the man before peering inside.

It was a large conference room with an oval table. The

special agent in charge, her analyst Simon Harris, Jami, and the Bureau's Bill Landry were seated. The SAIC stood as I entered, and the guard closed the door behind me. "My name is Lynne May," the woman said, extending her hand as she approached to introduce herself and then pulled out a chair between Jami and Landry. "Please have a seat, Mr. Jordan."

"Am I being detained?" I asked, still standing as May went to the head of the table and looked back at me.

She shot me a look, then briefly shifted her eyes over to Bill Landry as if to make sure that they were on the same page before her eyes returned to mine. "Agent Davis filled me in on who you are and what you do for the president," she replied as she eased into the office chair. Once settled in, May rested her arms on the table in front of her, brought her hands together, and interlocked her fingers before continuing. "Executive Office of the President. A good enough cover, I suppose. Hiding in plain sight can be effective."

"I asked you a question," I said, growing impatient with the woman. "Am I being detained—yes or no?"

"You are *not* being detained, Mr. Jordan." She paused as I pulled the chair out and reluctantly took a seat. "And I apologize that it took a while to clear you, but as a former special agent in charge, I'm sure you can understand the situation." May turned to Simon. "Harris reviewed the footage of the garage before the blast."

Simon looked up from his laptop and glared at me. "Trust, but verify," he said and kept his eyes on me.

There was something about Simon that bothered me, but I wasn't sure what it was. Landry leaned in and cocked his head toward me. "The Bureau's taking point on the bombing while DDC stays focused on the ransomware attack." He pointed toward the door. "My men swept the garage and the rest of the building."

I turned back to May. "Where's the rest of your team?" I asked, trying to understand where they had gone.

"Working from the Hoover Building," replied May. "Bill has the space for us, and my team can connect directly to the DDC systems remotely. We decided that until we stop the cyberattack and we can figure out what happened here and why, it would be better to have our people work together and focus our efforts on keeping one building and the area around it secure."

I narrowed my eyes and shook my head slowly. "Lynne," I began, trying to make sense of the situation, "what about the guy on the motorcycle?" I looked around the room. "Did you look into him?"

May nodded to Jami, who answered, "Blake, right after the blast, you asked me to take you to Simon's desk. Simon was talking to Morgan Lennox, and I heard you tell Morgan about the man on the bike that you said you saw outside the building when you arrived." She turned from me to Harris. "I had Simon access the CCTV cameras across the street that you mentioned. We saw the man you were talking about."

"Then," interrupted Landry, "Lynne asked Simon to access another camera and roll back the footage. We saw you approach the building. A car was following you. When you turned into DDC, the vehicle kept moving south past the Hoover Building. We pulled more footage farther back all the way to Alexandria."

I shook my head. "Are you telling me that someone followed me here all the way from my apartment?"

"Well, it sure as hell looks like it," snapped Landry. "Black Lincoln Town Car. Dark, tinted windows."

I leaned back in my chair and thought about Sammy and the call I had made to my friend Charlie. Whoever was looking for me might not have known where I lived, but they knew where my SUV was parked and waited for me to use it. "We need to pull more footage, figure out where the car came from."

"I tried," replied Simon. "There weren't any other cameras to pull from. The footage starts in Alexandria."

"What about the guy on the motorcycle? We need to know where he went and figure out if he's involved."

"Simon's on it," said May, shifting her eyes to Harris sitting next to her. "I've asked Morgan Lennox to focus on the ransomware attack with the Bureau's Cyber Division while Simon tries to locate the biker."

"Where's Chris Reed?" I asked, turning back to Landry. "I was supposed to meet him here to help him."

Bill Landry stood. "Lynne, I'll let you fill him in on the rest. I'll see you across the street in a few minutes."

May nodded as Landry left the room. "Mr. Jordan, the White House has made it clear that I am not to detain you. Seeing how you've apparently done nothing wrong, I won't. However," she glanced at Jami, "Agent Davis will take you to Reed and accompany you until this investigation is resolved. Understood?"

I thought about it and realized that I'd better play ball with the SAIC. "Understood," I replied and stood.

17

After Lynne May dismissed Jami and me, she told Simon to pack up his things and be ready to leave in five minutes. She advised him that they would be going across the street to work out of the Hoover Building. Jami went back to her cubicle, closed the lid to her laptop, and stuffed it inside a thin laptop bag. Strapping it over her shoulder, Jami passed her boss's office and asked Lynne May for a DDC loaner vehicle. May retrieved the keys to one of the SUVs parked on the ground floor and handed them to Jami.

The Bureau guys cleared the way for us to exit and allowed me to grab my messenger bag from my SUV.

Taking the stairs at the corner of the garage next to where I had parked my vehicle, we descended to the ground floor, and Jami pressed a button on the keychain as we approached a row of black, unmarked SUVs. We saw the parking lights illuminate on one of them as the doors unlocked, and we climbed inside.

Jami grabbed her phone, searched for a message she had received, and entered the address from the phone into the GPS system inside the vehicle. A woman's voice announced the address in east DC and said it would take fifteen minutes for us to arrive. I placed my messenger bag in between my feet, buckled the seatbelt, and held on tight as Jami threw the SUV into gear and navigated us out of the dark garage.

I tried calling the White House, but Emma Ross didn't answer her cell immediately, so I left a message for her to call me back. Turning to my left, I looked at Jami and said, "Fill me in, Jami. Where are we going?"

She glared at me again before turning her attention back to the road. "The Bureau got wind of some information a little over an hour ago, right before the bomb went off at DDC. Simon and Morgan were making progress on the ransomware when Chris called and said he wouldn't be able to help us out."

"Why not?"

"He said he'd been reassigned by Landry. Metro Police got an anonymous tip that they passed on to the Bureau, and Landry called Reed and told him to meet up with Mark Reynolds at the place we're going to."

"Landry has plenty of agents out in the field. Why call Chris if he was assigned to the ransomware attack?"

"I guess because he needed his experience."

Narrowing my eyes, I asked, "What's *that* supposed to mean?"

Jami shook her head. "All I know is that they found explosives. We'll know more when we get there."

I turned back to watch the road. There was a sharpness to Jami's voice, and I understood why it was there. Looking out the window at the passing buildings as we raced through the streets of Washington, I thought about the conversation with Lynne May a few minutes earlier. "You shouldn't have told her."

"What?"

"You shouldn't have told May about what I do for Keller. That's on a need-to-know basis, Jami."

"Blake, you showed up minutes before the field office was bombed. And I'm the one that let you inside. Besides," she said and paused before making a sharp right turn, "if I hadn't told her, Landry would have."

"Maybe," I said. "But knowing Landry, he'd have done anything he could to keep me detained."

Jami stepped hard on the accelerator and reached up to flip on the overhead police lights. I held on tight as she swerved around traffic. I tried to calm myself down, but my heart was racing. I wasn't sure if it was from the way Jami was driving or from being partnered with a woman I hadn't thought I'd work with again.

"If you were going to tell her, then why'd you let her detain me? Why didn't you say something while I was standing at Simon's desk?" I asked as she took another turn. "Instead, you just let her men take me away."

Jami looked to her left before turning again and starting to slow down as we approached the neighborhood we were headed to. Up ahead, I saw a cluster of police vehicles and a line of black SUVs and knew we had arrived. Jami took a deep breath before she finally answered me. "I wanted you to know how it felt."

I turned back. "How what felt?"

"Having someone walk away from you," she replied as she slowed to a stop and put the vehicle in park. "But you know what? At least I changed my mind. I made a bad decision, but I made up for it. I told May the truth, I told her that I let you in, and yes, I also told her about what you do for the president, Blake."

I kept my eyes on her. Jami's glare was gone and she just

looked me over with what felt like indifference. "Jami, I know you don't understand why I walked away from us. I don't expect you to. But the truth is—"

"The truth?" interrupted Jami. "The truth is, what you did to me is unforgivable, Blake." She paused, turned the police lights off, and unbuckled her seatbelt. "The truth is, you never really cared about me."

"That's not true, Jami."

"Could have fooled me," she said. "You don't walk away from someone you care about, someone you love."

I removed my seatbelt and rested my hands in my lap. I felt the outline of the ring in my pocket. The ring I had carried with me for six months now. The ring I had planned to give Jami underneath the fireworks at Navy Pier in Chicago on New Year's Eve. I remembered what her sister, Kate, had told me—that I could have the girl or the job, but I couldn't have both. She said that I was going to have to decide. And I had.

Jami and I sat in silence for what felt like an eternity. I wanted to tell her everything. I wanted to explain to her why I had walked away. But nothing came out. Jami shook her head slowly, and I could see the pain she had lived with since that night. She finally looked away, reached for the handle, and pulled it.

"Maybe when this is all over, we can—"

"I'm busy that day," she said sharply, then paused to regain her composure. Jami tucked a lock of brown hair behind an ear and dropped her gaze. "Sorry. I'm just stressed out over what happened at DDC."

"I know, we all are," I replied and reached over to put a hand on Jami's shoulder, but she pulled away from me. "One day you'll understand," I said and watched her slide out of the seat and stand at the door.

"Yeah." She sighed. "And by then, it won't matter anymore, will it?" Jami paused and looked me over. "I've said what needed to be said, and I'm over it now. See you inside," she said and slammed the door.

I watched the afternoon sunlight hit her dark brown hair as she stepped across the street, spoke with a couple of Bureau guys standing at the door, and went inside to meet with Chris Reed and Mark Reynolds.

I stepped out into the DC heat and jogged across the street to talk with the Bureau men so I could join her and the rest of the team. As I approached, I thought hard about what Jami had said, and my heart sank when I realized that she was right: by the time she understood, it wouldn't matter anymore.

18

DIMITRI AND HIS MEN WAITED ON REPORTS TO COME IN ON THE bombing of the Washington DDC field office, located just three miles southeast of their current location. Makar continued scanning various news websites as Andrei discussed next steps with Dimitri, who had taken a seat at the table across from him.

Andrei rummaged through a backpack and found a notepad and pencil. He leaned forward on the desk as Dimitri watched him outline the situation so he could offer a recommendation. "Dimitri," began Andrei, still maintaining his gaze on the notepad, "we do not yet have a report from inside DDC, but we can safely assume that the explosives were detonated as planned here," he said, sketching out the DDC floor plan. "The ransomware continues to spread, with two instances deployed, one in Chicago and the other here."

Dimitri remained expressionless, eyeing Andrei as he asked, "And our two assets? Where are they now?"

Before Andrei could respond, Makar turned his laptop around to show his screen to the two men sitting at the other end of the table. "We have confirmation, Dimitri. The *Washington Post* is reporting activity on D Street, just outside the Hoover Building." Makar turned the laptop back around and scrolled through the story before he continued. "Pedestrians reported hearing a loud explosion from the building directly across from the Navy Memorial Plaza," he said and glanced up at Dimitri. "No word on casualties yet."

"What else does it say?" asked Dimitri as he stood and walked behind Makar to read over his shoulder.

"Police and unmarked vehicles arrived immediately," replied Makar, still scrolling through the story. "Federal agents rushed the parking garage on the lower floor of the building that serves as the Washington field office of the Department of Domestic Counterterrorism." Scanning further, he added, "Plainclothes men and women, directed by Bureau agents, emerged and then proceeded to walk across Ninth Street, carrying computer equipment, then proceeded to enter the J. Edgar Hoover Building across the street."

"Why have we not heard from our asset on the ground? We should not have to rely on the media, Makar."

The man shook his head. "Something must be wrong. Or maybe—"

Andrei's cell phone rang from across the table, and the man answered immediately. "Yes?" he asked and listened carefully as Dimitri stepped away from Makar and rounded the table, staring intensely at Andrei, who pulled the phone down, away from his face. "Our man is now inside the Hoover Building."

"Let me speak with him," demanded Dimitri as Andrei held a hand up to caution the young man.

"Remember, Dimitri—the plan was for him to only speak with me. You and I both know how this works."

Dimitri nodded, remembering the conversation on the drive back to DC, when Andrei had advised that voice signature technology could help the Americans figure out what was going on if they were not careful. "Ask him about the explosives," Dimitri said softly so his voice would not get picked up in the background.

Andrei brought the phone back up and asked, "Is everything in place for the delivery?" trying to conceal the actual question due to the keyword triggers that he knew were monitored by agencies such as the NSA.

A smile grew on Andrei's face as he nodded his acknowledgement to Dimitri. "Excellent," he said, keeping his eyes set on the young man. "The transport is ready. Delivery is expected to take place within the hour."

But the smile was short-lived. A concerned look appeared on his face and Andrei shook his head quickly. "What kind of problem? What happened?"

He pushed himself away from the table and stood, pressing the burner phone harder against his ear. Andrei turned and looked over his shoulder at Dimitri and Makar as he started walking around the large room before saying something into the phone out of earshot of the other men. Dimitri stepped closer and watched as the man finished his conversation with the caller and returned to his partners a minute later.

Disconnecting the call, Andrei threw the phone on the table and said, "Jordan and the woman are safe. There were two casualties. I was unable to infer who they were, but I trust that it does not matter to us."

"What else?" asked Dimitri.

Andrei remained standing and placed both hands on the back of his chair. "He also confirmed the report that

Makar read to us. It seems that the two agencies have their people together. The plan is on track."

"So they are now one team working jointly from the Hoover Building?"

"Yes."

"Excellent," said Dimitri. "What about Mr. Jordan and the woman? Are they together?"

Andrei nodded that they were.

"Good. It will be more meaningful if he is present. We need to find them now."

"He said they were sent to the address to meet with Bureau agents and help with the investigation. They're either there now or will be arriving shortly." Andrei paused for several seconds before adding, "Dimitri, he said he will not call us again and asked me not to make any further contact at this time. He is worried about our communications being intercepted. But he will continue to do his part as we do ours."

Dimitri nodded to himself. He picked up the phone from the table and tossed it to Andrei. "He has done us a great service, Andrei. Quick—contact our men. Send them to go find Jordan and the girl right away."

"How?" asked Makar, still seated at the end of the table as he lowered the lid to his laptop again.

"There is no doubt that they are looking for our man on the bike," replied Dimitri. "So let them find him."

"And then what?" pressed Makar.

"They will go after him. Have our other asset ready to take out their vehicle from behind. Surprise them."

Andrei held onto his phone, thinking through the plan that Dimitri was suggesting to them. Looking up, he asked, "How do you want us to play this, Dimitri? Capture them and take them both to the safe house?"

"Is that what you suggest?" he asked as Andrei's eyes darted to Makar, then back to Dimitri.

Andrei nodded, and the younger man shook his head slowly, disappointed with the response Andrei had given him.

"That is not how you convince a man to do something for you, my brother." Dimitri let his words hang in the air before he continued. "Bring Jordan to the safe house. I will visit him and tell him what I want."

"And the woman? What do you want to do with her once Jordan is taken?" asked Andrei.

Dimitri thought about it. He brought his hands behind his back and began pacing the room again.

Andrei kept his eyes on the young man pacing the floor, deciding the fate of the woman. "Dimitri?" repeated Andrei, becoming impatient. "Tell me what it is that you want our man to do with Agent Davis."

Dimitri turned back. "Have him wait until Jordan has been taken away first." He paused. "Then kill her."

19

I CLIMBED THE STEPS OUTSIDE THE HOME, STEPPED UP TO THE open doorway, and showed my credentials to the men who were posted just outside the door as I approached. Inside, I saw a frenzy of ATF and Bureau agents from the Explosives Unit loading up boxes. Two of them walked past me. I turned and watched them place the boxes into a large truck parked at the curb as another set of agents oversaw the process.

The guys at the door let me inside, and I scanned the home as I entered. It was small and unoccupied. There was no furniture in the main room, and the kitchen was empty. The air conditioner was blowing hard, keeping the place cool from the extreme summertime Washington heat, and the lights were on.

Standing in the foyer, I saw Jami near the kitchen, talking with Mark Reynolds, Chris Reed's partner at the FBI. From a room to my right, I recognized Chris's voice. I stepped through the doorway as Reed looked over, nodded to me, wrapped up his conversation with an ATF agent, and walked over to talk with me.

"Hey, man," said Reed as he extended his hand. "Landry called about the DDC bombing. What happened?"

I shook my head. "DDC's looking into it. They evacuated the building, and Landry suggested that Lynne May move her people over to the Hoover Building." I paused for a moment and added, "It went off right as I stepped into the field office, Chris. Knocked Jami and me over. If it had gone off a few seconds earlier..."

I didn't finish my sentence. I didn't have to. Looking past Chris, I saw a small stack of C-4 explosives in the corner of the room. The ATF agent along with a Bureau counterpart stepped back into the room with a few more boxes and carefully lifted the explosives, one brick at a time, until a box was filled and taken out.

"What are we dealing with here, Chris?" I asked, and he nodded to the doorway.

"Let's get out of their way and I'll fill you in."

I followed Chris into the kitchen. We joined Jami and Mark, and I shook the man's hand and crossed my arms as the four of us huddled together for Reed to bring Jami and me up to speed on the situation.

"Ninety minutes ago, DC Metro Police received an anonymous tip. An intruder was apparently breaking into homes throughout the neighborhood, looking to make a quick buck." Reed paused before continuing. "Apparently, he broke into this one sometime this morning. Said he noticed it was empty, but when he checked that room—" Reed pointed to the room we had just exited from "—he found the explosives."

"An honest criminal," said Jami with a tone of voice that said she was skeptical. "So the place is vacant?"

"Yeah," replied Reed.

"Then why's the power on?" I asked. "We have lights and air-conditioning."

Reynolds cleared his throat and said, "We looked into that. The house is owned by an older couple living in Florida. They've been trying to sell the place and had to keep the power on for showings. We contacted them, and they said they recently fired their realtor and were planning on coming back next month." He turned to look behind him briefly before adding, "My guess is someone's been watching the place and saw it's been empty for a while. It had air-conditioning to keep the explosives cool, so they decided to use it."

"But why store it here?" I asked as the ATF and Bureau agents walked outside to transfer more explosives into the vehicle out at the curb while another pair of agents stepped inside with more boxes and entered the room to collect the remaining explosives. "Chris, how much are you guys seizing here?"

"Hard to say," replied Reed. "We also found bomb-making equipment, weapons, clothing, wigs, and photographs of DC buildings along with maps of the city. Somebody was planning something big."

I looked past Jami, out the open front door, and fixed my eyes on the men carefully loading the boxes inside the large truck, and turned back to Reed. I nodded to the truck. "Where are you guys taking it?"

"Hoover Building before we send it off to TEDAC," he replied, referring to the Terrorist Explosive Device Analytical Center, an interagency organization located in Huntsville, responsible for assisting with acquiring, analyzing, and linking explosives to the terrorists that made them. "Landry's having our Explosives Unit document whatever we were able to secure here and make it safe for transport—"

Before Reed could continue, I heard the sound of my cell ringing in my back pocket. At the same time, Jami's cell rang, and she moved toward the front door to take the call. I checked the screen and saw that it was Morgan. "Go ahead, Morgan. I'm here with Chris Reed and Mark Reynolds. You're on speakerphone."

"Glad to hear that you and Jami are okay," said Lennox before sharing the reason behind his call. "Blake, I think I may have figured out how to stop the ransomware attack from spreading. I'm still validating, but from what I can tell, the rate of its spread seems to have decreased dramatically over the last ten minutes."

I looked up at Chris and Mark and saw that we all shared the same relieved expression. "How'd you do it?"

"When I finally got Simon out of my hair, I started looking at the code a little more closely, and I think I found a way to slow it down. And I may have even stopped it—not sure yet. And all it took was ten bucks."

"Explain," I said.

Morgan paused before continuing. "I was reverse-engineering the code and noticed that the ransomware's programmers had added a module to check whether a certain gibberish URL led to a live website or not. I stared at the thing for twenty minutes, curious about why that piece of code was there. I copied the URL and plugged it into my web browser to see what was there. The URL wouldn't resolve, the site wasn't live."

Trying to understand, I asked, "So what did you do?"

"I registered the bloody domain, went back into the code, and executed it in our sandbox environment. The thing wouldn't work anymore. It seems that the people who stole this from the NSA had added a kill switch and embedded it into the code in a way that wasn't easy to spot at first. I'm guessing it was there so they could rein in the monster they had created if they ever needed to after deploying the thing. As long as the domain wasn't active, the module had no effect on the ransomware's spread." Morgan paused. "Actually, mate, I'm surprised that Simon didn't notice it. It was hard to miss once you found the module."

"So then we're good?" asked Chris Reed, taking a step closer to me. "The threat is over now, Morgan?"

"No," replied Lennox. "Activating the kill switch seems to have stopped the spread. But the damage has already been done. Computer systems already infected with the malware are still rendered useless. The ransomware is still demanding money, which still isn't working, even if you pay it. I tried paying the ransom in our sandbox environment after I registered the domain, and that had no effect, it seems."

I looked up and noticed Jami across the room. She had a concerned look to her. I thanked Morgan and told him I'd call him later. Jami ended her call and stepped closer to me. "Blake, we need to go right now."

"You got something?" I asked as I walked around the kitchen counter and approached the door.

"Simon thinks he's found the biker."

20

Meg Taylor sat quietly as the taxi driver headed northwest into the Washington suburbs. Prior to leaving the White House Press Corps offices, Meg had taken her time to write a story that would capture *New York Times* readers' attention—really the attention of half the nation who wanted President Keller out—making sure that she had accounted for all of the talking points her informant had given her earlier.

She knew the story would rock the nation and damage the president's image as a by-the-book leader.

Before leaving the White House, Meg saved the story to a thumb drive, printed a hard copy, and started to email a copy to her boss, Robert King. But before sending the file, Taylor began to have second thoughts.

If what her informant had told her was true, the ramifications for the sitting president would be explosive. There would be an investigation. If the report gained enough traction and media attention, a special prosecutor might be appointed. And like Woodward and Bernstein, she'd be at the center of the investigation. For better or worse, if King ran with the story, she knew her life would be changed forever.

Meg's cell phone rang as the cab entered the residential neighborhood of Crestwood. Glancing at the number, Meg sent the caller to voicemail to avoid discussing what she was about to do and risk being overheard by the taxi driver. Besides, she figured she could just call the man back as soon as she was done. She had enough to worry about and was trying to convince herself that she was doing the right thing.

One thought remained constant in Taylor's mind that she could not let go: she was at the *New York Times*. And she was young. The men and women she rubbed shoulders with every day had worked for twenty, even thirty years to get a position with the *Times*, and she couldn't imagine having to go back to her hometown or, worse, a paper in a small town and try working her way back up. She had to save her career.

Taylor reached out and placed a hand on the back of the seat in front of her to steady herself as the taxi driver brought the vehicle to an abrupt stop at Varnum Street and turned around. "Is this it?" he asked.

Meg checked the address on her phone, turned to her right to confirm the house number, and nodded. After paying the fare, Taylor climbed out and began to walk up the steps rising from the sidewalk and stopped at the door. Turning back, she saw the red glow of the taxi's brake lights as it navigated a dip in the road and disappeared beyond the trees that lined the street as the late afternoon sun started to set.

She knocked three times and waited, but there was no answer at the door. She knocked three more times. There was still no response. Meg heard the sound of a car approaching from down the street and turned to look at it.

The vehicle turned into the alleyway that ran to the right of the house. Taylor caught a glimpse of the driver's face as he pulled into the driveway and slowed long enough to acknowledge Meg's presence.

It was Robert King.

Taylor descended the stairs, clutching a manila folder, and folded her arms across her chest as she stepped onto the sidewalk and curiously followed the vehicle into the alleyway to catch up with her boss.

"What are you doing here?" asked King as he stepped out of the driver's seat and closed his car door.

Looking sideways, still trying to convince herself that she was doing the right thing—and likely the only thing she *could* do right now to get back into her boss's good graces—Meg stepped forward and stretched out her hand. "Mr. King, I'm sorry to bother you at your home, but I need you to read this."

King cocked his head to one side and furrowed his brow as his eyes ran up and down Taylor's body.

"Please," added Taylor, taking another step closer. "Just read it and then I'll leave you alone, Mr. King."

King reached out and took the folder, opened it, and stared at the headline that Meg had come up with. "President Keller's black ops team," he said sarcastically as his eyes flicked across the top of the first page. He continued to read through the story she had written, licked a thumb to wet it, and turned the page. "What is this, Megan?" the man asked, keeping his gaze downward as he scanned the report.

Hesitating for a moment, Taylor collected her thoughts and said, "You wanted dirt on Keller. Here it is."

With that, King glanced up briefly to acknowledge the severity of the statement she had just made. Lowering his gaze, he began to read excerpts from the report out loud.

"For the past eighteen months, President Keller has been running a secret black ops team headed by his senior advisor on issues of domestic counterterrorism, Blake Jordan." King continued to scan through the report and licked his thumb again to flip the page before adding, "Megan, you're making some pretty serious accusations here."

"I know."

"This man, Jordan—" King shook his head and paused before continuing "—according to what you have here, he's saved Keller's life twice." King flipped back to the prior page to find the spot he was looking for. "Jordan was responsible for figuring out where then-Senator Keller was being held hostage after being kidnapped the night Keller was set to accept his party's nomination for president. Megan, he saved his life." Taylor started to speak, but King held a hand up so he could continue. "Same thing a few months later," said King. Another lick of the thumb. Another page turned. King pointed at the passage. "Jordan and his team, consisting of select members from the Department of Domestic Counterterrorism and the FBI, saved Keller again—along with his incoming administration—from an improvised explosive device on Inauguration Day." King closed the file. "I want to know who your source is for all of this information."

Taylor crossed her arms and bit her lip out of nervousness. "Sir, my source is anonymous and will stay—"

"The hell they are," snapped King.

"There's more," said Meg, looking down to the closed folder in her boss's hand. "This guy—Jordan—he's the man behind the situation in New York six months ago. One of his black ops team members was being forced to dismantle an NSA surveillance program. Jordan found out and stopped it. That's what really—"

King held a hand up again and lifted the folder with the other. "Ms. Taylor, I don't know where you're getting your information from, but the *New York Times* will not be running this story." He paused before adding, "If what you're saying is true, then this man Jordan is a hero, and that will overshadow any misconduct by the president. Americans are greatly divided when it comes to politics, but after thirty years in this business, I know there are two things they come together on: fighting terrorism and the safety and security of a sitting president, regardless of party affiliation. That's what sets us apart from other nations."

"There's one more thing you need to know," added Meg, followed by a brief pause to collect her thoughts as she decided the best way to reveal the last bit of information she needed to share. It was a last-ditch effort to attempt to gain favor with her boss. She took a deep breath and said, "Blake Jordan is a personal friend of the president's." This raised King's interest, but he kept a straight face. "Jordan's known him since he was a kid. When Keller was preparing to run for senate and Jordan was still in high school, he trained the man to help improve his chances of becoming a SEAL. They trained at four in the morning every day for a year." She paused. "I know how you feel about Keller. This can and will hurt him."

King maintained his composure. "Ms. Taylor, I needed dirt on the president. Instead, what you've given me is anything but. No need to clean out your desk on Monday, we'll mail your belongings back to you."

"But, Mr. King—" said Meg as the man turned and smiled to himself. This was just what he was looking for.

21

I HELD ON TIGHT AS JAMI RACED THROUGH THE STREETS OF the Woodbridge neighborhood, headed east. She passed her cell to me, and I helped navigate as Simon Harris monitored the location of the man on the bike. I put the call on speakerphone and Simon shouted out the biker's location as we raced to catch him.

"Turn right," he said, and Jami followed the command, taking the next turn and stepping hard on the accelerator. "Looks like he's about ten blocks northwest of you now. I'm going to try to close the gap between the two of you as fast as I can, but I'm relying on CCTV cameras in the area, so I don't have the guy's exact location in real time. Not enough time to retask a satellite," he said as Jami accelerated again.

"Simon," I said, keeping an eye on traffic from side streets, "where'd the guy go after the bombing?"

There was a pause on the other end of the line as the sound of typing filled the interior of Jami's SUV. "Not sure," he replied. "After I got to the Hoover Building, I started looking for the guy based on his last known location, the spot where I lost him. I isolated the footage from some of the cameras in the area and I began expanding my search in greater concentric circles until I finally—" He paused. "Hang on a sec."

I looked at Jami, and she turned to me. "Simon? What's wrong?" she asked as I looked at the phone.

"The guy turned again; now he's headed west. Jami, make the turn as soon as you can, okay?"

"On it," she replied and turned the wheel hard at the next street, forcing me against the passenger door.

"Okay, he's about ten blocks ahead of you. I think you're on the same street. Pick up speed if you can."

Jami stepped on the gas again as I reached for the grab handle above with my right hand, still clutching Jami's phone with my left. "Slow down—you're gonna kill us both," I said as she began weaving in and out of traffic and slowed only when we came up to a light at an intersection that had just turned red. I looked into the passenger-side mirror and noticed a dark vehicle a few blocks behind us, picking up speed, fast.

After getting through the intersection, Jami picked up speed again, and I looked over to Jami to tell her about the car behind us when I saw the guy on the bike momentarily at the next intersection before he disappeared again. I let go of the grab handle and pointed to my left. "Jami, he's one block over from us."

She nodded and slowed at the next intersection and turned the wheel hard. Her tires screeched as she quickly navigated the turn to get us one block over so we could catch up to the biker. I reached for the grab handle again and looked in the mirror to check on the dark vehicle. The car that I thought might have been following us was gone, so I refocused my attention on the guy on the bike, who was now in front of us.

"Any idea where this guy is going?" asked Jami as we watched the biker five or six blocks ahead of us bob and weave between vehicles with ease, and she tried to do the same, waiting for Simon to answer. "Simon, talk to me," she yelled to get his attention. I looked down and saw that the line had been disconnected.

"The call dropped," I said as I turned my gaze from the phone back to the biker up ahead and pulling farther away from us. I kept my eyes trained on the single taillight that continued to appear every few seconds as the guy weaved in and out of traffic, trying to go faster as Jami followed suit, starting to close the gap.

In the mirror to my right, I saw headlights approaching fast. I leaned forward and confirmed that it was the same car I'd seen earlier. "Jami—I think we have a problem," I said, maintaining my stare.

"What is it?"

"The Town Car Landry told us about earlier—the one he said followed me from Alexandria—I think it's tailing us."

Jami looked into the rearview mirror and saw what I was talking about as we both watched the vehicle bobbing and weaving in and out of traffic to catch up to us, just as we were doing.

Jami's cell rang, and I answered the call, again on speakerphone. "Lost him," said Simon as Jami and I looked farther down the street, trying to see the biker again. "Jami, do you have a visual?" asked Simon.

She looked at me briefly before turning back to the road. "No," she said. "How could he just disappear?"

"Jami, look," I said as the car following us got to a clear straightaway, gunned it, and headed straight for us. Her eyes switched between the rearview mirror and the road ahead. "Jami, what are you thinking?"

As the driver got closer, she responded, "Just hold on, okay?" and as he closed the gap even more, Jami slammed on the brakes. The driver did the same, but not fast enough. Turning back to look behind us, I watched as the car skidded along the road, his tires trying to gain traction, before hitting the back of Jami's SUV. The guy's airbag deployed as Jami stepped on the accelerator. "Who *is* this guy?" she asked.

"I don't know, but we need to find out," I said as I saw the car get rolling again and start to pick up speed.

Two blocks ahead, I saw the entrance to a parking garage. Remembering the garage at DDC, I had an idea. "Pull into that garage," I yelled, pointing at the entrance as we approached, and I looked behind me again.

"Why? We'll be pinned if I do that," she said as I noticed that the call with Simon had dropped again.

"Just trust me, okay?" I said as Jami slowed and yanked the steering wheel to the right, causing her wheels to skid again as she did. She drove through a white bar that was lowered and turned right. Before she made the first turn, I looked over my shoulder and saw the car enter the garage, following us inside. "Go faster," I said and—after being slammed against the door as Jami took the next turn—I steadied myself and reached into the messenger bag between my feet, found my Glock, and checked the magazine.

Jami slowed as we approached the next turn. "What are you going to do, Blake?"

"Tuck and roll," I replied.

Jami looked confused.

"I have to figure out who this guy is and what he wants."

Jami paused and asked, "What do you want me to do?"

I looked up ahead and confirmed that there were enough parked cars for my plan to have a chance at working. "Stop up ahead and let him catch up to you," I replied and unbuckled my seatbelt and gripped the Glock tight as I waited for Jami to take the next curve. "Don't worry, I'll be right behind you."

As soon as she took the curve, I used my other hand to open the door, and the force of the movement from the vehicle pushed me out onto the concrete pavement. I landed on my shoulder and immediately knew something was wrong. Rolling several times, I stopped rolling in an empty space between two parked cars.

Looking back, I saw the passenger door slam shut after Jami straightened out the vehicle and accelerated.

A few seconds later, the black Town Car buzzed by me and took the same curve.

With both cars out of my direct line of sight, I got to my feet as I heard the sound of Jami braking hard, followed by the Town Car doing the same a moment later. I winced in pain as I realized that I was injured from hitting the pavement at such a high rate of speed. Gripping my weapon, I ran after the two vehicles stopped around the corner. In that moment, I thought about the fault in my plan and knew that my worst fear was about to come true. Jami was in trouble, and I only had one chance to do something about it.

22

I KEPT MOVING FORWARD, KNOWING THAT EVERY SECOND counted. Aiming my weapon toward the ground, I climbed the ramp to the next level, approached the corner, and rested my back against the cold concrete. Trying to slow my breathing, I closed my eyes and listened to what was happening around the corner. I waited. A car door opened, then slammed shut. I gripped my weapon even tighter and opened my eyes.

Peeking around the corner, aiming my Glock at the floor, I carefully checked to see what was happening. The Town Car was stopped behind Jami's SUV, engine still running, and pinning her to the edge of the garage with nothing but a concrete wall at the end of the top level. There was nowhere else for her to go.

Jami kept her foot on the brakes, causing a bright red glow against the surrounding area behind her. I watched the driver aiming his weapon at the driver's side door and taking careful steps as he moved in.

I turned the corner, lifted my weapon, and trained it on the man, approaching from behind as Jami kept the SUV running. The engine masked my steps as I moved quickly to get to the driver before he could realize what was going on. The pain from my shoulder was unbearable, but I had to keep moving.

"Lower the window!" he shouted as he approached, and I detected a faint Russian accent. "Lower it!" he repeated, and finally, I saw her window lower the whole way as the guy took a wider path as he got nearer to make sure there wouldn't be any surprises from inside the SUV. "Now show me your hands."

I continued to move farther behind him so Jami could see what I was doing. The man approached the window, aimed his weapon inside the cab, and tilted his head to the left as he looked past Jami and into the backseat. "Where's Jordan?" the man asked, taking two steps closer to Jami as she kept her hands up.

With two hands, I raised my weapon high and brought the butt of my gun down hard on the back of the man's skull, causing him to collapse immediately and fall to the ground. "Right behind you," I answered.

The man had let go of his weapon, and I kicked it away as I stuffed mine in the small of my back and grabbed the guy. "Jami, help me out," I said as I dragged the man to a nearby column at the end of a parking space. Three cars were parked along the last row next to the column. Business people, I guessed, working late on a Friday night. Jami stepped out and looked at me, concerned.

"Throw me your cuffs," I said

She nodded, reached into a pocket and threw me her handcuffs, and I secured the guy to the column.

The driver slouched, and I stood next to Jami as his head started to move and he regained consciousness.

"Who is this guy?" she whispered, both of us staring at the now defenseless driver, and I shook my head.

"Let's find out."

I stepped to the man and crouched as Jami remained standing behind me. The guy blinked several times, but wouldn't acknowledge me and instead continued to look down at the ground. "Who are you?" I asked.

The driver blinked some more and then looked up to me before eyeing Jami over my shoulder.

Grabbing his face to force him to look at me, I got even closer to the guy. "Hey—I asked a question—who are you?"

There was no response, only a blank stare. After several seconds, he opened his mouth and started to say something. I let go of his face and waited to see what the man would say. "Screw you," he finally grunted.

I reached behind and grabbed my weapon. I lowered the barrel and rested it on his leg. I was breathing hard. "Let's try this again," I said in a low, gruff voice. "Who are you, and why are you following me?"

Jami walked around behind him and checked his pockets. She found a wallet and cell phone and stepped to the side as I kept the barrel of my weapon resting on his leg. "Why are you following me?" I asked again with no response. I raised the Glock, aimed it to the right of the man's head, and fired it. "Who sent you!"

I inched closer as the man looked up and spit in my face. I was stunned for a moment, but wiped it away and smiled as I moved the weapon back down, this time setting it on his kneecap. I pulled the trigger.

The man thrashed in pain and twisted around as a dark puddle of crimson formed by his outstretched leg.

"Who sent you!" I asked again, but he didn't answer, just writhed in pain as beads of sweat formed on his forehead.

"Don't make me do this, you son of a bitch," I said, moving the gun to the other kneecap. "Talk."

"Okay," he said between quick breaths as the sweat from his forehead started to stream down his face. "Been trying to find you for a week." He sucked in air as his eyes moved down to his leg. I followed his gaze and watched as the crimson puddle grew larger. "I was hired by somebody to bring you in."

"Why me?"

The guy shook his head quickly. "I don't know."

"Who sent you?"

He shook his head again. "Don't know that, either."

"You're lying," I said and pressed the gun harder on his other kneecap, ready to pull the trigger again.

"Stop!" he yelled, panting even harder now as more sweat dripped from his face onto his shirt. "Please, I'm telling you the truth. I work for an intermediary." He panted some more. "I don't know who he takes his orders from. All I know is I was told to find you and bring you in." He closed his eyes to bear the pain.

"And the other guy? The one on the bike?"

Keeping his eyes closed, he shook his head. "He works for the same man I work for."

"The intermediary," I said as I kept the barrel in place. "I want a name."

He shook his head again. "He'll kill me if I give it to you."

"I'll kill you if you don't."

Before he could answer, I heard Jami gasp behind me. "Blake?" she said as I realized that I was so focused on trying to get information out of the driver that I hadn't noticed the sound she had heard.

The rumble of the motorcycle's loud engine echoed from the lower levels of the parking garage as the biker made his ascent and approached. "Quick," I said, turning to Jami and handing her my phone. "There's an address I put in Maps earlier. Go there and see a man named Charlie Redding. He'll help you."

I could hear that the guy on the bike was now two floors below us. "Get under that car," I said, pointing at the vehicle parked farthest away from us. Jami ran to it and looked back to me one last time. "Call Morgan when you get to Charlie's. Turn your phone off, and do not contact Simon again. Do you understand?"

Jami nodded and dropped to the floor. I pulled the trigger once more, and the driver's body slumped over.

23

"WHAT ARE YOU DOING?" YELLED JAMI AS I STOOD BEHIND THE Town Car and next to the dead man's body. Turning back, I saw her on her knees, deciding if she was going to go underneath the car to hide or not.

"Please, just go to Charlie's," I yelled over the sound of two car engines running and the squeals from the motorcycle's tires. "They want me for some reason. It's time to find out why."

"I can take him out," she argued. "We can at least try to get some information out of him."

Turning to my right, I looked at the driver's lifeless body. "We already tried that. Get under the car now!"

As I faced forward, I saw the man on the motorcycle hook around the corner. Dressed in black and wearing an all-black helmet with a smoked-out face shield, he had his weapon out and trained on me.

I held both hands in the air, my right still gripping the Glock as the man carefully twisted the throttle and closed the gap between us until he was twenty feet in front of me. He killed the ignition and climbed off.

It was a Beretta M9 trained on me. The man used his free hand to remove the helmet and set it down. Shifting his gaze for the first time, he looked to his left and saw the dead man still handcuffed to the concrete column. "Put the weapon down, Mr. Jordan," he said as he took another step closer and stopped.

Lowering my body, I carefully brought my right hand down and set my weapon on the concrete floor before standing back up again, maintaining eye contact with the guy the whole time. "What do you want?"

He looked past me, past the Town Car, back toward Jami's SUV. "Where is the woman?" he asked as I noticed over the rumble of two engines the same accent. Another Russian. It was in that moment that I knew that my past had finally caught up to me, the haunting words of a dead man echoing in my mind.

"Ivanov sent you, didn't he?" I asked, referring to the man who I had killed six months earlier and remembering once again the words he had spoken before his death. "Russia has a very long memory, Mr. Jordan. We're going to keep coming after you," he had said after telling me he had already told his affiliates who I was and who I worked for. I knew it was only a matter of time until they found me.

"Ivanov?" he said, turning his head sideways with a surprised look. "You catch on quickly, Mr. Jordan." He looked past me again. "But you still did not answer my question." He paused. "Tell me where she is."

"I'm alone," I lied, glaring at the man as he took another step closer to me. "There's no one here but me."

A smile crept across his face as he looked down and shook his head. "Agent Jordan," he said and took another step closer, resting the barrel of his M9 in the middle of my forehead, "I am told that the two of you left together, so I suggest that you be truthful unless you want to end up like my comrade over there."

My heart was pounding out of control. The only thing I had wanted for the last six months was to stay away from Jami so she wouldn't be involved in any of this and to keep her safe. I thought about Jami on the floor just a few feet away from us and what the guy would do if he found her. Then I had an idea.

"She got a head start on you," I said.

Keeping my eyes on the man, I saw a bright exit sign from the corner of my eye. Quickly, I glanced at it.

When the man turned to look at the stairwell next to me, I brought my right hand up and grabbed the barrel of the gun and pushed it aside. He squeezed the trigger and fired a round into the wall, sending chunks of concrete and dust into the air. He brought his other hand up to punch me, but I blocked the blow instead. In frustration, the guy fired again as I knocked the gun out of his hand and onto the floor.

Drawing his hand away, he made a fist and lunged at me as I sidestepped him, bringing my knee into his stomach and throwing him onto the trunk of the Town Car. I grabbed the back of his head and slammed it onto the trunk as he brought his elbow back and jammed it into my chest, knocking the wind out of me.

I took a step backward and let the man kick me in the stomach. The blow sent me to the ground, fast.

Gasping for air, I struggled to push myself backward with my legs. I was too hurt to get back on my feet.

I watched the man reach down to pick up his gun, kick mine underneath the Town Car, and walk to the driver's side door. Still on the floor, I looked past him and saw Jami. She stared at me, and I held a hand up, telling her to stay where she was as the man popped the trunk and walked behind the vehicle.

He reached inside, found a collection of zip ties, and peeled one off as he stepped over my body. Turning me over, he rested a foot on my neck and brought my hands behind me so he could secure them together. "Do not worry," he said. "We will find her, eventually. And when we do—" he grabbed the back of my shirt to lift me up "—I will make sure that she suffers the same fate as my friend here," he said, pointing at the man handcuffed to the column as he spun me around and pushed me toward the back of the Town Car.

"Where are you taking me?" I asked, knowing that Jami was listening, still trying to catch my breath.

I felt the cold barrel of the M9 touch the back of my neck to encourage me to keep moving. "Get in."

"Not until you tell me where we're going and what you want from me."

After a brief pause, he said, "Mr. Jordan, there's somebody who's waited a very long time to see you."

He pushed the M9 harder against my neck, and I stepped closer to the back of the Town Car until he pulled the weapon away, grabbed me by my right shoulder, and pushed me down toward the open trunk. I winced in pain from the pressure of his grasp on my already injured shoulder, but I tried not to show that I was hurt.

As I stepped inside, the driver slammed the trunk shut, causing everything to go black.

The car rocked as he climbed inside, turned the vehicle around, and accelerated down the ramp.

I knew that the guy would take me alive, and I had managed to make him think that Jami had escaped. Still, the man had asked where she was and even called Jami by name. He knew who she was, knew somehow that we were together, and said they'd find her and kill her as soon as they caught up to her.

After the vehicle took the final turn out of the garage and picked up speed, I thought about Jami staring at me on the cold concrete floor. I thought about what I had told her to do—get to Charlie's and contact Morgan.

I breathed harder as I started to catch my breath from the wind being knocked out of me. As the man driving the Town Car twisted and turned down the dark streets of DC, I couldn't help but think about the last time I'd been zip tied and left inside the trunk of a car. I had tried so desperately to escape, and I had.

But this time was different. This time, I remained perfectly still. I knew I had to conserve my energy.

I was being taken farther away from Jami and getting closer to knowing who was looking for me and why.

24

Jami waited until the sound of the tires disappeared before crawling out from underneath the car. She picked up the Glock, grabbed her cell, and climbed into the still-running SUV before calling Morgan. Jami kept the cell against her ear with a shoulder as she held the other phone to find the address in Maps.

"Lennox," he said, sounding annoyed and typing in the background as Jami found the address for Charlie.

"It's me," she said, still balancing her phone against an ear while pulling up the Maps application and touching the screen with a thumb to navigate her to the address. "I need your help, Morgan."

The typing stopped. "What's wrong, love?"

Jami programmed the Rosslyn address into her vehicle's GPS and dropped the phone into the messenger bag next to her. "I need you to run a plate for me, see if you can figure out who owns the vehicle, and..." Jami paused. Having finished backing the vehicle out, she pulled around the motorcycle and stopped next to it. "Actually, I have two plates I need you to run for me," she added and gave Morgan the numbers.

"I'll look them up for you; give me a few seconds," he replied a beat later. "You don't sound like yourself."

Jami stepped on the accelerator. She navigated the vehicle down to the first floor, drove out through the exit she had busted through earlier, and turned left onto the road, following the GPS's directions. It told her that she was just over three miles and eleven minutes away from the address in Rosslyn, Virginia. "Simon called us earlier and said he had located the guy on the motorcycle who was at DDC earlier."

"Bloody hell. Why didn't I know about that?"

"I don't know, Morgan. We were with Chris and Mark when we got the call, so we left to track it down."

Jami went on to explain everything that had happened as she headed west on Constitution Avenue. She explained that the motorcycle was back at the top floor of the parking garage, but that they needed to locate the Town Car immediately. She said she couldn't talk long, that she needed to turn her phone off.

"I'm entering the plate number you gave me into Veri-Plate to see if I can pick up the vehicle using the Automatic License Plate Recognition database," he said, referring to the license-plate-scanning technology being used on major roads and highways by law enforcement. "I'll let you know if I pick up anything. In the meantime, I'll see if I can figure out where the car's been lately." He paused and added, "I can also try to get access to the Bureau's Stingray program and try to ping Blake's phone if it's still turned on, Jami."

She paused for a moment before saying, "It's still on, Morgan. I have it here with me."

There was silence on the other end of the line. "I'm sorry, love. We'll get him back. Don't worry, okay?"

Jami looked to her left and stared at the empty National Mall as she approached the Theodore Roosevelt Bridge. Before she could answer, she heard the cell ringing from the messenger bag on the seat next to her. "I have to go. Call me as soon as you get something. And, Morgan—don't share anything with Simon."

She set her phone down and, with one hand, fished around inside the bag for the other one still ringing. Bringing it up to her face, she saw that the incoming call was from Chris Reed. She answered and explained what was happening and asked if Chris could meet her at the Rosslyn address she'd be arriving at in two minutes. He said he was with Mark at the Hoover Building and about to meet with Bill Landry, but would bring the man up to speed and head right over.

After giving Chris the Rosslyn address, Jami disconnected the call and exited onto Interstate 66 and took it to North Fort Myer Drive. Two more short turns later and Jami arrived at the corner of Ode Street and North Colonial Court. She brought her vehicle to a stop in the driveway immediately behind a red-bricked townhome and checked the address before she killed the ignition and proceeded to turn off both phones.

Large willow oak trees lined the pristine street. Their branches darkened many of the streetlights, creating a menacing feel. She sat silently in her car and heard the rumble of thunder close by.

Jami thought about Lynne May. If Reed was going to give Landry a heads-up that he and Reynolds were going to meet her in Rosslyn, it was just a matter of time until May found out. Jami thought about the warning she'd been given about

Simon and wanted to keep him and May in the dark as long as possible.

She stepped out of the vehicle, closed the door, and headed to the front of the townhome. Looking up to the darkening sky, Jami saw the storm clouds rolling in, remembered the heavy downpour from the night before, and knew that another round of thunderstorms was about to hit DC. As she approached the door, she looked up at the old building. Unlike the connected townhomes across the street, this one was a stand-alone. Three stories tall, red brick, red front door. Jami climbed the steps and knocked three times.

Through the window next to the door, she watched as a strange orange glow from a lamp somewhere inside turned off quickly. She cupped two hands on the window to look inside, but it was too dark to see anything.

She knocked on the door again, but the result was the same. "Charlie, please open the door," she said. Jami crossed her arms and turned her back as a strong wind from the approaching storm passed over her.

Straightening her hair back in place, Jami heard a voice from the other side of the door. "Who are you?"

It was a warm, kind voice. Jami stepped closer. "You don't know me," she said softly to the man.

He paused for several seconds. "What do you want from me?"

"Blake sent me. He's in trouble, and I need your help," she said and turned as the wind picked up again.

A moment later, she heard a latch being twisted, a deadbolt unlocked, and the click of the doorknob turning fast. The door opened and an older gentleman with a short, graying beard ushered her inside.

He flipped the lights on and locked up again before turning around to face Jami, who tucked a lock of her hair behind an ear again as she looked up at the large broad-shouldered man in his mid-sixties. "Charlie Redding," he said, extending his hand, which Jami took and squeezed as she nodded to him.

"Jami Davis," she said. Her eyes broke away from the man as she checked out the home. "I'm with DDC."

Charlie held onto her hand. She turned back and saw him tilt his head at her. "You're wrong," he said.

Jami furrowed her brow, just staring back at him. "About what?"

"I *do* know you."

Jami's eyes narrowed, and she shook her head slowly as Charlie let go of her hand.

"Follow me, Agent Davis," he added and walked past her into a large study and flipped on another set of lights as Jami walked behind Redding and entered the room. He gestured for her to take a seat as he walked around to an adjacent chair, eased into it, and leaned forward. "What kind of trouble is Blake in?"

Jami sat down. "I don't know. A couple of guys were after him. One of them took him twenty minutes ago."

Charlie nodded. "He's right, I can help you," he said and stood, moving to his desk to share what he knew.

25

TWENTY MINUTES INTO THE RIDE, THE TOWN CAR STARTED TO slow. I figured we were still in Washington. The car rocked with each turn the man took as I tried to keep myself steady inside the trunk of the car.

The pain from my right shoulder was unbearable. But the vehicle was driving slower as we approached our destination, and the turns the guy was taking were becoming smoother. I felt the car come to a stop and heard the engine turn off as I waited in the darkness to find out what the guy was going to do to me.

A minute later, I felt the car rock back and forth from the weight of the man stepping out of the car. He popped the trunk as I looked up to the sky and saw the bright orange glow of a streetlight overhead.

"Come on. Get out," the guy said as he appeared from the side and reached down into the trunk to grab my arm. I winced in pain and tried to hide my injury from him, but he noticed and grabbed my arm even tighter. Climbing out, I pulled away from him and quickly took in my surroundings to try to figure out where he had taken me while the man grabbed the back of my shirt and slammed the trunk closed. Turning to my right, I saw that we were at Thirty-Fourth and Garfield. *Northwest Washington*, I thought.

"Move," he barked and pushed me to the sidewalk as I looked up to see the building we were entering.

It was three stories tall, with faded yellow bricks on the outside of the building. It looked like it had been abandoned for some time, but I couldn't understand why. It was a nice, upscale neighborhood, and the Naval Observatory—where Vice President Billings lived—was nearby. It shouldn't have been abandoned.

The guy ushered me up ten short steps and knocked twice when we got to the wooden double doors.

"Yes?" a voice called from the other side.

"I have Jordan. Open the door," the guy grunted.

I heard the deadbolt turn; then the door creaked open. We stepped into complete darkness and I closed my eyes. The heat was intense from the building baking in the summer heat of Washington all day without air-conditioning. That was when I noticed a man on the other side of the room with a flashlight in his hand. The man who had let us in flicked his on as well and shined it in my face as the door was locked behind us.

"Where is Dimitri?" asked the man who had ushered me inside, still holding onto the back of my shirt.

The guy kept the light shining in my face as I heard a low rumble of thunder somewhere in the distance. "He's on his way," he replied, lowering the light and moving it to offer a path to the other side of the room. "He wants us to prepare the prisoner," he added, referring to me as I tried to figure out who Dimitri was.

The man holding onto my shirt pushed me forward, forcing me to walk through the dark foyer and into an open space as the other guy guarding the entrance remained at the door and shined his flashlight in the direction we were to follow. His light briefly caught what looked like metal hooks hanging from the ceiling. I looked up, waiting for the light to catch them again, before I noticed another light coming from the left of me, from the other man I'd seen pass by moments earlier when I had entered the building.

"Keep moving," the guy holding onto me said as I approached the center of the room, and the man to my left lifted his hand and sent a strong white beam of light across the room, following me as I walked.

I kept my eyes fixed on the dark objects hanging from the ceiling as they became clearer the closer I got. When I arrived at the center of the room, a chill ran up my spine as I understood what I was looking at.

Two ropes hung from the ceiling, secured to two metal rings holding them in place. Stopping underneath, I heard the man behind me stuff his weapon in his belt before he cut the zip tie off my wrists and secured one hand to one of the ropes. I was in over my head and knew I had to do something to get out of this.

When he was done with the first rope, the man moved to my right and lifted my arm as I writhed in pain. He laughed to himself as he started to fasten my other wrist to the rope. After a few seconds passed, I noticed that the man was struggling to secure it. The other guy, somewhere behind me, moved his light up to the rope and asked the guy if he needed help. The man ignored the question and kept working on it.

When he was done, he checked his work and then wiped sweat away from his forehead. Quickly, I grabbed the ropes and held on tight as I jumped, twisted my body, and wrapped my legs around the guy's neck.

He struggled to breathe as I squeezed tighter and heard shouts from the other two men in the building—the man somewhere behind me and the guy posted at the door. I twisted my legs hard, breaking his neck.

The guy's body went limp and, as I loosened my legs, he fell onto the floor. I let go of the ropes as I breathed hard, and the light from behind me lowered onto the man's body. Now two of them were dead—the driver of the Town Car and the guy on the bike. I felt a fist held to my back followed by a sharp piercing sensation. I twisted my body from the pain, not fully understanding what was happening to me.

The fist was held in place for a long time, then removed. The shouts became muffled. My legs grew numb.

My body went limp and I hung from the two ropes as I looked up and saw streams of white as the guy at the door ran toward me, still holding his light. Sounds became distorted. I tried to stay focused on the light as it swirled in front of me. It left a long trail as it moved, and I blinked several times as I watched it. The two men stood in front of me, and I felt one of them kick me in the stomach as I hung there, helpless.

Another kick to my stomach knocked the wind out of me. My body swung back. I struggled to breathe.

I tried to look up again. As I did, a fist struck the left side of my face. I immediately felt the taste of blood in my mouth as I dropped my head and felt one of the men grab my hair and bring a knee into my chest.

"What do you want from me?" I said in a low whisper, unsure if anyone could hear me. My own voice sounded loud in my head and echoed as the man holding onto my hair forced me to look up at him.

My head was spinning—and looking the man in the face—I spat blood on him as he let go of my head.

Taking a step back, he barked an order. "Fill the syringe and double the dosage."

The words were muffled, but I heard them. They echoed in my mind as I wondered what the hell they had done to me. I tried to get to my feet, but all I could do was hang there. I felt one of the guys check the ropes secured to my wrists. I looked up, and the other guy moved his light to my face, and I looked away.

"I said fill the syringe and double the dosage—do it now!" he yelled as I felt myself losing consciousness.

"No," the other guy said. "Dimitri will be here shortly."

The voices overlapped each other in my head as whatever they had given me continued to work its way throughout my body. It was becoming harder to keep my eyes open. I managed to look up one more time.

"Fine," the other guy said and stepped forward, taking one more swing against my face.

My head snapped to the right and my body went limp. The sounds, the lights—everything went dark.

26

Charlie Redding pointed at an image that had been enlarged on one of the two large monitors on his desk. Jami stood next to him and shook her head in disbelief. "Those are the men from today," she said as she tapped the face of one of the guys. "He was the driver of the Town Car." Jami pointed at the other guy. "And this was the man on the motorcycle who put Blake in the back of the Town Car earlier." Turning back, she looked Charlie over and asked, "How'd you get access to this image?"

Redding stood back, one hand tucked under an arm and the other touching his beard as he studied the image. "Blake called me earlier. Said he needed my help. Told me that a couple of guys were near his apartment looking for him a few days ago. They roughed up some homeless guy, trying to figure out where he lived." Charlie kept rubbing his short, graying beard as his eyes shifted to Jami. "He asked if I could call in a favor and get access to the CCTV footage from that area from one of my former intelligence buddies. Guess he didn't want to go through DDC or the FBI because of their focus on the ransomware attack."

"May I?" asked Jami as she gestured to the desk chair.

Charlie nodded and pulled the chair out as Jami grabbed her phone and sat down. "Morgan," she said a few moments later, cradling the phone against her ear while typing on the keyboard, "I'm sending you an image of the two men from tonight. The guy on the left was the driver of the Town Car that Blake killed. The one on the right is the biker who took him away in the car. Can you ID the men based on this photo?"

Morgan said he'd get to it after he tracked down the vehicle. After disconnecting the call, Jami stood and turned to Redding. "I have DDC looking into the image." She slipped her cell into a pocket and pulled back her sleeve to look at her watch. "Two men will be arriving shortly to meet up with me here, if that's okay."

"That's fine," replied Redding as he motioned to the two empty chairs. Jami forced a smile and sat down.

She looked up at the man as he took a seat, and asked, "Mr. Redding, how do you know Blake?"

"Call me Charlie. And can I get you anything?" Jami shook her head as Charlie paused before continuing. "I've known Blake a very long time. Family friend. Worked with his father at the ATF back in Chicago."

"Ben," said Jami softly.

Redding nodded. "Ben Jordan. A great man." Charlie paused, his eyes moving away from Jami as he looked across the room and a flood of memories rushed over him. "I believe I met you at the funeral."

Jami thought about it. "Maybe. There were so many people there. I'm sorry, I really don't remember."

"Don't be sorry," said Charlie. "Standing room only—most people I think I've ever seen crammed into a church outside of a Christmas Eve service." He smiled. "Showed how many people loved Ben Jordan."

Jami nodded slowly and knowingly. "So you know President Keller, too? From the Chicago ATF office?"

Charlie smiled. "It's been a while since we've spoken—at the funeral, I guess—but yes, I know Jim well." Redding reached over and grabbed a glass of water and took a long drink. Setting it down, he said, "I moved out here a few months back. Been doing some contract work since retiring. Blake's been stopping by a lot." His eyes moved back to Jami. "He hasn't been himself since his dad passed away. I'm sure it's been hard on him. He mentions you sometimes." Charlie paused. "He won't say it, but he misses you."

"Then he shouldn't have..." Jami stopped herself and just looked at Redding. "Never mind. It's nothing."

Charlie remained quiet, tapped a hand on the armrest, and stroked his beard with the other, thinking.

Jami maintained eye contact, sensing there was something Charlie wasn't telling her. "What?"

He shook his head slowly and dropped his gaze. "You're right, he shouldn't have walked away, but he did." After several seconds, Redding added, "You know, it's really not my place to share this, but—" he looked over to an old black-and-white photograph on his desk of a younger, slimmer version of himself with an arm wrapped around a woman as Jami followed his gaze "—you need to know that he had good reason to."

Jami's eyes narrowed as he picked up the old picture and brought it closer. "What aren't you telling me?"

Charlie took a deep breath and let it out slowly. "He loves you, Jami." He dropped his gaze once again. "Bought a beautiful ring for you. Showed it to me before leaving for Chicago last Christmas. Said he was going to give it to you on New Year's Eve." He looked up to gauge Jami's reaction to what he had shared.

She looked away. "He was staying with me for a few weeks. We had plans to go to Navy Pier that night." Pausing briefly, she continued, feeling like she was talking to an old friend instead of a perfect stranger. "But something happened. We had to go to New York and—" she took a breath "—everything changed."

"I'll tell you what happened," he said as he grabbed his glass of water and took another long drink from it. "He wouldn't go into specifics, but did tell me he'd been warned that night in New York, Jami."

"Warned?"

Redding nodded. "He said that who he was and who he worked for had been compromised. Right before he killed the man, he told Blake that he couldn't stop what was already in motion. That it wouldn't end with him." Charlie looked up, trying to recall the specific words. "Russia has a very long memory."

Jami let the words hang in the air for a few moments before she spoke again. "What does that mean?"

Redding thought about it for a moment. "They said they would keep coming after him. I guess they were right," he said, looking back at the image of the two men still displayed on the large monitor on his desk.

The two sat in silence for a few moments before Jami said, "So that's what this is all about. Revenge."

Shaking his head slowly, Charlie said, "Seems like it, doesn't it?" and then paused before looking at Jami. "He still carries it."

Jami's eyes narrowed.

"The ring," he clarified. "A reminder of what's at stake, I guess."

"He should have stayed," she said in a soft voice as Charlie set the old picture down carefully on his desk.

He nodded again. "Sometimes we do the wrong thing in the moment," he said with regret in his voice as he kept his eyes on the photograph. "But that doesn't mean you can't go back and make things right, does it?"

There were three loud knocks at the front door as Redding turned to look at it. "The guys," said Jami as she stood and walked to the front of the home to meet Reed and Reynolds as Charlie followed her there.

"Jami," said Redding before they reached the door, and she turned and looked up at the man. "Tell him."

She narrowed her eyes again and shook her head. "Tell him what?"

Charlie unlocked the door, grabbed the handle, and turned to her before twisting it open. "Whatever's in your heart, whatever's left to be said, you have to say it. Blake is just like his father—he's a good man."

27

Lynne May locked her laptop screen. She stood and left the cubicles where Simon and the rest of her DDC team were working at the Hoover Building. May walked down a dark corridor to find Landry's office and, as she got closer, noticed that his door was slightly ajar. She approached slowly and heard him talking. Trying to see if Landry was in a meeting before interrupting, she stopped at the door and listened.

"It'll be okay," she heard him whisper. "Come over to my place. I'll give you the address," he said and gave it to the caller. "There's a key hidden in a sprinkler head by the front door. Text me when you're there and I'll disarm the security system from my phone. Make yourself at home, okay? I'll be there in a few hours."

May heard the sound of the receiver being set down quietly and knocked twice on Landry's office door.

"Come in," he said.

"I'm sorry to interrupt. I can come back."

"Please come in," repeated Landry. "Just dealing with my daughter. It's always something, you know?"

May nodded in agreement. Landry's fingers were interlaced and rested on top of his desk. She didn't know the man had children. She looked for a wedding band and didn't see one. She looked around the office for pictures, but saw none. Landry gestured to a chair across his desk, and May pulled it out and sat down.

"Bill, we have a problem."

"What is it?"

"We've lost contact with Agent Davis. Simon tried to reach out to her several times with no response."

"Where's Jordan?"

"He's with her," said May as Landry just stared at her. "I asked Simon to ping their cell phones earlier; they were at the same location before they went offline." She paused and looked around Landry's office again, feeling uneasy about the conversation she'd overheard. "We believe their phones were turned off."

"Okay," he said, nodding to himself. "Last known location?"

"An address out in Rosslyn. We looked up the owner, a man named Charles Redding. A retired ATF man."

Landry held a hand up to May as he became more relaxed, leaned back in his chair, and crossed his legs. "Okay, I spoke with Agent Reed a little while ago. Said that he and Reynolds were headed out to Rosslyn. Davis probably stumbled onto a lead and called him for assistance. I wouldn't worry about it, Lynne."

"Bill," pressed the DDC woman, "I haven't known Davis for long, but I do know how she operates." May paused. "It's not like her to go dark like this. Why would she contact Reed and not check in with me?"

Landry maintained his gaze from across the desk and slowly shook his head. "Lynne, if it makes you feel any better, I'll reach out to Reed and Reynolds and ask for a situation report. I'll have them relay the message for Davis to check in with you. And I'll have my people begin tracking their movements, okay?"

May glared at Landry, feeling like this was becoming the Bureau's show to run instead of a joint operation with the Department of Domestic Counterterrorism to find their only lead on the field office bombing.

As May remained silent, Landry asked, "How's the investigation going across the street? Any updates?"

"We're close. I'm told that the vehicle where the explosive originated from should be identified shortly."

"Already?" asked Landry skeptically with an overly concerned expression on his face.

"Well, that's what I'm hearing. We may be able to move our operations back by morning, if not sooner. I'm expecting to hear from them any minute now." She paused again. "Thanks for all of your help so far."

Landry sat up straight. "Of course. You and your team are welcome to stay here as long as you need to."

"And I appreciate that, Bill," said May as she pushed her chair away from the desk and stood.

"In fact, I insist that you stay," he added, joining her at the door. "At least until we get through all of this."

May looked past Landry and slowly turned around, taking one more look around his office. His intense, direct style made her feel uncomfortable. She thought about his offer. "Fine," she said, turning back to him. "Our people are working well together out there. It's best we let them do their jobs without—"

Before Lynne May could finish, Landry's landline started to ring. "I better get that," he said, sitting back down behind his desk and checking the caller ID. "Let me know what they find across the street. I'll get in touch with my guys shortly, and I'll have them tell Davis to give you a call as soon as they arrive. Okay?"

Landry placed a hand on the receiver, waiting for May's response.

She nodded and let herself out, closing the door behind her and hearing the Bureau man's muffled voice as he answered the phone in his office.

May remained outside his office. "Why would his kid not know where he lives?" she whispered to herself.

Simon Harris appeared from around the corner and called for her. "What do you have?" she asked as she approached and walked with him back to the cubicles where the Bureau and DDC analysts were working.

"The ATF is on the line for you, ma'am," he said, short of breath. "I'll have them transferred over to you."

She nodded as she entered the cubicle directly across from Simon and grabbed a pen and a yellow sticky note, writing a reminder to herself about something she wanted to follow up on when she had a moment. "Put him through, Simon," she said after she set the pen down and pulled the landline closer to her. "Looks like extension thirty-two fifty-seven."

Simon repeated the extension for the desk that May was working from to a Bureau analyst next to him.

A moment later, the phone at May's desk started to ring. "This is Lynne May," she said as Simon approached and stood at the entrance to her cubicle. May held a hand up and listened intently to the information being given to her from the ATF man across the street. "That doesn't make any sense at all."

The man on the other end of the line continued to speak. When he had finished relaying what he knew, May said, “Thank you for the update. Rest assured that we will fully cooperate with the investigation.” She went on to give the caller her cell number and asked that he call as soon as they were cleared to return to the office so they could resume normal operations. May disconnected the call and looked up at Simon.

“What did he say?” he asked as May stood to return to Landry’s office to fill him in on the news.

“They identified the vehicle where the explosives originated,” replied May, still in shock. “It was Jami’s.”

28

Chris and Mark stood with Jami in Charlie's home office as she brought the men up to speed on the current situation. Operational planning wasn't typically discussed in the presence of civilians, but Jami explained the concerns she had with DDC and, more specifically, analyst Simon Harris. And the fact that Charlie Redding was a retired ATF man and had managed to obtain an image of the only suspect they had in the agency bombing—not to mention was a personal friend of Jordan's—made him a part of the discussion.

"So that's him?" asked Mark, pointing at the man on the left of the image taken from a CCTV camera.

Chris crossed his arms and stared at the large monitor. "And the other one was taken out in the garage?"

Jami nodded her response to both of the questions as Reed grabbed his phone and started to place a call. "Who are you calling, Chris?" she asked.

"Landry."

"I told you, we have to cut off all communication until we understand what we're dealing with here."

Reed shook his head. "There's a dead man handcuffed to a concrete column on the top floor of a parking garage. Think about it, Jami. How long until he's discovered? Someone's probably found the guy already."

Jami was becoming frustrated and sighed heavily. "Then what are you suggesting?"

"I'll call it in. Landry will get some Bureau guys over there to claim the body and figure out who he is."

"No," argued Jami. "I already sent the image to Morgan. I'm having him ID both of the guys already."

"Metro PD will be swarming all over that place, if they're not there already, Jami." Chris turned to Mark Reynolds, who nodded in agreement. "It'll be all over the news, and that could tip off whoever took Blake."

"Chris is right," said Mark. "We should call it in. If Metro PD gets there first, this will get ugly real fast."

Jami's phone started to ring, and she reached into her pocket to fish it out. "It's Morgan," she said and looked back up to Chris. "Go ahead and call Landry. Explain to him the situation with Simon Harris and DDC. Tell him what happened, but tell him he's got to keep this between us—he can't go to May about it."

Chris nodded as Jami's cell continued to ring. "Morgan," she said and stepped toward the front door.

"I think I've found him, love," he said as Jami turned back to look behind her and saw Reed across the room, talking on his phone, as Mark and Charlie stood together, studying the image on the monitor.

"Are you sure?"

"I think so," the Chicago DDC analyst replied. "I was able to reposition one of the joint agency satellites when you first called me, so I had it taking snapshots of the area already. I was able to pinpoint the parking garage based on your phone's GPS when you called. I located the garage and went from there."

Jami's heart started racing. She heard the sound of rain starting to come down hard outside. It hit the window next to the door, forcing Jami to press the cell harder against her other ear to hear him better. "Where is he?" she asked and placed her free hand to her forehead as Morgan typed in the background.

"Four miles north of you, love. Thirty-four ten Garfield Street Northwest, about fifteen minutes away."

Jami nodded to herself.

"Hold on a sec." A few seconds of silence passed. "Bloody hell," he finally said.

"Morgan? What's wrong?"

"The satellite's refreshing every ninety seconds, Jami. Another vehicle just showed up at the location."

"What kind of vehicle?"

After a few more seconds of silence, Morgan said, "It's too dark; the picture's grainy. But I'm positive that the vehicle I'm looking at right now wasn't there a few seconds ago. It's parked right behind the first one."

Jami got the attention of the others and quickly filled them in on everything that Morgan had told her. Then she put Morgan on speakerphone so they could continue the discussion with the rest of the team. Morgan cleared his throat. "Okay, guys. The vehicles are parked in front of the building at Garfield. I'm going to need you guys to come in from the south. Actually, hang on a sec." Morgan paused as Jami heard the sound of typing again as she raised the volume on her phone so they could hear him better. "Got it. You'll want to come up Fulton Street and approach from Thirty-Fourth. Yes, I think that would be best."

Jami was still concerned with the second vehicle that

had arrived at the building. "Any way to figure out where that vehicle came from, Morgan?" she asked and looked up at the men all huddled around her.

"I can try, love. It took me a while to locate the first vehicle because of the way this satellite is refreshing and because there are still a lot of cars out tonight." He thought about it some more and added, "I'd say the first priority is to get over there before it leaves, and we can get a plate number so I can run it for us."

"Okay," said Jami. "I'll call you back from the road, and you can talk us in as we approach the building."

Jami disconnected the call and began planning the next steps with Chris and Mark. The team decided that Jami would lead them into the neighborhood, with the Bureau guys following close behind. A bright flash of lightning lit the window by the front door, closely followed by a loud crack of thunder a second later. The lightning strike and accompanying thunder were so close that it put all of them on edge as they realized that the storm was getting worse and the conditions were less than ideal to perform a tactical operation. But they had no time to wait it out, and the team got ready to leave for the address immediately.

"Stop short of the building," said Mark as he and Chris moved closer to the door. "We'll pull Chris's SUV behind yours and pop the hatch to shield us from the rain so we can make our final plans and get ready to move in, okay?"

Jami nodded as Mark turned to Chris. "We have enough gear for all of us, man?"

Reed thought about it. "We should be good." He turned to his left to look at Jami and started to share the news that had just been given to him from Bill Landry, but changed his mind, deciding to hold off for now.

Charlie Redding moved past them, grabbed the doorknob, and twisted it. When he pulled the door open, the sound of rain engulfed the entrance to his home as the two Bureau agents brushed past him and Jami.

They headed outside, carefully jogged down the steps, and turned left to get to their parked vehicle.

Jami turned to look at Charlie before heading out into the storm herself. "Thanks for your help."

Redding kept a hand on the door and nodded. "Get him back, okay?"

Jami extended her hand, which Charlie clasped, and the two smiled briefly as Jami maintained eye contact with the man. "I have to," she replied over the sound of the rain. "There's still a lot left to be said."

29

I FELT THE SENSATION OF SOMEONE SLAPPING MY FACE repeatedly, trying to wake me up, while shining a bright light in my eyes. As I opened my eyes, I remembered where I was and immediately felt pain in my wrists as my limp body hung from the ropes. I slowly stood to relieve the pressure as the light continued to shine in my eyes, and I closed them and looked away, trying to understand what was happening to me.

"Time to wake up, Mr. Jordan," a man said as he grabbed my face and forced me to look at him.

The light moved from my face to his, and I had to blink several times to get my eyes to adjust. A young man stared back at me as he held the flashlight at the bottom of his face, creating shadows over his eyes as the top of his head remained darkened. The man looked like he was in his early twenties. He kept a stoic demeanor and just stared at me blankly for several seconds before he let go of my face and stepped back.

"Who are you?" I managed to ask, breathing deeply and still feeling drowsy as I tried to stay focused.

He smiled, dropped the flashlight, and started to pace around me. He circled me once before answering.

"My name is Dimitri," he said with a Russian accent, confirming what I already knew—that my past was finally catching up to me as the words of the man I killed six months ago echoed inside my mind. "Dimitri *Ivanov*," the man added, putting emphasis on his last name as he completed a circle around me.

"Ivanov," I whispered to myself, trying to process what the young man had just said.

"Six months ago, my father—Nikolai Ivanov—attempted to put a stop to your government's surveillance of the people of my country. And he would have been successful if it had not been for you stopping him."

"Is that what this is all about?" I asked the young man. "I killed your father, so now you want to kill me?"

I heard him laugh to himself. "But the truth is, Mr. Jordan, he never really could have stopped that surveillance program. In his mind, bringing down that NSA substation hidden in plain sight in New York would have put an end to the American government's program—" he paused briefly "—but you and I both know that's not how it works. Another substation would have gone online and taken over. You can never fully stop a powerful force like the American government. No, the only thing that is effective is violence."

"What do you want from me?" I asked.

"But not just any kind of violence," he continued, ignoring me. "It must be focused, unconventional, like the attack on nine-eleven. My father's intentions were on target—but it was his approach that was flawed."

My eyes were adjusting, and I could see the outline of a man in the far corner of the room. I imagined that the other one, who had injected the hallucinogenic earlier, was somewhere behind me. I watched Ivanov continue to pace the floor, circling me slowly and stepping around the body of the man I had killed earlier.

"I will tell you what I want from you, Mr. Jordan," he said as he came around my right, stepped closer, and crouched down on the floor in front of me. "I want you to bring my father back to me by daybreak."

I shook my head. "I don't know what you're talking about," I replied. "Your father is dead. He was killed in the explosion at the top of the TITANPOINTE building in New York six months ago. He didn't survive."

Dimitri brought the flashlight to my face, and I turned away. "My father is certainly *not* dead, Mr. Jordan."

The man let his words hang in the air before he lowered the light and began pacing again. I turned as he came around me again. "If he wasn't dead," I said, my eyes following him as he moved, "I would know."

"I would have thought that someone in your position within the government would have known better," he replied. "You are, after all, a senior advisor to the president —are you not?" When I didn't respond, he said, "At the very least, I would think that someone with your background would acknowledge that your country has underground prisons for so-called terrorists that are presumed to be dead. Men and women detained in facilities hidden far away from the public's view. 'Black sites,' as your government calls them."

I shook my head. "Black sites don't exist anymore. President Rouse terminated the CIA program well before leaving office. You're kidding yourself if you think your father is being held inside one of them."

Ivanov stopped again, reached inside a pocket, and retrieved a cell phone. The light illuminated his face as I watched his thumb flick across the screen several times before he held the phone up for me to see. Staring at the screen, I studied an image of a bearded man wearing an orange jumpsuit. I focused on the eyes of the man and felt the hair on the back of my neck stand on end. I looked up at the man's dark face. "Where did you get that?" I asked as I realized for the first time that Ivanov might be telling me the truth.

He pulled the phone away from my face and shoved it back into one of his pockets. "Mr. Jordan," he said, this time remaining still, his dark outline visible to me as my eyes readjusted to the room, "my father had many contacts within this country's government. Friends, I would call them. A few held positions within the intelligence community. When I learned the news about what had happened to my father in New York, I was saddened, until I received this picture," he said, keeping his hand on the phone inside his pocket.

"I'm not going to help you," I said, dropping my head and feeling weak as I felt my body go limp again. The ropes cut into my wrists, but I didn't care anymore. I was getting used to the pain. "I'll never help you."

Dimitri laughed again. "Mr. Jordan, I told you that my father has friends—supporters—in government positions. So it should come as no surprise that I know everything about you." He took a step closer, and as I looked up, he grabbed my face and held it straight. "I've read your file. I know about your friendship with President Keller." He paused before adding, "I think I may know you better than you know yourself."

I narrowed my eyes. "What are you talking about?"

I sensed that the man was now smiling. "The woman—Agent Davis—I know everything about her, too." He let go of my face as I found my footing and stood taller. "Of course, none of this is in your file. I had to rely on my people on the inside to fully understand who you are and what matters most to you. It's always the girl, isn't it, Mr. Jordan? The women we want that we know we can't have. The women we want to protect."

I gripped the ropes, squeezing them tight as a rush of adrenaline surged through me. "You son of a bitch."

Ivanov laughed. "That's right," he whispered. "The feeling you have right now—anger, vengeance, like you're not in control anymore—use it like I have." He paused and added, "My people on the inside, they know even more about her than they know about you. They know exactly where she is at any point in time. You have until dawn," he said, slipping the phone into my pocket. "And if you decide *not* to comply—" he grabbed my throat and squeezed, gripping it tight as I struggled for air "—I'll go after the girl. Understand? And before I kill her, I will explain to her that you had a chance to stop it from happening."

I watched as the man in the corner of the room approached quickly and whispered something into Dimitri's ear. As he left, Ivanov said, "Your people are on their way. They will be here in five minutes."

"I don't know where your father is."

"Ask your friend President Keller. He's been lying to you, but knows the truth. You have until daybreak."

30

After Ivanov left, followed by the man guarding the door and the other guy who had been lurking in the dark somewhere behind me, I waited alone, expecting agents to arrive at any moment, as Dimitri had suggested. The storm I had heard battering the outside of the building just a few minutes earlier seemed to be moving out. All I could hear now was a light sprinkle against the windows near the front entrance.

I waited, scanning the dark and thinking, until finally the front door was kicked in and three figures entered, each with tactical flashlights shining their path as they stepped inside and approached quickly. One broke off and moved to the left, another to the right, as the third one headed straight for me, illuminating my face briefly before the light checked each of the corners of the large room surrounding me and then stopped on the dead man at my feet. I heard the voice of Mark Reynolds as he got closer to me.

"Clear," he yelled, his deep voice echoing throughout the large empty room. I heard Chris and Jami repeat the word as they came into view and shined their lights in my direction, joining Mark as he fished a knife out of a pocket. He set his light on the floor as Chris and Jami lit my wrists to help Mark see.

"Blake," said Jami with a gasp as she raised her light to my chest and kept it there. I looked down at my shirt and saw a splattering of blood. "Are you okay?" she asked as Mark cut through the first, then second rope. I grabbed my wrists and massaged them. She approached and put her arms around me and held me.

"I think so," I replied, wincing in pain from my hurt arm as it adjusted to its new position after being held upright for so long. I wrapped my other arm around Jami as Chris shined the light on the dead man.

"Who's this guy?" asked Chris as he turned the body over, studied the dead man's face, and got his answer. "Looks like one of the guys Redding showed us," he said, and I knew he had visited Charlie.

Jami shined her flashlight around the old, abandoned building as she tried to understand what she was looking at. "What *is* this place? Looks like it's been deserted for thirty years," she said before turning back to me. "I went to your friend's house, Blake. Charlie Redding—he had an image taken from the CCTV footage you asked him to get. The two people talking to the homeless guy were the man you killed back at the parking garage and this guy here," she said, looking at the body of the man who Chris had turned over.

The three of them moved their flashlights around, checking out the building. My eyes were starting to adjust to the light as I looked around, trying to understand why it was abandoned. Mark turned to me. "Blake, what's this all about, brother?" he asked, knowing that the chances of the guy on the floor being able to tie me up by himself were slim and wanting to understand what had happened before they arrived.

Before I could answer, I noticed Jami pulling her cell phone from a pocket. The screen was illuminated, and I could tell that she had an active call in progress. Jami held it up, and I asked who was on the line.

"Morgan," she said, and I realized he had likely helped her and the guys find my location.

"Morgan, can you hear me?" I asked, making sure the DDC analyst was still on the line.

"I'm here, mate. Glad you're okay."

I nodded to myself and paused to collect my thoughts before I began. "What I'm about to share with you all must stay between the five of us," I said and looked at Jami before turning to Mark and Chris to make sure I had their agreement. They nodded as I put a hand on my hurt shoulder and held it there for a moment, deciding where to begin. "Nikolai Ivanov—the man who was killed at the NSA substation in New York six months ago—" I paused briefly and looked each of them in the eye "—the man is very much alive."

"How do you know that, Blake?" asked Chris, a question I knew the rest of the team shared.

"Because I just came face-to-face with his son, Dimitri Ivanov. He was here less than five minutes ago."

Silence filled the room. A few seconds later, I heard the sound of typing coming from Jami's cell phone. "Listen, mate," said Morgan. "I'm looking in our database, but not seeing anything on a Dimitri Ivanov." He paused. "And, Jami, the other two guys that you wanted me to ID, they're not in the database, either."

"What does he want?" asked Mark as Jami handed my phone back to me, and I slid it in my back pocket.

I thought about how to answer, weighing the pros and cons of sharing what I knew, given the threat Dimitri had made against Jami. "He said that his father survived the explosion at the NSA substation back in New York and is being detained at a black site," I replied. "And I have until daybreak to get him out."

"A black site?" asked Jami. "I thought President Rouse shut them all down before he left office."

"I did, too. And if I don't get him out by daybreak, he said there will be more bombings," I lied.

We stood in silence for a few moments before Chris spoke. "Jami," he said, "I need to tell you something." She turned to him as he continued. "When I called Bill Landry right before we left Redding's home, he said that Lynne May had just left his office. The ATF guys finished their preliminary analysis at DDC." Chris glanced over to me, then turned back to her. "It was your vehicle that exploded in the garage, Jami."

"What?" she asked and shook her head in disbelief. "How is that even possible, Chris?"

"There's something else you all need to know," said Morgan as Jami turned up the volume on her phone. "The ransomware attack from earlier—I traced it back to Palos Community Hospital, south of Chicago."

"I know that hospital," I said.

"I know you do, mate. The malware was introduced into that specific hospital followed by two others in Washington later in the day. But Palos Community is where it all started. There have already been several deaths there because of the malware. Aside from the Washington hospitals, it has the most fatalities."

Jami stepped closer to me. "That's the hospital where you and Keller were taken after you rescued him."

I nodded to myself. "But that's not why the ransomware was introduced into Palos Community," I said. "It's because that's the hospital where my father died." I heard Morgan stop typing as the line went silent.

"Ben," Jami said softly as she rested a hand on my back and looked down. "How could I forget? I'm sorry."

"The hospital—the bombing at DDC—it's all related. This is personal," I said and grabbed my wrists, massaging them to help with the pain from the ropes digging into my skin, leaving them raw and tender. "It's not gonna stop until Ivanov gets what he wants," I said, thinking about the threat the man had made against Jami that I had decided to keep to myself. "He said he's getting help from someone on the inside. Until we figure out what's going on, this stays between us. No contact with anyone at the Bureau or DDC." I paused to look at the others before adding, "I need to get his father out. Then I'll deal with both of them."

"I'll try to find the location of the black site," said Morgan as I heard the sound of typing start back up.

"No, find Dimitri. I'll go see Keller. He knows about this. It's time to learn the truth about Nikolai Ivanov."

31

PRESIDENT JAMES KELLER SAT IN HIS STUDY, ONE LEG CROSSED over the other, studying the newspaper he'd been meaning to read since breakfast. Still wearing dress pants and a white dress shirt, he loosened his tie with one hand while continuing to scan the paper and slowly shaking his head to himself.

There was something about the *New York Times* story that bothered Keller. *How'd they get tipped off?* the president asked himself, turning his gaze back to the headline. "Russian spy ship patrolling off America's east coast," he muttered as he set the newspaper on the table next to his roomy easy chair, removed his reading glasses, and placed the arm against his lips as he stared across the room, thinking.

The White House leaks had become rampant over the last six months, yet the people Keller had surrounded himself with since the beginning of his presidency eighteen months earlier had, for the most part, remained unchanged. Glancing back to the paper on his left, he began to wonder who the *Times* was getting their information from. Keller began replaying conversations he'd had over the last few months in his mind, trying to connect the dots between the various leaks coming from the White House, but couldn't pin any of them on a specific person within his administration. Keller tossed his glasses on the paper out of frustration just as there was a knock at the door behind him. "Come in," he said as he turned.

The door slowly opened, and a Secret Service agent looked inside. "Emma Ross for you, sir," he said as the president nodded and motioned that it was okay for the man to let his chief of staff enter the room. The agent nodded, disappeared from view, and Ross stepped inside with a paper tucked under her arm. Keller saw the paper, decided it was the same one he'd been reading, and forced a smile as she entered.

"I'm sorry to bother you so late, Mr. President," said Ross as the agent closed the door once she entered.

"It's no bother, Emma," said Keller as he began twisting his wedding band, something the man had started to do out of habit whenever he thought about his late wife. "I don't get much sleep anymore." He looked down briefly before deciding to walk over to the window to look out into the darkness. "It's just a cold, empty bed waiting for me at the end of every day." He turned back to Ross and forced another smile.

Ross furrowed her brow as she studied her boss from across the room. "Are you okay? You look worried," she said as her eyes narrowed.

"It's nothing, Emma. It's just late, and I..." Keller looked at his chief of staff for a few moments, realized that she wasn't buying his story, and nodded to himself before stepping closer to her. The president gestured to the newspaper tucked under her arm. "I had a meeting with the joint chiefs about an hour ago, Emma." Keller crossed his arms. "That Russian ship was doing more than just trying to intimidate us."

"What do you mean?"

The president looked up at the ceiling, trying to recall the conversation so he could relay the facts back to Ross just as he had heard them. "When the *Viktor Leonov* left port in Cuba and started to make its way up the east coast, we began surveilling its movements with satellites, Emma. Tracked the damn thing all the way up to Boston before it veered off into the Atlantic." Keller pointed at the paper Ross was holding. "We don't believe it was seeding the US coastline, though we are going to check just to be absolutely sure."

Ross maintained eye contact with Keller and asked, "Then what's the concern?"

"The concern," replied Keller, "is what one of our satellites picked up last night as the vessel passed by just east of Delaware." Ross slowly shook her head as Keller checked his watch. "Just about twenty-four hours ago, our people detected a bright light one mile behind the ship, right along the same path it had taken."

"Lightning?" said Ross, and Keller shook his head.

"It lasted for several seconds." He paused before adding, "It was a distress flare, Emma. A call for help."

Ross was becoming anxious. "Why? Who was out there?"

Keller placed his hands in his pockets, looked down, and shook his head. "We don't know yet. But they applied a layer and picked up what we believe to have been a small watercraft that immediately went to that location. Several minutes later, the boat made its way back to a pier located in Ocean City, Maryland."

"We need to find out who was out there and what they were doing."

"We're trying," replied Keller. "We have good people working on it right now. They think they found the vehicle leaving the Ocean City pier as it headed to Washington, but lost it once it got onto the interstate. They're going back over the imagery now in an attempt to try to locate it again." Keller looked down at the paper that Ross was now holding with two hands, and gestured toward it. "So I appreciate you coming to see me—" he pointed at his own copy resting next to his chair "—but I'm already aware of the situation."

Emma remained silent as Keller turned, went back to the window to look outside, and crossed his arms. Several seconds passed in silence. Sensing that something was amiss, he turned back to his chief of staff.

"Mr. President," she said, concern in her voice, "thank you for the update, but that's not why I'm here."

Keller stared at the woman over his shoulder from his position at the window. "There's something else?"

Ross nodded.

"What is it, Emma?" he asked, but she didn't answer, so the president stepped toward her.

"Sir, I suggest you have a seat."

Keller lifted a hand to caution the woman. "Stop tiptoeing around this, and tell me what the problem is."

She maintained her gaze and finally said, "It's about Blake Jordan."

"Blake? What about him?" asked Keller. "I just spoke with him. He's on his way here now to meet with me and sounded concerned." He paused. "Does that have anything to do with what you're about to tell me?"

Ross slowly shook her head. "I doubt it, sir," she replied and handed Keller the newspaper.

The president took it and kept his eyes on the woman as he unfolded it and slowly lowered his gaze.

"It's an early copy of tomorrow's paper. I have a friend at the *Times* that called me about an hour ago, saying that there was a lot of excitement at the New York office. She heard a few people talking about a story that would finally be the smoking gun needed to bring down the president. It's another leak, sir."

Keller stepped over to the table next to his easy chair and grabbed his reading glasses. Putting them on, he stared at the headline with disbelief before he began scanning the accompanying story that followed. "Good God," he whispered to himself as he finished scanning the story that was just a few hours away from being distributed to six hundred thousand households and digitally to two and a half million email inboxes—a story sure to be picked up by every news and media outlet on the other side of the aisle.

"We have to get in front of this," said Ross.

The president folded the paper, dropped it on the table, and removed his glasses. "How can we stop this?"

32

Lynne May stood next to her analyst and leaned in closer to the speakerphone. "Morgan, you there?" she asked and pressed a button to turn up the volume as Simon Harris's counterpart in Chicago replied.

"I can hear you just fine," said Lennox, sounding disinterested in speaking with the Washington SAIC.

"The three of us need to get on the same page," said May as Simon Harris turned in his chair and looked up at his boss. "Morgan, as you know, Agent Davis left DDC with Blake Jordan a few hours ago. After the motorcycle chase, they spent a considerable amount of time at a parking garage. Landry got word from Agents Reed and Reynolds that something went down over there, so he's sending people over there now." May looked up and watched Bill Landry appear from down the hallway. He stopped briefly to answer a question from one of his Bureau analysts before he disappeared again. May lowered her head to continue. "Simon and I have been monitoring their movements, and we tracked them to an address in Rosslyn registered to a retired ATF man. We know that Davis met up with Reed and Reynolds at the home. A short time later, we tracked them as they left for another location, and now their phones are turned off again." May looked at Harris and paused a beat before she continued. "Morgan, what the hell's going on here?"

Morgan remained silent as the special agent in charge crossed her arms and looked at Simon, confused.

After several seconds, Simon grew tired of the awkward silence. "The last time I had contact was during the pursuit of the man on the motorcycle," he said. "The call dropped, and I couldn't reach them again."

"You led them into a trap," snapped Morgan as May raised her eyebrows in surprise at the accusation.

Simon shook his head vigorously. "I did *not* lead them into a trap. Morgan, why would you think that?"

"Because of the approach you brought them in on. You were a block off target, Jami had to make the correction, and by the time she did, the guy on the motorcycle was too far out for her to catch up to."

Simon shook his head at May in shock, then returned to his laptop, determined to prove his innocence.

"And then the ransomware," continued Lennox as May reached over and lowered the volume after seeing a few Bureau analysts poke their heads over their cubicles to see what the commotion was with the visiting DDC team. "Simon, you were responsible for analyzing the malware. I took that task over from you, and within minutes, I found the kill switch embedded in the middle of the code. It was in plain sight, mate."

May looked up and saw Landry appear again from the dark corridor. He turned and headed her way.

"Morgan, is Roger Shapiro up to speed?" she asked, referring to Morgan's boss at the Chicago field office.

"Yes. He's letting you run this if you're sure you can still effectively handle it from the Hoover Building."

"Good. Then I need you to find another way to track Davis and Jordan."

Simon stopped typing and pointed at his screen. "I just did."

May leaned in to take a look.

"She took one of the field office's loaner vehicles, right? I confirmed that there weren't any others checked out. And DDC uses a fleet-tracking system for our vehicles at both the Chicago and Washington field offices."

May pointed at a blip on the screen that was slowly moving toward the center of the city. "Is that them?"

Simon nodded.

May stood up straight. "Good work. Let me know when they stop so we can intercept."

"Lynne," said Bill Landry as he approached Simon's cubicle, "can you come see me when you're done?"

"Yes, give me a few minutes and I'll stop by your office."

Landry nodded and turned as May watched him walk back through the maze of cubicles and disappear into the dark corridor again. "Morgan, are you still there?" she asked and dropped her eyes to the landline.

"I'm here."

"The Bureau's Cyber Division is currently working on a patch for impacted healthcare and government systems. Since you seem to be more proficient with the code, I want you available in case they need help."

"Fine," grunted Lennox from the speakerphone as May looked up to the corridor toward Landry's office.

"I'm going to go chat with Bill and see what he wants. I'll be back shortly." She looked down at Simon. "And I'll bring him up to speed on Reed and Reynolds and see if we can find out what's going on out there. I might need someone from his Bureau team to intercept Davis and Jordan, and it can't be those two."

May disconnected the call, eyed Simon's screen briefly, and walked back to her cubicle. After taking a seat, she drew in a deep breath and slowly let it out, her cheeks puffing out as she did, and unlocked her screen. Pinching the bridge of her nose with her thumb and forefinger, she closed her eyes and tried to will the headache she felt coming on to go away. Opening her eyes, May glanced at her watch to check the time.

She minimized her email program after confirming that no new urgent communications had come through over the last several minutes that she had spent at Simon Harris's desk. Once she did, all that remained on her screen was the instant messaging program that the Department of Domestic Counterterrorism used to communicate within and between the two teams in Chicago and Washington.

Scrolling through the online contacts, May found Morgan Lennox. She double-clicked on his name.

The cursor blinked inside a new chat window, waiting for her to type a message to the analyst she'd only met once, back when the Washington field office had been formed three months earlier. She didn't know Lennox very well. But from her initial meeting, she had learned two things about Morgan. One, he was intelligent and underutilized by his boss, Roger Shapiro, and definitely one of the better analysts she'd come across in her long career. And two, the Australian seemed to be an excellent judge of character and wasn't afraid to speak his mind when needed. May thought long and hard about those two points.

And it was Morgan's outburst with Simon moments earlier that bothered May and prompted her to open the chat window. May let go of the mouse, placed her hands on the keyboard, and thought about how she should phrase her question to him. Following a few seconds of hesitation, May typed her message: 'Morgan, is there something going on with Simon that I need to know about?'

Her finger lingered above the enter key for several seconds. Then she hit it and stared at her screen.

May's eyes focused on the instant message chat window and waited thirty seconds before the program indicated that Morgan was typing a reply. May folded her arms across the desk, waiting for the response.

'Please call me,' replied Morgan.

May typed her response: 'Ping me your personal cell number. Will call you after touching base with Bill.' She hit enter and then typed another message. 'Also need your help on a private matter, Morgan. Okay?'

Lennox replied with his number, which May entered into her cell, then stood to go meet with Landry.

33

I DROVE JAMI'S SUV OVER TO THE WHITE HOUSE AND PARKED it along the Ellipse, the street that runs along the circumference of the fifty-two-acre park where many of the president's staffers park each day. Jami didn't say much on the short drive over, except for asking me twice if I was feeling okay. I figured that I was looking pretty rough and she was maybe feeling a little guilty about our heated exchange earlier. I wasn't sure what it was, but there was something different about her now.

After pulling into an empty spot close to E Street, I climbed out and reached for my messenger bag. I took off my shirt with the blood splattered on the front of it, wiped my face with the clean part, and threw it in the backseat. I reached into my bag and found one of the shirts I had packed when I was planning on spending a few days at Charlie's, and pulled it over my head. Jami handed my Glock back to me. I stuffed it inside my bag and left it in the vehicle as I closed the door and walked toward the White House with Jami.

Chris and Mark were circling Washington, on standby

with Morgan back in Chicago as he tried to figure out where Dimitri Ivanov had gone. That was plan A. The conversation I was about to have with President Keller was plan B and—unless Morgan could find Dimitri's location quickly—would be the only other option that I could see to get Nikolai and Dimitri Ivanov out in the open so I could keep Jami safe.

I showed my White House staff credentials at the guard post. After contacting the president and telling him that I needed to see him, I told him that Jami was with me and she'd need clearance to enter with me. Keller had asked me what the visit was about, and I told him I'd explain everything when we got there. The guard verified Jami's name on the list, studied her identification, and escorted us onto the property.

Ten minutes later, Jami and I were ushered to the presidential study upstairs. With a knock at the door, the agent posted there pushed it open and gestured for us to enter, saying that Keller was expecting us.

"Mr. President," said Jami as she walked in first and shook his hand before greeting Emma Ross, whom Jami had met eighteen months prior when there was a credible threat against Keller on inauguration day.

"My God," said Keller as I stepped in behind Jami and he looked at me. "What the hell happened to you?"

My eyes darted over to Ross, then back to the president. "I need to speak with you alone," I said.

The president crossed his arms. "Blake, anything you have to say to me can be said in front of Emma."

"Please," I said.

Keller turned to his chief of staff and nodded. I watched as Ross gestured to the door, grabbed a newspaper from the table next to the president's chair, and walked out of the study with Jami.

"What's this all about?" said Keller as I turned back once the door had been closed and we were alone.

"Nikolai Ivanov."

"Ivanov?" he repeated and turned his back to me as he approached the window. "What about him?"

I took a few steps closer and looked him over before responding. "Where is he, Mr. President?"

Keller turned back with a surprised expression on his face. "I don't know what you're talking about."

"Sir, I need to know where he's being held," I said, paying close attention to his facial expression and body language. Based on my training as a SEAL and as a counterterrorism operative, I knew he was lying.

"Don't lie to me, Mr. President," I said as he turned back to the window. "I deserve to know the truth."

Keller remained at the window. He dropped his head and, after several seconds, started to nod to himself. "You're right," he said softly. "You do deserve to know the truth." The president paused again as he collected his thoughts. "Early morning on New Year's Day, I had an intelligence briefing on the events in New York." Keller slipped his hands into his pockets with his head still hung low before he continued. "The FBI had gone into TITANPOINTE and went up to the top floor and found the two men who tried to bring down the intelligence-gathering system." He looked over his shoulder to me. "Ivanov was alive."

"That's not possible," I said. "There was enough C-4 up there to destroy the entire floor of the building."

Keller began walking to me slowly. "From what I read, it was piled up in a corner on the opposite side of the building. He was trapped inside an elevator. The blast reached him, but it just didn't kill him, Blake."

Neither of us spoke for several seconds as I thought about that night in the city. "Why didn't you tell me?"

The president looked past me and shrugged. "There are protocols for situations like this, Blake. Processes. Procedures. The American people don't need to see terrorists within our own country brought to trial, only to have it drawn out for months if not years until these people are exonerated or brought to justice." He took in a deep breath and let it out slowly. "Far better for the public to believe he's dead."

"I'm not the public. I'm your counterterrorism advisor," I said and paused a beat. "And I'm your friend."

"Blake, don't—"

"Sir," I said, interrupting him, "you should have told me. I could have done things differently."

"It doesn't matter," replied Keller. "For all intents and purposes, the American people believe he's dead. And he might as well be. Nikolai Ivanov will never again see the light of day, I can promise you that."

I crossed my arms, took a step forward, and stared at the president as he looked back at me. "Where is he?"

"It doesn't matter," he said again after a few seconds of silence, deciding to end the conversation there.

"Mr. President," I said as I winced in pain and grabbed my right shoulder from the stress of the situation. "Please. I need to know where he is. It's important."

Keller dropped his gaze and shook his head. Finally he spoke. "Mount Weather. Sixty miles west of us."

I looked away, recognizing the name of the facility, but unaware of what it was. "What's Mount Weather?"

"As far as the American people are concerned, it's

nothing out of the ordinary. A civilian command facility," he said and shrugged again. "Center of operations for FEMA, a site controlled by Homeland Security." Keller's eyes remained fixed on mine. "But the truth—" he said, looking past me to the door before glancing back "—is that Mount Weather is the location for a shadow government. Precautions for a doomsday scenario, a program put in place by Reagan. Several buildings on the surface, but three hundred feet underground—" he pointed at the floor "—is a massive complex. A subterranean fortress carved deep into the mountain. Twenty multistory buildings. Fresh water reservoirs two hundred feet across. A hospital. A broadcast studio where I—or my successor—could keep Americans posted on events. Enough supplies for two hundred government officials to survive for a month. Enough bunks for two thousand. In the event of a nuclear war, should Washington get wiped out, any surviving members of our government would be taken there." The president took in another breath, and after letting it out, he added, "And there's a prison down there where people like Nikolai Ivanov are kept. That's where he is, Blake."

34

The president's words cut right through me as I realized what he was trying to tell me—that there was no way I could ever get inside a facility like Mount Weather. I imagined the kind of security that would surround such an off-the-record government installation. I needed to find another way to get to Ivanov.

"I need you to make a phone call," I said to the president.

Keller laughed to himself at the suggestion. "And do what exactly, Blake? Ask them to let the guy go?"

"You have to do something."

"Why?" he pressed and took a step closer to me. "First, I need you to explain to me what this is all about."

I shook my head and looked away. I took a deep breath in and let it out slowly, trying to calm my nerves. "Jami," I replied. "If I can't free Nikolai Ivanov by daybreak, they're going to come after her."

"*Who's* going to come after her?" he asked, his voice now lower than it was just moments earlier.

"Dimitri Ivanov," I replied. "His son. He's responsible for

everything that's happened today. The ransomware that targeted Chicago and Washington hospitals. The DDC bombing. This is personal, sir."

Keller's eyes stayed fixed on mine. "Is that who did this to you?" he asked, looking me over. "Dimitri?"

I nodded. "Like I said, I have until daybreak to bring his father to him. Please. I need your help."

He watched as I walked past him, put my hands on the back of my head, and slowly slid them down my neck.

"Does she know?"

I stared at the floor and shook my head.

"Then I think you need to tell her, son."

"Mr. President, I've just spent the last six months of my life looking over my shoulder. Waiting for these people to find me. Wondering who they were. Where they were. When they'd show up." I stopped walking and looked up when I got to the window. "I don't want that life for her. That's why I've pushed her away from me for so long." I turned back to look at my friend. "If I don't deal with this, they will come after her. The rules of engagement don't apply to these people, sir. Please," I said again. "I'm asking for your help."

Keller crossed his arms and looked down to the floor. "I can't do it, Blake."

"Can't or won't?"

"Can't," he repeated. "Ivanov is under the Bureau's control along with Homeland. They call the shots."

"Then call Bill Landry. Call the FBI director."

He looked up and thought about it.

"Just make one call."

"Alright," he said, once again stuffing his hands in his pockets. "I'll do what I can to help. But first, we—"

Before Keller could continue, I heard a knock at the door

behind us. It opened slowly. I turned as Jami entered with Ross following close behind. Jami looked pale and was carrying the newspaper that Emma had been holding when they had left us just a few minutes earlier. "You okay? What's wrong?" I asked.

"I'm sorry to interrupt," said Jami, walking past the president and unfolding the newspaper she carried. She looked down at the paper, turned it around for me, and extended her hand so I could take it from her.

I read the headline, started scanning the rest of the story, and looked up in disbelief. "What is this?"

"Another leak," replied the president's chief of staff as I looked back down and continued to read the story.

The *New York Times* was not fond of the president and didn't go out of their way to hide it. Over the last eighteen months, they had ripped his presidency apart. First, claiming he had won the office out of sympathy due to his kidnapping. Then they claimed voter fraud. Since the beginning of the year, there had been multiple leaks coming out of the White House, with Keller unable to control the flow of information.

The author of the story had their facts straight. It was a public outing, revealing that the president had his own black ops team at his disposal, handling domestic counterintelligence missions for him. The story centered on me and my past with Keller. It had details all the way back to high school, Keller training me to help me become a SEAL, my unusual rise to become a presidential advisor, and how it was just a cover.

It explained in detail how I had saved the president's life on the night he was set to receive his party's nomination for president and again on inauguration day. It exposed what I had done in New York City six months ago, revealing the details about the NSA operation at the site called TITAN-POINTE that should have remained a secret. I finally got to the end. "We can't let this get out," I said. "We have to stop this."

"Third major leak so far and we're only halfway through the year," said Ross.

"All from the *Times?*" I asked, and Emma nodded her answer. I looked at the byline. "Who's Meg Taylor?"

Ross folded one arm under the other and brought a hand up under her chin, resting it there to think. "Been filling in for David O'Malley. Young, ambitious woman. Currently in the White House press corps."

"How would she get these kinds of details on Blake?" asked Jami, but the chief of staff just shrugged.

"You said she's part of the press corps?"

"Temporarily," Ross clarified. "She's been working from O'Malley's desk downstairs until he returns."

"Do you have any contact information for Taylor?" I pressed.

Emma shook her head.

I looked at Jami for a moment, then turned back to Ross. "Can we see her desk?"

Emma deferred to the president, who considered the request. "What are you thinking, Blake?" he asked.

"I'm thinking that whoever's leaking information to the *New York Times* might be the same person leaking information to Dimitri Ivanov about his father." I paused, looking at each of them before continuing. "They're using people like Taylor to try to bring down your presidency. The leaks are coming from the intelligence community, not from inside the White House," I said, thinking about Simon Harris.

"How can you be so sure?" asked Keller.

"Because Dimitri Ivanov said he had people on the inside. It's the only thing that makes sense right now."

Keller nodded to Ross. "Take them downstairs. Help them any way you can, Emma." The president stretched out his arm and brought his wrist up to his eyes to check the time. "I have some calls to make. Blake, I'll reach out as soon as I have some answers," he added as Jami and I followed Ross out the door.

35

EMMA ESCORTED US DOWN TO THE PRESS CORPS OFFICES. AS soon as we walked through the doorway, the overhead lights automatically came on, revealing several rows of desks. Ross stepped forward, crossed her arms, and narrowed her eyes as she searched the room to find O'Malley's desk.

"It's here somewhere," she whispered to herself as she brought a finger to her lips and tapped it slowly as her eyes flicked back and forth across the empty room. "I think it's back there in the corner somewhere."

She began walking through the maze of desks as Jami and I followed. Once she reached the corner desk, Ross lifted a few papers to reveal an old wooden nameplate with O'MALLEY embossed on the front of it.

The room had a distinct old-house smell to it and reminded me of my father's office from when I was a kid. The scent was a combination of cluttered papers, mildew, and stagnant air inside the cramped space. I couldn't help but look around the old office and acknowledge the history that the room represented.

"Blake," said Jami as I looked down and saw that she was holding onto something and handed it to me.

It was a picture of me along with fourteen of the president's aides and closest advisors. My eyes grew wide. "This was from the night we bombed the Shayrat air base." I brought the picture closer to my eyes. My face had been circled and someone, Taylor, I guessed, had written my name right on the photograph.

Handing it back to Jami, I started to sift through some of the papers spread across the desk that Meg Taylor had been working from as Jami looked it over. "Why's your name written on this picture, Blake?"

I was wondering the same thing myself. "Maybe Taylor came across the picture and started going through the list of Keller's team present the night of the airstrike. Maybe she didn't recognize me and decided I was worth checking out," I said as I continued to sift through the loose papers on the desk.

Jami handed the picture over to Ross, who stood behind us as Jami joined me at the desk and began going through the loose papers, receipts, and other paperwork carelessly left on top of it. Then I found something that looked promising, held it up, turned it so the overhead light could catch it, and started to read it over.

"I think this is a receipt," I said, scanning the paper and turning it over to look at the back side.

Emma took a step closer and looked at it over my shoulder. "It's for a temporary parking pass," she said. "With O'Malley being out, standard operating procedure is to issue a temporary pass to anyone that fills in from the *Times*. We wouldn't want to issue anything longer than two weeks for someone filling in, but wouldn't want to put a reporter through the hassle of having to get a new parking pass every day, either."

"You make them pay for a pass?" asked Jami as I turned around to look at Ross, who shook her head.

"No, but as you can imagine, security is tight. We require photo identification, social security number, and a pretty extensive background check, so we need to know in advance when one of the news outlets will have someone filling in. We expedite wherever we can. But—" she pointed at the paper I was holding "—we make them sign that privacy notice for the background check and mail a copy to their home address."

I studied the information written on the privacy notice. I recognized the Federal Flats temporary housing address in Georgetown. "This isn't far from here," I said, turning the paper to show Jami. "Let's head out."

Jami nodded. But as I folded the paper in half and turned to leave, Emma stood in our path, blocking it. "Blake," she said, sounding concerned as she turned from Jami to me, "we need to talk about something."

"What is it?" I asked.

Ross tilted her head slightly, trying to find the right words to say. "As chief of staff, it's my job not only to lead and direct Keller's team, but also—" she paused for a moment "—to protect the president as well."

I shook my head slowly. "Protect him? I don't understand. What are you trying to say, Emma?"

"The story that's coming out in the *Times* just a few hours from now," she said, lifting her wrist and checking her watch. "It's bad, Blake. Really bad." She took a step closer and crossed her arms as she did. "You and I both know that when this story hits, it's going to create a firestorm we haven't seen in years." She turned to Jami. "A black ops team, not only green-lit, but directed by a sitting president."

"It's not like that," I said and turned to Jami. "I haven't worked with Jami in six months now. Two Bureau agents," I said, referring to Chris Reed and Mark Reynolds, "a Chicago analyst. They just let me work with them on occasion. Emma, when the American people find out about this, I don't think it'll be—"

"They'll go after him," said Ross, interrupting me. "They'll appoint a special counsel to investigate. They'll issue subpoenas and will start identifying witnesses. They won't care why Keller did it. And if they decide to move forward, they'll go to the Bureau to bring criminal charges against him. Do you want that?"

I thought about Bill Landry at the Bureau and how much he had opposed me over the years, clearly not a supporter of the president or me. "No," I said and looked down at the floor for several seconds, thinking.

When I looked back up, Ross was still staring at me. "And then they're going to come after you," she said. "A special prosecutor will be named by the Justice Department. You'll be questioned as if you were on trial. Everything you've done to help Keller over the last eighteen months will be looked at, Blake."

"Emma," I said as both of our voices were getting louder and beginning to echo inside the room, "I've done nothing but serve this country, and I've given it everything I've had. I've saved the president's life. *Twice*," I said with emphasis. "I lost my job at DDC, I lost my wife, and I lost my father because of my service to this country. Everything I've ever cared about has been taken away from me," I said. "This job is all I have left now. There's nowhere else for me to go. There's nothing else I want to do but serve the president,

Emma. I'll help him fight this. The American people will understand what we were doing here."

Jami remained silent. Ross looked down at the floor for several seconds before replying in a whisper. "That's not how it will be portrayed," she said. "You and I both know that. They'll try to impeach him. They'll say he sidestepped the process, took the law into his own hands. The beginning of the end, Blake."

I shook my head and tried to calm myself down as I thought about what Keller's chief of staff was saying. "Then what do you suggest?" I asked in a soft, low voice, trying to find a third option, but not seeing one.

Emma paused for a few moments, glancing at Jami, then back over to me. "The president would never fire you, Blake. That's why you need to resign."

I was taken aback by the suggestion, but it didn't stop there.

"I've already called in a favor. I can have a private jet ready within an hour to take you out of the country."

"Out of the country?" I repeated. "You want me to disappear?"

Ross nodded.

I took a step closer. "I appreciate what you're trying to do, but I'm not leaving my job and I'm not going anywhere, Emma." Turning to Jami, I motioned to the door. "Come on, let's get out of here."

"Thanks for your help," said Jami as we walked through the doorway and passed by a Secret Service agent.

"Think about it, Blake," called Ross from behind. I ignored her and kept moving. I had to find Meg Taylor.

36

Simon Harris returned to his cubicle with an ice-cold soda in his hand that he had purchased in the Hoover Building's third-floor break room just a few moments earlier. Checking his watch, Harris saw that it was four thirty in the morning. He wouldn't be getting sleep anytime soon and needed to stay alert. He unlocked his computer, pulled the tab on top of the can of soda, and took a sip as his eyes glanced up at the computer monitor, and he saw that something had changed since he'd gotten up from the desk he was working from temporarily—Agent Davis's loaner vehicle was now moving again.

He carefully set the soda down, keeping his eyes glued to the monitor, and leaned in closer to the screen.

Locking his workstation, Harris stood, left the cubicles where he, Lynne May, and the rest of his DDC colleagues were working, and headed down the hall toward where he thought Bill Landry's office was located. Passing through the dark corridor, he found an office with Landry's name posted outside it.

The door was closed, so Simon knocked three times.

There was no answer. "Mr. Landry?" he said, knocking again and waiting for an answer, but there was still no response. Simon turned to look back down the corridor and saw a couple of Bureau agents pass by, headed to one of their coworkers' desks or maybe to the break room to get some caffeine to help get them through the next several hours of work.

Simon reached for the door handle, turned it slowly, and pushed the door open. The office was empty.

Taking a look farther down the opposite side of the corridor, three offices past Landry's, he noticed a light on and started walking toward it. As he approached, he saw another nameplate posted outside the office, with MULVANEY on it. It was the FBI director's office, and as he stepped closer, he saw that it was twice the size of Landry's. Peter Mulvaney was wearing a white dress shirt, his sleeves rolled up, and his tie loosened. Glancing inside, Simon saw that the director's suit jacket was folded over a chair across the room. Mulvaney was hovering over his phone, glancing over to his computer monitor, and pressed a button on his landline to get a dial tone so he could enter in the conference call number to join a meeting.

Harris knocked on the door as the director looked over his shoulder. "Yes?" he asked, sounding rushed.

"Director Mulvaney," began Harris, who paused and looked back to his left towards Landry's office, "I'm Simon Harris, part of the DDC team that's working down the hall." The sound of the dial tone awaiting a number to be punched in filled the room, and Mulvaney turned back to disconnect the call while Harris continued. "I'm looking for Lynne May. She was meeting with Bill Landry, but they're not in his office."

"Nice to meet you, Simon," said Director Mulvaney. "I

just spoke with them a little while ago. Bill may have taken Lynne down to the cafeteria. Give them a few minutes, okay? They should be back in a bit."

Mulvaney flashed a reassuring smile and pointed at the door. "Can you get that for me?"

Simon returned the smile, reached in to pull the door closed, and headed back toward his cubicle. When he returned, Simon unlocked his screen and reached for the soda, but saw that something else had changed besides Davis's vehicle moving. Two notifications flashed on his screen from the cellular tracking system he had set as soon as Davis's and Jordan's phones had turned off. Both phones were now on.

Deciding that he needed to tell someone what he knew, Simon pulled up the instant messenger program and began to ping Morgan Lennox, but decided he'd better have the conversation over the phone. Simon clicked on Lennox's name, saw the phone number to his direct line displayed, and reached for the phone.

"Lennox," he said, answering on the first ring.

"Morgan, it's Simon."

Harris heard the man take a deep breath and let it out. "What do you want?" he asked, still annoyed.

"Jami's vehicle is on the move," replied Harris. "It was parked near the White House for close to an hour. Her cell phone is back online now. So is Jordan's. I was supposed to alert Mrs. May, but I can't find her."

There was silence on the other end of the line. "What do you mean you can't find her, Simon?"

Harris rested both elbows on top of his desk, lowered his head, and closed his eyes as he thought through the last several minutes. "I don't know," he replied. "She hasn't returned to the desk she's working from. You were on the phone with us when Landry stopped by and said they needed to talk. I went to his office, and it was empty with the lights turned off. I found Director Mulvaney; he said not to worry about it."

There was more silence from Morgan's side of the line before he finally decided to speak. "Simon," he said, "she pinged me a while ago. Said she needed to talk, but she never called. I thought it was her calling me."

Simon jumped in his chair, startled by two hard knocks that came from overhead. He looked up and saw Bill Landry hovering over his desk. "Mr. Landry," said Harris, pulling the phone away and keeping it out of Landry's direct line of sight as he looked up at the man standing on the other side of the cubicle wall.

"Any progress?" the Bureau man grunted.

Simon pointed at his screen. "Agent Davis's vehicle is on the move. And her cell phone's back online, so is Jordan's." Harris looked up at Landry. "I stopped by your office earlier. I can't find Mrs. May anywhere."

Landry nodded. "Lynne's not feeling well, Simon. I told her there was a privacy room located inside each of the restrooms, where she could sit down and rest her eyes for a while." Landry paused for a beat. "Not sure how long she'll be gone. Go ahead and send what you have to my screen. I'm taking over until she feels better. And I'll give you access to the Bureau's fleet-tracking system as well. I need you to monitor Chris Reed's vehicle for me, too." Simon stared blankly at Landry, who raised his eyebrows. "Got it?"

Harris nodded slowly. "Got it," he replied. "Sending the details over to your screen right now."

"Good. I'll be in my office. If anything changes, I need to be aware of it. Hell of a time for her to get sick."

Simon watched as Landry turned and stepped toward

the dark corridor. He grabbed the receiver he had set on his desk and brought it back to his ear. "Morgan? Still there?"

Lennox replied that he was.

Harris cradled the phone against his ear and used two hands to get back to work. "You get all that?"

Morgan said that he did and walked Simon through the steps to send the tracking details from the DDC system to the Bureau's so that Landry could grab it and see what Simon was viewing on his own screen.

"Simon, I need you to do me a favor, mate. Dial zero, talk to security, and confirm for me that May didn't leave the building. As a visitor, she'd have had to sign out." He paused before adding, "Something doesn't feel right. I just want to make sure Landry didn't escort her out of the building."

After agreeing, Harris disconnected, heard a dial tone and hit zero. "Security," a voice said immediately.

"This is Simon Harris, one of the visiting DDC analysts. Can you tell me if Lynne May stepped out?"

"No, sir," the man on the other end of the line said. "None of the visitors have signed out yet, Mr. Harris."

Simon thanked the man, disconnected the line, and pinged Morgan to tell him that May was still there. Morgan didn't reply, but Simon decided that if he didn't see May within the hour, he'd go check on her.

37

Jami and I knocked on the door to Meg Taylor's apartment. When she didn't answer, I used a knife and started working on the lock. About a minute later, I heard it click, turned the handle, and pushed it open. We stepped inside and flicked the light switch on. With my weapon aimed at the floor, I signaled with my left hand for Jami to go and check out the room to our left as I headed to the one located on my right. Thirty seconds later, the apartment was clear, and we met in the kitchen area to figure out our next steps.

"Where do you think she is?" asked Jami. "It's almost five in the morning. You'd think she'd be here."

I shook my head and turned around, scanning the home as I looked for anything that seemed out of place. "Maybe at a boyfriend's house." I rubbed my hand over my face and felt my stubble starting to grow in, realizing I'd been awake for close to twenty-four hours and feeling tired as I continued to look around.

Jami made a face. "Or maybe she's out celebrating. Biggest story of her life hits the newsstands this morning."

I nodded and stepped past Jami, entering the room she had cleared. I came out and checked the other one again. "I see clothes on the bed," I said and paused to think. "Maybe she was packing to go somewhere."

Jami shrugged. "So what do we do?"

"Keep moving," I said and started for the door. "I'll call the White House and see if Keller's made progress. You call Chris and Mark, make sure they're close by. We need to plan how we'll handle Nikolai Ivanov."

Before I got to the door, I noticed a yellow sticky note with a pen next to it on the kitchen counter. I picked it up and saw that there were large marks on the top sheet. Taylor had written something down quickly.

"What is it?" asked Jami as I stepped into the kitchen and walked under one of the fluorescent lights.

Tilting the notepad, I confirmed what I thought I had seen and showed it to Jami. "Help me find a pencil," I said, setting the notepad down and opening the drawers in the kitchen until I found a dull number two. I used the pencil to gently apply a light coat of lead over the deep grooves that covered the notepad until the entire square was covered. I held it to my eyes and nodded to myself before I gave it to Jami to look at.

Jami took the pen from the counter and filled in the grooves that were now easier to see. "It's an address."

"Northwest Washington," I confirmed as she handed it back to me and I motioned for the door. "Let's go."

We headed out to Jami's SUV and I climbed into the driver's seat. I plugged the address into the GPS, folded the note in half, and stuffed it into my pocket. I felt the ring as I shoved it in and turned to Jami. "Call the guys," I said and pointed at the address on the navigation screen. "Have them meet us there."

Jami put her seatbelt on and started digging for her phone as I pulled the vehicle out onto P Street. I made a turn north on Wisconsin and looked over to Jami and saw her scrolling through her phone to call Chris. "It's Jami," she said as she looked out the passenger window. I got into the right-hand lane as the traffic light up ahead turned red. I slowed the SUV so I could check the traffic on the cross street to make sure it was clear before driving through the light. I flipped on the overhead police lights and crossed the intersection as Jami brought Reed up to speed with our visit to Keller and our search of Meg Taylor's apartment. "Chris, we're at Wisconsin and Q Street, heading north. We need you to meet us at..." Jami paused.

I looked over and saw Jami lean forward, staring into the side mirror.

"Blake! Look out!"

I looked up and saw in the rearview mirror a vehicle with its headlights off headed straight for us.

I twisted the steering wheel to the right, stepped on the gas, and pulled the SUV halfway onto the sidewalk to get out of its way. "Hold on!" I yelled as I stretched my arm across Jami and closed my eyes.

We braced for impact, but the vehicle sped past us through the intersection and made a sharp turn several blocks down the road. I looked at Jami. We were both breathing hard, shaken by what happened.

"Drunk?" asked Jami, and I shrugged.

Looking into the driver's side mirror, I checked the road again. Before I could pull out, I heard a cell phone ringing. I looked down and picked up my phone, but realized the sound was coming from my pocket. Jami and I exchanged a look as I dug for the phone.

"Jordan," I said and looked into the rearview mirror

again as I waited for a response. Several seconds passed as I heard Jami tell Chris she was going to have to call him back. She stared at me and asked who was on the phone, but I just ignored her. "This is Jordan," I said into the phone Dimitri had given me.

"Mr. Jordan," came the voice, loud enough that I knew Jami could hear what was being said. "I believe you know the reason why I am calling." He paused for several seconds as Jami continued to stare at me. "You have exactly one hour before daybreak to deliver my father to me. Have you made any progress?"

I checked the side mirror and then faced forward again. "The president says he's being held at Mount Weather, sixty miles west of DC." I stretched out my arm and looked at my watch. "I need more time."

"You've had plenty of time, Mr. Jordan. You don't need more time—you just need a little motivation."

There was a sound of the phone being moved, followed by heavy breathing. "Don't listen to him, Blake," came a familiar voice on the other end of the line. "Don't do it. Take Jami and get the hell out of there."

Dimitri started laughing, distant at first, but it became louder as he moved the phone back to his face. "One hour, Jordan. If you want Redding back alive, you'll bring my father to me. And if not—" I heard the young man take another deep breath and let it out slowly "—don't make the old man pay for your crimes. Because when I'm done with him, I'm coming after Agent Davis."

I looked to my right. My eyes locked with Jami's. They were wide as she stared blankly at me, hearing everything.

"Then I'm coming for you."

I turned away from Jami and looked out the driver's side window, thinking. "How do I find you?"

"I will find you," he replied. "Get my father back, Mr. Jordan. You do that, and I will give you the old man. And if you don't..." I heard Charlie scream in pain. "One hour," he repeated, and the line went dead.

I pulled the phone away to confirm that the call was disconnected and turned to look at Jami.

"Dimitri," she began. "You said that if he doesn't get his father back by daybreak, there'll be another bombing."

"That's what he said, Jami," I replied and turned away as I stuffed Ivanov's phone back into my pocket.

She stared at me. "You're lying." We sat in silence for several seconds. "I heard what he said, Blake."

I set an arm against the door and rested my head in my hand. I looked over to her, took in a deep breath, and thought about what Dimitri had said. "He's coming after you," I admitted. "If I don't get his father back to him by daybreak, he's going to kill Charlie Redding. Then he's going to hunt you down, Jami." I paused for several seconds. "I shouldn't have told you to go to Charlie's. They followed you over there. Took him as insurance to make sure I follow through with what he wants. There's no way out of this now."

Jami shook her head. Several more seconds passed before she spoke again. "What are we going to do?"

Before I could respond, her cell started to ring, and I thought about our options as she answered the call.

38

It was Chris Reed calling Jami back. She gave him our location, and Reed said that he and Reynolds were only five minutes out and would meet up with us so we could regroup before heading out to the northwest Washington address together. I was familiar with the area and told Jami that I needed to call Morgan to see what he could find out about who lived there and ask what the best approach in would be.

As I started to dial, Jami reached over and grabbed my arm. "We need to talk." She paused. "About us."

"Not now," I said.

"If not now, when?"

I shook my head. "Chris and Mark will be here any minute now, I have to call Morgan before we head out, and I still need to call the White House to see if Keller's made any progress with Nikolai Ivanov, Jami."

"Why?" she asked. We sat in silence for several seconds. "Why'd you walk away? I just need to know."

I looked out the driver's side window, took in a deep breath, and let it out slowly. "It's complicated."

"Try me."

I thought about how much I should share with her. She was a smart girl. That was what I loved about her. Jami deserved to know why I left, and I knew she wouldn't let it go until I told her the truth—all of it. I looked away, thinking. "Dimitri has the same connections as his father. He knows everything about me—who I am, what I do for the president." I looked at Jami. "And he knows that you meant something to me."

"Meant?" she whispered and looked away. "I'm a big girl, Blake. I can take care of myself."

"I know that."

"Really?" She paused before continuing. "Mark told me what Nikolai Ivanov said that night after you left. That his people would keep coming after you. I didn't care. Being with you was my choice, Blake."

I looked down and nodded to myself. "Jami, this is all my fault. I should have made sure that Nikolai Ivanov was dead, but I didn't." I paused and added, "I'm going to get Dimitri's father released, and then I'm going to take them both out. That's the only way I can fix this. I have no other choice."

"You're wrong. We always have a choice. Six months ago, you walked away from me. That was a choice."

"Jami, I had to walk away from you. The last thing Nikolai Ivanov said to me was that it wouldn't stop with him. That he had already told his affiliates about me. He said they'd never stop coming after me." Pausing again as Jami turned back to me, I added, "That meant I had to leave if I wanted to protect you."

"And how's that working out for you, Blake?" she asked sharply. "Were you trying to keep Charlie safe, too? Did you really think you could keep me safe by walking away? Because in case you haven't noticed—"

"Jami—"

"No, let me finish," she said as she started to breathe hard, and I felt my heart start to race. "You never gave me a chance that night, Blake. You just walked away. Like I didn't matter. Like *we* didn't matter."

I started to speak, but Jami held up a hand for me to stop. I stared into her eyes, seeing for the first time what the decision I had made that night had done to her. A decision I had questioned for the last six months.

"I really thought we had something," she said softly. A car passed us slowly from the opposite direction. I watched it pass by, and when I turned back to Jami, she was looking out the window, blinking, trying to keep the tears away. "But I guess I was wrong about what I thought we had, the life we had together."

"That's not true," I said.

"Well, that's what it felt like."

"Jami, you just don't understand. Maybe if you did—"

"Why don't you explain it to me, then? I've waited six months for an explanation."

My heart was beating harder. I didn't think I could say anything to fix this. So I just spoke what I was feeling. "I've lost everyone I ever cared about, Jami. My wife was murdered. My father died because of me. All because of what I do and who I am. Try living with that," I said and turned back to her. "Try living with that kind of burden, knowing you've done the right thing for your country, but you lost what mattered most to you. Try sleeping at night knowing you'd never have another chance to tell someone you loved her. How much they mattered to you. Maybe then you'd understand why I walked away from you."

"Why didn't you just tell me that?"

"It's complicated."

"That's something people say when they don't want to tell the truth."

"Because I love you," I said before correcting myself. "Loved you. I didn't want anything to happen to you. I thought if I could walk away and keep you out of my life, any fallout from what happened with Nikolai Ivanov would just be on me. When I found out that those guys came looking for me, I knew that my past had finally caught up to me, Jami. And I was okay with that because I thought they had left you out of it."

We were both silent for several seconds before Jami finally spoke. "I'm sure they knew," she whispered. "Your wife. Your father. They knew you loved them." She was silent again before adding, "One night, I arrived at the hospital before you. Ben told me how proud he was of you." She looked down for a moment. "That was the one and only time we were alone together. We could have talked about anything. But he talked about you." She paused and looked at me. "Life is all about living with the decisions that we make."

I let the words sink in and nodded vaguely. "I just want you to understand—"

"I do understand now," she said and nodded reassuringly. "I do. But you need to understand that you're not in control. You never could have stopped what happened to your wife or Ben. And the way you saved Keller—that's something to be proud of, Blake. Your father died knowing that you saved his best friend."

She looked past me and watched Chris slow down, cross the intersection, and park across the street. Turning back to Jami one last time, I looked into her eyes. "I'm sorry," I said, keeping my eyes on her for a long moment before reaching for the door handle. As I opened the door, Jami grabbed my arm again.

"You only live once," she said. Her words sent a chill down my spine as I realized that they echoed what the president had said almost twenty-four hours ago. "Don't push the people that you care about away."

I paused and said, "We have to go." I pulled on the door handle and stepped out to meet Chris and Mark.

39

THE FOUR OF US HUDDLED BEHIND JAMI'S VEHICLE AS I brought the Bureau guys up to speed on Keller, Nikolai Ivanov, and the threat from his son, Dimitri. I explained that he now had Charlie Redding and what would happen if I didn't deliver Dimitri's father to him by daybreak. Jami glanced at me. She knew the rest of it, the part I wasn't sharing with Chris and Mark—that Dimitri would be coming after her, too.

"How'd he know about Redding?" asked Mark Reynolds.

I shook my head. "I don't know. Jami had my phone." I paused and thought about it some more. "Maybe he was tracking me and went to find out why my phone was in Rosslyn when he had me back at the abandoned building. Maybe they got inside Charlie's house and figured out that he was a friend of mine."

"Maybe they found the image of the two Russian men on his screen and decided to take him," added Jami.

Mark took a step closer. "You need to lose the phone, brother," he said and nodded to a nearby trash can.

Before I could explain why I had to keep it, my cell

started to ring. I reached into my back pocket, grabbed it, and answered the call. "This is Jordan," I said as I stepped to the sidewalk. "This is Jordan," I repeated.

"Jordan, this is Bill Landry," the Bureau's deputy director said, his voice firm and sharp.

I turned back to Chris and Mark. "What do you have, Bill?" I said so the guys would know I had their boss on the line with me. "Did the president get in touch with you about Nikolai Ivanov?"

"Keller called Mulvaney. He pulled me into his office a short while ago," replied Landry. "He explained the situation, and I took point on making contact with the officials over at Mount Weather. What's your location?"

"Wisconsin and Q."

"Good. That'll work." Landry paused before adding, "They're putting Ivanov on a chopper as we speak."

I lifted my wrist so I could check the time. "Where are they taking him, Bill?"

"Bolling Air Force Base. There's a small heliport just past the guardhouse right off the main road."

"When?"

"We're sending a Bureau chopper to get him. Could be an hour to pick him up and get over to Bolling."

I shook my head as I stared at my watch. "Bill, that puts us past six o'clock. That's not gonna work."

"Well, it'll have to. Can't get him there any sooner," barked Landry, growing impatient. "This is a terrorist that's not even supposed to be alive, Jordan. It's a damn miracle I was able to even pull this off." Landry paused again. "I've already called ahead; they're expecting you at Bolling. I'm going to have my men stage the area now and set up a perimeter so that once they're inside, we can pick up both of the Ivanov men."

"Damn it, Bill. You know how this works. His son isn't going to be at the exchange. He'll send someone in his place. I have to hand over his father and follow him back to Dimitri if I want to get to both of them."

"Jordan, you listen to me," said Landry. "There's no way in hell I'm letting this guy loose in Washington."

"I have Reed and Reynolds with me," I said and stepped back to the team. "So you'll have Bureau men on the ground. And I have Davis and Morgan Lennox helping me. I'll make a call and get a drone in the area." I rubbed the back of my head, trying to stay calm. "Bill, we won't lose him. Just don't send anyone else in."

Landry didn't respond for several moments. "Fine," he replied. "You screw this up, you lose this guy—"

"I won't," I said, interrupting the man. "I give you my word, I won't let Nikolai Ivanov out of my sight."

"You call me with an update as soon as he touches down and the exchange takes place. Understand me?"

"Fine. We need to move out," I said as I disconnected the line and turned to Chris, Mark, and Jami.

"What happened?" asked Jami.

I dropped my phone into my back pocket and crossed my arms as the four of us stood in a small circle. "Landry contacted Mount Weather. They're getting a chopper ready so they can bring us Nikolai Ivanov."

"Where are they dropping him?" asked Chris.

"Small heliport over at Bolling."

Mark thought about it. "That's about twenty minutes south of us," he said, and I nodded.

"We need to figure out how we're going to play this," I said. "I told Landry I'd work with Morgan to get a drone. They'll bring Redding to the exchange. Once they hand him over, we'll need to follow them back."

Mark Reynolds laughed. "Good luck with that, brother. They're gonna take you out on the spot, man."

I put my hands on the back of my head and slid them down my neck as I tried to think of another way.

Jami took a step back, turned, and opened the hatch of her SUV. She pulled out one of the large drawers in the back and rummaged around inside it. She finally pulled out a Kevlar vest and handed it to me. "Here," she said. "Take this."

I shook my head. "No, you'll need it."

"I have another one," she said and pushed the vest against my chest. "Besides, I'm not going with you."

"Why not?" I asked as she put on a thin jacket because the temperature was dropping.

Jami shrugged. "I'll go to the address we got at Taylor's apartment. See if I can find her and try to figure out how she knows so much." She kept her eyes on me. "Besides, you don't need my help. Do you, Blake?"

I thought back to the conversation we'd had inside her SUV a few minutes earlier before the guys showed up. I didn't want her anywhere near Dimitri Ivanov or his people. And Meg Taylor was a loose end we needed to tie up. I shook my head and reached down into my pocket. I felt the ring I still carried with me, but grabbed the note with the address and pulled it out. I tried to hand it over, but Jami shook her head.

"Still in the GPS," she said as she reached for my messenger bag and handed it to me. "I'll call you later."

"Put on the other vest, Jami," I yelled as I walked across the street. Chris stepped into his SUV, and I got in next to him as Mark climbed into the backseat. I handed the vest to Mark and watched Jami drive away.

40

TWENTY MINUTES AFTER LEAVING, JAMI ARRIVED AT THE Forest Hills neighborhood in northwest DC. The street was lined with old, majestic-looking trees that stretched across like a canopy, shielding it from the moonlight. Jami turned off her headlights and lowered her window. She slowed the vehicle as she approached the address programmed into her GPS and took in the large expensive homes as she drove.

She saw the house. It was large and set back far from the street. Jami passed slowly as she checked it out.

Then she faced forward, raised the window, and continued to drive until she reached the end of the street. She turned around at the cul-de-sac, parked the vehicle two houses from the end, and turned off the ignition. Jami looked out the back and side windows. The few streetlights that lined the road cast an orange glow against the perfectly manicured lawns. Jami shuddered as she reached for her phone and placed a call.

It rang several times until she was finally sent to voicemail. She tried again and heard, "Morgan Lennox."

"It's me," said Jami.

"Sorry, love. I'm trying to reposition a drone over Bolling, and I don't have much time to get it over there."

Jami nodded to herself. "Morgan, I have an address I'm checking out. We found it at Meg Taylor's apartment. I was hoping you might be able to look it up for me. Maybe tell me who I'm dealing with."

Morgan sighed, didn't speak for several seconds, then finally asked, "Okay, Jami. What's the address?"

She glanced down to the GPS system and stared at the screen. "Twenty-eight forty-five Allendale Place," she said and waited. She heard Morgan type the address into one of the DDC systems and then sigh again.

"That's strange. Nothing's coming up," he said. "I'll have to try getting to it another way. Hang on a sec."

"Don't worry about it, Morgan," she said and unbuckled her seatbelt. "Just focus on moving that drone."

"Are you sure?"

Jami said that she was and admitted that getting the drone over to the meeting place was more important. She disconnected the call, silenced her phone, slid it into a pocket, and reached for her Glock 17. She climbed out and stepped to the back of the vehicle, opened the hatch, pulled out a drawer, and inserted a fresh magazine. She chambered a round and grabbed one more item that she had brought from the White House. Stepping onto the sidewalk, Jami tucked the weapon into the small of her back and walked quickly.

When she got to the house, she turned up the pathway that led to the front door and slowed her approach.

The front of the home had two large doors, each made from textured glass to allow light to come in from the outside. Getting closer, Jami cupped two hands against the glass and tried to look inside the house, but couldn't see anything. It was dark, but Jami thought she could see flickering light from a TV on inside.

She turned around to look back at the street. Still quiet. No movement on the sleepy, oak-lined cul-de-sac.

Turning back to the front door, Jami knocked three times. Moving her right hand behind her back and gripping the butt of her Glock, she cupped her left hand on the glass to shield the orange light reflecting from the street behind her. She looked for any signs of movement as she waited, but nobody came to the door.

Jami knocked again, louder this time. The flickering light inside turned off and everything went dark. She was just about to ring the doorbell when she saw movement. She took a step back, kept her right hand on her weapon, and gripped it tight as a dark, shadowy figure approached the other side of the glass.

"Who is it?" a woman asked.

"My name is Agent Davis with the Department of Domestic Counterterrorism," replied Jami.

There was no response for several seconds. Then the woman said, "What do you want?"

Jami thought about it and replied, "I'm looking for someone."

"Well, he's not home right now," replied the woman. "Come back later, okay? He should be back by—"

"I'm looking for Meg Taylor with the *Times*."

The woman was silent.

"Please open the door, Ms. Taylor."

Several more seconds passed before the woman on the other side of the door spoke again. "Your badge," she finally said and, with a fingernail, tapped twice on the glass in the middle of the door. "Let me see it."

Jami reached inside a pocket, retrieved her DDC credentials, and flipped it open. She pressed the badge against the glass and held it there for a beat. The woman stepped to the side and a light came on overhead. Jami heard the deadbolt turn until it clicked, and the door cracked open as Jami put her badge away.

"How'd you find me?" a blonde woman asked softly as she looked Jami over. The question caught Jami off guard. She maintained her gaze on the woman and studied her. She was fully dressed and looked like she might have been wearing the same clothes from the day before. The blonde cocked her head to one side and raised her eyebrows. "I want to know how you found me," she repeated.

"Doesn't matter," replied Jami.

Looking her over, the woman finally asked, "What do you want?"

"I need to ask you some questions, Ms. Taylor."

"At five thirty in the morning?"

Jami looked past the woman, saw the dark foyer behind her, and gestured toward it. "Can we talk inside?"

"No," she replied sharply. "I told you, it's not my house. Whatever you need to ask, you can ask out here."

"It's concerning your story about the president's black ops team that's hitting newsstands this morning."

"What are you talking about?" the woman asked, sounding genuinely confused by what Jami had said.

Jami tilted her head, let go of her weapon, and grabbed the folded newspaper she had tucked under her arm. She handed it to the woman. They exchanged a look as she accepted the paper and held it to the light. Jami watched her look it over in shock, then looked up to the top to see the date and the byline. Seeing her own name listed as the writer, she looked up at Jami, confused, and shook her head slowly.

"I'll let you in," she said softly. "But you leave your weapon out here." She held her gaze until Jami nodded, reached for her Glock, and set it inside one of the two large flowerpots that lined the entrance. She followed the blonde inside, and she locked the door again. "Follow me," she said and went to the kitchen.

41

Simon Harris was at his desk in the cluster of cubicles that he and the rest of the visiting DDC team had been working from, sipping a third can of soda to fight off the drowsiness that was trying to overtake him. Simon kept watch over Agent Davis's loaner vehicle he'd been tracking and watched it come to a stop and tried to figure out what Jami was doing. Pulling up DDC's proprietary Maps application, he began to check each of the addresses of the nearby houses one by one to understand who she was meeting with in the Forest Hills neighborhood, when an instant message popped up on his screen.

It was Morgan Lennox. 'Simon, please call me,' the message read along with the number to his direct line.

Reaching for the landline, Harris lifted the receiver, punched in the number, and heard it ring once before Morgan answered. "It's me," said Harris, still upset with his counterpart for his earlier accusation.

"Simon, is Lynne May back yet? She's still showing as being away on Messenger."

Looking over his shoulder, Harris moved the phone to

his other ear and looked at the desk May had been working from since arriving at the Hoover Building. "She's still in the privacy room, resting," he replied.

"I need you to go in there and get her for me right now."

Harris turned back around to face his screen and stared at the dot on Maps that represented Jami's SUV. "Sure, after you tell me where Agent Davis went," he said. "I think you're the one that's hiding something."

"Simon, please."

"First tell me what's going on," demanded Harris. "May asked me to track her. Well, now I'm tracking her. Now you tell me what she's doing up in Forest Hills because that's the first thing May's going to ask me."

"She's running down a lead, Simon. Jami found an address and she's checking it out. Now go get May."

Simon stood and looked beyond the cubicles to the dark corridor that led to Landry's and Mulvaney's offices. At the end, close to the cubicles, were the Bureau's restrooms. From Simon's desk, he could see the women's restroom clearly and watched as a woman approached, opened the door, and disappeared inside.

Simon shrank back into his seat, rested an elbow on the desk and rubbed his forehead with his hand. "Morgan, I don't know if I can go in there. What's so urgent that you need me to go get her right now?"

Lennox sighed. "I'm going to take control of one of the Bureau's Predator drones. I don't have time to do the paperwork. I need May to know what I'm doing so she doesn't get blindsided with Bill Landry, okay?"

"You mean so you don't get in trouble, right?"

Morgan sighed. "It's not just the drone. Something's about to go down, and I need to get her up to speed."

Harris thought about it. Earlier, after finishing his first

soda, he had gone into the men's room and saw a door with the words PRIVACY ROOM on it at the opposite end of the room. As he approached, he saw there was a horizontal slider sign, much like the kind of sign he'd seen outside countless conference rooms. The slider had been pushed to the left, showing the word VACANT on the right. Simon had opened the door and flipped on the light to understand what the inside of the small room looked like. He stood again and stared at the women's restroom across the floor, imagining an identical room inside.

"Simon?" asked Morgan, growing impatient.

"Okay," replied Harris as he looked down at the desk and noticed a wireless headset attached to the landline. Simon pulled it off the charger, pressed the green button on the landline marked "headset," and slid it over his ear. "Can you hear me?" he asked. Morgan said that he could, so he set the receiver down.

Stepping out of the cubicle, Simon approached the restroom. As he did, he saw the woman who had entered two minutes earlier exit the room and walk past him down to the other end of the floor where she and a team of Bureau analysts were working. Simon stopped when he got to the entrance.

He looked up and down the corridor, both ways, and saw that it was clear. "This is embarrassing," he said, and stepped forward, pushing open the door to the women's restroom, and stepped inside.

He saw a row of sinks on his left and three stalls on the opposite side of the room. They were all empty. Simon looked straight ahead and saw what he was looking for. Harris moved quickly toward the privacy room, trying to get the task over with as fast as he could, but stopped when he reached the door. He saw the same kind of slider he'd seen in the men's room. Only this time, the slider was on the right side, revealing the words IN USE on the left. Simon lifted his hand, hesitated for a moment, then knocked.

"Mrs. May, it's Simon Harris. I'm sorry to bother you, ma'am, but we need you out on the floor, please." He lowered his hand and waited for a response, but there was no reply. He raised his hand to knock again.

"Oh, for the love of Pete, just go in there, Simon," yelled Lennox from the headset, growing impatient.

Harris reached for the handle and tried to turn it, but it wouldn't budge. He began to twist the handle up and down quickly, thinking maybe it was just stuck, but realized that it wasn't. He knocked again, harder this time. "Mrs. May, please wake up, ma'am." There was still no response, and Simon stepped backward. "Morgan, I don't know what to do," he said, still staring at the door. "She's not answering."

"Does it take a key?" asked Lennox.

Harris looked down at the door handle. "Yeah," he replied. "I think so. I see an opening on the handle."

"Simon, go into the men's room and check the handle. See if you can lock it from the inside for me."

Turning to leave, Simon walked to the end of the women's restroom, pulled open the door, and lowered his head in embarrassment as he walked past two female analysts who noticed what he had done. Entering the men's room on the other side of the corridor, Simon walked to the privacy room door, pulled it open, and flicked on the light. "Okay, I'm in," he said. "Looks like it does lock from the inside, Morgan."

"Bloody hell." Morgan sighed. "Something's wrong if she's not answering. Can you go get Bill Landry?"

"No, he's not here. I just looked for him a little while ago, Morgan. Can't find him. These people show up and disappear whenever they want," he said, frustrated. "Mulvaney's here, but he's on a conference call."

"Then go get Mulvaney, Simon. Tell him what's going on. You might have to break that handle to get in."

Simon stepped out of the men's room and turned toward Mulvaney's office. He was breathing hard. "Morgan, both of them are gone. Landry and Mulvaney," he said after checking both offices, and he stood in the corridor, thinking. "I'll call security and tell them what's going on, and I'll call you right back, okay?"

"Good. I'll go reposition that drone, mate. You get security to open that door and make sure she's okay." He paused and heard Simon still breathing hard as he went back to his desk and disconnected the call.

42

SIMON TAPPED THE SWITCH HOOK ON THE LANDLINE AND heard a dial tone in his wireless headset. He dialed security, who answered immediately. "This is Simon Harris," he began. "I need help on the third floor."

"What's the problem?" asked the woman on the other end of the line.

"I think someone may be trapped in the privacy room. She's not answering the door and it's locked."

"Are you sure someone's in there?"

"Yes," he replied. "Lynne May from DDC. She wasn't feeling well, and now she's not answering the door."

There was a pause. "Okay, privacy room in the women's restroom," she said curiously. "We'll be right up."

Simon started to call Morgan back, but decided to give him a few minutes so he could focus on the drone. Instead, he walked back to the corridor and stood in front of the restrooms and waited. Three minutes later, he heard movement from the adjacent corridor and looked around the corner, where he saw two members of the security team—a man and a woman—approaching. They were dressed in white shirts and black slacks. The man held a large silver toolbox. Simon stepped into the corridor to wave them down.

"Harris?" the woman asked.

"Yes. Please hurry," he replied.

The man gestured to his counterpart. She knocked on the door twice, announced for anyone inside that security was entering, and pushed the door open. The man followed, bringing the toolbox inside with him. Simon watched as some of the workers heard the commotion and stood to peer over their cubicle walls at what was going on. A few of them stepped out from their desks and stared at Simon as he stood alone.

Following them inside, Simon watched as the woman approached the privacy room door and knocked on it. There was no response. She tried the handle and confirmed that it was locked. Turning back, she nodded to the man, who set the toolbox on the tile floor, opened it, and fished around inside for a tool that looked like a screwdriver but was much skinnier. He grabbed a hammer, approached the door, and inserted the tool through the small hole and twisted it for several seconds, but couldn't get the door open.

Frustrated, the man stepped back, dropped the tool into the toolbox, and grabbed a hammer. He stepped back to the door, rested the end of the hammer on the base of the handle, and lifted it to eye level. The man brought it down hard twice. On the third strike, the handle broke off and he pushed the door open. It was dark inside the room. The man flipped on the light and stepped inside, followed by the woman officer.

"It's empty," the man said after taking a look inside and stepping back out, followed by the other officer.

The man looked at Simon, shrugged, and pointed at a

sign inside the door. "Unlock the door before you leave," the officer read aloud and shook his head. "Happens sometimes, never had anyone locked inside, though. Always had time to pick it." He paused. "Maybe now they'll finally change the damn doorknobs."

"We still have a problem," said Simon. "I was told that Lynne May was here resting. Now she's missing."

The woman gestured toward the exit and followed Simon out. "You called earlier," she said from behind him. "I told you Mrs. May has not left the building. If she had, we'd know about it. Visitors must sign out."

When he had exited, Simon turned back around to speak to the woman. "Don't you have cameras here?"

"Of course," she replied as her counterpart exited the restroom and stood next to the woman.

"Can you check them? See where she may have gone?"

She put her hands on her hips. "What exactly is the concern, Mr. Harris?"

Simon didn't respond, just looked out at the Bureau employees as they continued to stare in their direction from their cubicles.

The officer took in a deep breath and sighed. "Have you checked the cafeteria? Looked inside any of the conference rooms that are up here?"

Simon shook his head.

"Then I suggest you start there, Mr. Harris."

"Irene," said the man, still holding onto the toolbox, "it wouldn't hurt to take a look and see what we find." He looked at his watch. "My shift is ending, but I'll stay a little longer so I can check the tape." The man turned to Simon. "Where are you sitting?"

Simon pointed to the cluster of cubicles against the wall.

The security guard nodded. "Alright. I have a few things I need to wrap up; then I'll take a look for you. Okay?"

Simon nodded back and turned to the woman, who had an annoyed expression on her face.

"Check the areas I suggested," she said. "Call us back when you find her so we don't waste our time."

Simon turned back to the cubicles and noticed that the onlookers had already sat down and went back to focusing on their work. Simon thanked the officers and headed back to his desk, pulled out his chair, and took a seat. He leaned back and just sat there, silent, listening to the sound of the people working around him for several seconds before turning back to his laptop. "Something's not right," he whispered to himself and unlocked his laptop. The screen illuminated, and his eyes grew wide at what he was seeing.

The mouse was moving. A command line prompt appeared. A command was entered into the window. There was more typing, more movement, and Simon couldn't stop it. Every time he moved his mouse and tried to take back control of his system, the mouse would move back and the typing would continue. Someone was controlling his system. Harris pressed a button on the landline and heard a dial tone. Lennox answered immediately. "Morgan, I stepped away to talk to security, and when I came back, my—"

"What happened?" interrupted Lennox. "Did they get in the room?"

Simon kept his eyes on his screen. "Um—" Simon paused "—she wasn't in there."

"Good instincts, mate. Now we just need to figure out what happened to her."

Simon continued to stare at his screen. "Morgan, someone's taken control of my system, and I can't—"

"It's me, Simon."

Harris grew silent. He narrowed his eyes and shook his head. "Morgan, what the hell are you doing?"

"I got the drone circling over Bolling. Now I'm trying to access the database archive for the Hoover Building's security camera footage." There was silence on Harris's end of the line, so Morgan elaborated. "I can't access anything directly from here, so I established a direct connection with your system through our DDC VPN. And since you're in the Hoover Building and on their network already..." He paused briefly so he could focus on what he was doing. "Done. I think we're in. Now we just need to find the archive."

"You repositioned the drone already?"

Morgan grunted affirmatively.

"Um, what do you need me to do?"

Morgan paused as he continued his search for the location of the archive. "Just watch and learn, Simon."

43

Meg Taylor held the front page of the *New York Times* to her eyes and shook her head from side to side in a small quick motion as she tried to process what she was looking at. "Where did you get this?" she asked as Jami checked her phone and set it on top of the kitchen counter and turned to the woman.

"Early edition of the paper that's being delivered—" she pulled back her sleeve to check the time "—right about now." Jami maintained her gaze on the woman, who was visibly shaken to see the story printed. "Why do you seem so surprised?" she asked, furrowing her brow. "You are Meg Taylor, aren't you?"

The woman nodded, slowly at first, then decisively as she folded the newspaper in half and set it down. "Just didn't expect to ever see this in print," said Taylor, still looking confused about the whole thing.

"Why not?"

Taylor crossed her arms and looked away briefly. "That's really none of your business."

Jami narrowed her eyes. "Ms. Taylor, I don't know what

your angle is on all of this or why you're trying to damage the president by exposing matters of national security, but the man you wrote about—" Jami paused to make sure she phrased what she wanted to say the right way "—you shouldn't have done this."

"Is that why you're here? Because of the man I wrote about?" Taylor paused. "Are you part of his team?"

Jami stepped closer. "I'm here, Ms. Taylor, because I want to know who your informant is."

Taylor shook her head quickly. "Not gonna happen. I never reveal my sources, Agent Davis."

Jami pointed at the paper. "You can't just publish libelous statements. Do you realize what you've done?"

Meg looked down her nose at Jami. "It's not libel if it's true. If Mr. Jordan wants to take me to court, he—"

"Ms. Taylor, you haven't just ruined a career or damaged the president because of this." Jami grabbed the newspaper from the kitchen counter and held it up to her face. "This is a death sentence. You crossed a line the media should never cross." Jami lowered her voice. "This man is a hero and doesn't deserve this."

Meg was silent for several seconds. She reached up and ran her fingers through her blonde hair, thinking. "The story wasn't supposed to run," she finally said and turned, pacing back and forth nervously in the large kitchen area. "My boss wanted me to find dirt on Keller. I noticed Jordan in a picture. He looked out of place. Something didn't seem right. I knew someone and called him up and got what I was looking for."

"Robert King," said Jami softly. "So he's behind this?"

"No," answered Meg. "That's just it. I showed up at his house last night and handed him the story I wrote."

Jami watched Taylor as she paced around the kitchen, arms crossed, thinking hard. "What happened?"

"He said the same things you're saying now, how the guy was a hero. Said he couldn't run the story." Taylor paused a beat before turning back to look at Jami. "He fired me," she said and furrowed her brow.

Jami narrowed her eyes again. "I don't understand. He fired you because of the story you wrote?"

"No, he fired me because I didn't get him the kind of dirt he wanted. That's what he told me, anyway." Taylor stopped pacing and kept her gaze on the ground. "I should have taken the story back from him. Instead, I just let him walk away with it." She took a deep breath and let it out fast. "I think he set me up."

Jami took a step closer to the woman. "After you left King's place, what did you do?" she asked gently.

Taylor thought about it. "I went home. Tried to sleep, but couldn't. Called a friend about what happened. Didn't want to be alone, you know? Only person I really know in this city. Just met him a few weeks ago."

Davis forced an understanding smile and looked around the room. "So this is your friend's house," she said gently, putting the pieces together and trying to create a bond with the woman. "What does he do?"

But Meg just stared blankly at Jami and shrugged. "He won't tell me. Says he has to keep a low profile."

Jami thought she heard, or maybe felt, a rumble outside the house, but she ignored it. "Your informant? Does he live here?" she asked, but Taylor didn't reply. Jami took a step closer. "Is this his house, Meg?"

A moment later, a mechanical sound came from the other side of the kitchen door. Taylor's eyes grew wide as she turned to the door. The sound continued for a few more seconds, then stopped abruptly. Meg's head snapped back to Jami. There was panic in her eyes. "He's home! You need to leave right now!"

They heard the sound again, and Jami realized what it was. The garage door had opened and was now being closed. The women turned back to the door and heard a muffled thud. A door being closed.

"Not enough time," said Jami, looking over her shoulder at the front door on the other side of the house.

"Then you need to hide," whispered Taylor desperately. "Right now. Go. He's got a temper. *Please.*"

Jami took a few steps backward, then turned and went into a dark, adjacent room. She leaned against the wall and heard a key inserted into the lock. The kitchen door creaked open and someone stepped inside.

"You're home," said Meg with a smile in her voice. The door was closed. Several seconds passed in silence. Then the faint sound of kissing, followed by another long period of silence. "What took you so long?"

"I told you I'd be a while," said the man. Jami's eyes grew wide. She felt her heart start to beat rapidly.

Jami heard them kiss again, followed by several more seconds of silence. Then there was an abrupt kicking sound on the tile. Jami furrowed her brow, trying to understand what she was hearing. The kicking stopped. There was movement in the kitchen. A drawer was opened, then closed, followed by a loud tearing sound. More movement. She heard the tearing sound again, louder and longer this time.

The kitchen door was opened; then Jami heard a dragging sound on the tile. Her heart beat even faster. The sound grew distant and disappeared. The kitchen door was closed. There was a thud. Then she heard something slam shut and the mechanical sound again. As the vehicle started, Jami had a realization.

Duct tape—that was what Jami had heard. She was sure of it. She reached for her weapon, but it wasn't there. Jami remembered that Meg hadn't let her inside with it on her. Ten more seconds passed and she heard the mechanical sound again, followed by a rumble from the car's engine as it navigated the driveway. Jami passed the kitchen and ran to the front door and looked out the textured glass. She saw the headlights turn on as the car backed into the street, stopped, and started to leave the neighborhood.

Jami opened the front door, retrieved her weapon from inside the flowerpot, and ran toward her vehicle parked close to the cul-de-sac. She knew who Taylor's informant was. *She had recognized the man's voice.*

44

I HEARD A CELL PHONE RINGING AND REACHED INTO MY BACK pocket before realizing that it was the other phone, the one Dimitri had slipped into my pocket, that was actually ringing. I dug it out and answered. "This is Jordan," I said and looked up at the dark sky, desperately searching for any sign of the chopper.

"Mr. Jordan, you have been stationary for quite a while now."

"I'm at Bolling Air Force Base," I said.

"I know where you are," Dimitri said. "I can see that you are positioned at the heliport three hundred meters inside the base." I wondered if he was tracking me from my phone or the one he'd given me. "Time's up, Mr. Jordan," he continued. "I'm assuming that my father has been delivered to you already?"

My heart started to beat faster as I continued to scan the night sky. "I have him," I lied. "Where are you?"

He paused. "Let me talk to him."

"You can talk to him when you get here," I replied, and as I spoke, I heard my cell ring in my back pocket. I kept the phone that Dimitri had given me pressed to my ear while I checked the call. It was Morgan. I silenced my phone and waited for Ivanov to respond. When he didn't, I asked again, "Where are you?"

There was another pause, longer this time. "Very well, Mr. Jordan. I will play this your way. But make no mistake —" the young man lowered his voice "—anything short of you turning my father over to me and—"

"You'll get him back," I lied again.

"Good. We will be there in two minutes. No games, Mr. Jordan," he said and disconnected the line.

"Damn it," I whispered to myself as I lowered Ivanov's phone and dropped it into another pocket. I reached for my cell and brought it to my eyes to check the missed call from Morgan. I saw he had left a voicemail, but I ignored it, and started to call Landry as Mark spoke into the earpiece I was wearing.

"Was that Ivanov?" he asked.

I brought my hand up to my ear as I looked south to where Reynolds was positioned behind a row of bushes that lined the street just inside the base. "He's two minutes out, Mark," I said. "And no sign of the chopper." I turned and looked to the west and saw Chris Reed at his position fifty meters away in between two of the military housing complexes. "Chris, do you copy?" I asked to make sure we were all on comm.

Reed said we were coming in clear. I lifted my cell and brought it to my ear as I waited through four rings before getting Bill Landry's voicemail. "Bill, this is Jordan. I need that chopper here right now. Call me back." I disconnected the line and tried to remain calm as I thought through my options. I tried not to panic and decided to dial another number and brought the phone to my ear as the line started to ring.

"Blake," Keller's chief of staff said softly, answering the call on the first ring.

"Emma, I need to talk to the president. Are you still with him?"

"Yes, hold on for me," she said. I heard her voice tremble slightly as she quickly moved to get to another room inside the White House. I waited thirty more seconds before she came back on. "Okay, here he is."

I heard a rustling sound as the president took the phone. "Blake, Emma told me about her plan to get you out of the country ahead of the news breaking, but the damn thing's on every cable news channel already. Son, I think you need to reconsider this. I've asked her to go ahead and make the arrangements so that—"

"Mr. President, that's not why I'm calling," I said, interrupting the man. "I'm standing on the heliport at Bolling Air Force Base. I can't get in touch with Bill Landry, and the exchange is taking place right now."

Keller didn't speak for several moments. "Exchange?" he asked. "Blake, what are you talking about?"

"The chopper that's transporting Nikolai Ivanov," I said. "It was supposed to have been here by now." There was more silence. I narrowed my eyes as I waited for a response. "Mr. President? Are you there?"

Keller said cautiously, "That is *not* the conversation I had with Bill Landry. There must be some kind of misunderstanding, because I just went over the whole thing with him. Landry said he'd call you with the update. I made a few phone calls, Blake. Got in touch with Mount Weather and spoke with officials stationed over there. Relayed what I learned to Landry and told him I would call you next.

Landry said he'd take care of it." He paused. "There's no chopper headed to Bolling, son. Nikolai Ivanov isn't coming."

"Why not?" I demanded and looked east, noticing the sky starting to become brighter.

Keller paused again. "Because Nikolai Ivanov is dead."

I felt like the air got knocked out of me. I couldn't speak for several seconds. I looked up and saw headlights from a vehicle slowly approaching down MacDill Boulevard, headed straight for my location. "When? How?" I finally asked as I kept my eyes fixed on the approaching headlights.

"They're telling me it happened about a month ago. Officially, it's been documented as a suicide." Keller paused before adding, "Unofficially, Ivanov's death was the result of enhanced interrogation methods used inside the Mount Weather prison. Remember, Blake, the world thinks this guy died six months ago."

"I get that, Mr. President. But I told you what's going to happen if I don't get Nikolai Ivanov back."

Keller was silent for a beat. Then he finally said, "You mentioned an exchange?"

I nodded to myself. "They have Charlie Redding," I said in a low voice as the vehicle got even closer.

"Redding?" asked Keller, recognizing the name of the man who he and my father had worked with at the ATF office in Chicago years ago, long before he left to run for the senate. "How the hell did that happen?"

"Long story," I said. "I'll get him back. I'll get Dimitri. Then I'm gonna find out why Landry set me up."

I heard Mark in my earpiece ask what the holdup was, as the Tangos were entering the base. I held up a hand to him. "And, Mr. President, about what Emma's suggesting, I'll defend my actions over the last eighteen months, and I'll take full responsibility for any actions I take today. I'm not going anywhere."

"I'm not trying to protect myself here, Blake, or my presidency. I'm showing you a way out of all of this."

"I have to go," I said and disconnected the call. I pressed the earpiece and watched the vehicle park thirty meters away from me. "Nikolai Ivanov's dead and Landry set me up. We're going to have to come up with another plan," I said and reached behind me briefly to check on the Glock tucked in the small of my back.

I watched the driver park and help a man with a bag over his head out of the trunk. *Charlie*, I thought. The driver prodded the man with his gun, forcing him to walk. "I have an idea," I said into my earpiece.

45

The man's eyes darted left to right as he and Charlie walked across the wet grass and met me at the concrete heliport, where I stood alone. "Where is he?" the man grunted, scanning the open field around us.

"Safe," I replied, wondering who the tall Russian man was and where Dimitri had called me from earlier.

Charlie stood motionless with the bag still covering his head. The man pushed his weapon against it. "Where?" he repeated. The man grew impatient and racked the slide on his weapon to chamber a round.

"My men have him," I said.

"That was not the deal. A life for a life, Mr. Jordan. You hand over Ivanov; we give you the old guy."

"How do I know that if I hand Ivanov over, you wouldn't take him and kill both of us right now?" I asked and nodded to Charlie as I continued. "You had insurance. Now I have insurance. This is the deal."

The man kept his eyes fixed on mine and the gun pressed hard against Charlie's head. "Explain."

"It's simple," I said and nodded to Charlie. "Let my

friend here go. Take me instead. A life for a life, right?" I stared at the man, watching his reaction to my proposal. "Once I know he's safe, I'll take you to Ivanov."

The guy looked past me and scanned the field again to make sure we were alone. His eyes went back to mine as he decided whether or not he could take the deal I was offering. "This will not be acceptable to Dimitri," he finally said. "If I do not return with Nikolai Ivanov, he will kill me. I cannot accept this deal."

As he looked away from me, I wiped my hands on my jeans to dry them. My heart was pounding fast. It had all unraveled so quickly. I looked at my friend standing there helpless in front of me. In that moment, time stood still. A million thoughts raced through my mind, memories of Charlie visiting my dad in Chicago when I was younger. It felt like a lifetime ago. They started to move, and I became present again.

As they stepped onto the grass, I began walking slowly to close the gap. "What are you doing?"

"Dimitri is not a stupid man, Mr. Jordan," the guy replied. "And neither am I." He kept walking backward. "He told you what the consequences would be if you did not get his father—you don't have him, do you?"

"I do."

He shook his head. "No, you—"

Before he could finish, I heard the sound of a branch snapping. The Russian man heard it too, and he turned quickly toward the sound. I followed his gaze over to the bushes where Mark Reynolds was hiding.

I turned back. The man moved his weapon from the back of Charlie's head to the bushes and fired a shot.

Reaching behind me, I grabbed my Glock and aimed it at the man. "Drop your weapon!" I yelled as I felt pain shoot down my arm from where I had hurt myself earlier. Reynolds returned fire, and the man grabbed the back of Charlie's shirt to use him as a human shield as he fired more rounds into the bushes.

He brought the gun to the side of Charlie's head and held him tight. "Show yourself," the man yelled as I held my weapon steady and slowly started to back away to get a better shot and avoid hitting my friend.

"Coming up the side," Reed said in my earpiece, but I ignored him and wanted to take this guy out myself.

I fired above his head to get his attention. He turned to look at me and was hit by a round from Reynolds. He took the blow, cursed, and fired back at Mark. Redding thrashed his body, trying to escape, but the man held on tight. Then he looked back at me to see what I was doing. He started to bring his weapon around. I closed an eye and squeezed the trigger just as he yanked Charlie to his right to shield himself.

The sound from the gunshot echoed off the surrounding buildings. My eyes grew wide. I stared at Charlie in disbelief and watched as his body went limp. He dropped to his knees and started to fall backwards onto the wet grass as the man holding onto the back of his shirt let go and swung his weapon toward me.

"No!" I yelled, realizing what I had just done. In an instant, I aimed and squeezed the trigger three more times. The bullets hit the terrorist's chest and the man fell backwards, landing right next to Charlie's body.

I kept my weapon aimed in the man's direction, and I stood there motionless as my eyes moved back and forth between the terrorist and Charlie. For a moment, I thought about my father. I saw him lying on his back in a field, bleeding out as I was standing over him, yelling for a medic.

It was happening all over again. I looked up and saw Chris Reed running toward me as I shook my head and became fully present.

Remembering the mistake I'd made with my father, I moved quickly past Charlie's body and went over to check the terrorist. Finding his weapon near his hand, I kicked it away and knelt down to check his pulse.

The man was dead. "Mark, you okay?" I asked and waited for a response as I saw Chris getting closer. I stood and went over to Charlie. I stuffed my weapon into the small of my back and knelt down next to him. I looked him over as I put my hands on the back of my head and exhaled. I was getting ready to pull off the hood when Chris ran past me. I watched him run over to Reynolds, and I knew that something was wrong.

"I think he's hit," yelled Chris as he knelt down next to the thick bushes and pulled Mark onto the grass.

I left Charlie and went to help with Mark. I saw him blinking and staring at the sky. "Chris, call for help," I yelled as I started to check Mark's body for the entry wound. Reed stood and called for an ambulance.

"Where does it hurt?" I asked, but Mark didn't respond. He just looked at me and twisted from the pain.

I unzipped his jacket and was about to pull open his shirt when I looked down and saw the blood pooling on the ground around Mark's leg. "I think you're going into shock," I said as I continued to examine him and found where he'd been shot. "It's your leg," I said as Mark looked down at his drenched jeans.

I stood and ran over to the dead terrorist's body and pulled off his belt. Returning, I lifted Mark's leg. He winced in pain as I pulled the belt underneath and secured it tight just above the entry point of the bullet.

"Help's on the way," said Chris as he walked back toward us, and we waited together for two minutes. I kept the belt tight until I heard the wail of a siren in the distance. I looked up and saw a police car appear.

"It hurts, man," Mark finally said as I continued to pull the belt tight and an ambulance entered the base.

"You're gonna be okay," I said, trying to reassure him.

Mark shook his head and, with a hand, slowly touched his chest. "No," he said, his voice sounding weaker. "It hurts here, too," he said and tapped below his chest as the ambulance jumped the curb and got closer.

I looked up and said, "Chris, hold this for me."

Reed crouched down and grabbed the belt, keeping it taut. I unzipped the jacket, ripped open his shirt, and froze.

"I need help!" I yelled as the paramedics ran to us.

46

MARK WAS HIT JUST BELOW THE BOTTOM OF THE KEVLAR VEST I had given him. The paramedics quickly applied a dressing to his wound to slow the bleeding. They asked about the men on the ground behind me. I said that they were dead, and they told me they would send another unit back to get them. As they got ready to move Mark, one of the men turned to me and said they'd take him to Inova Alexandria Hospital.

"That's too far," I said as I watched Mark get lifted onto a gurney and quickly moved into the ambulance.

"It won't take long," the paramedic said before he jogged over to the passenger door and stepped inside.

The vehicle pulled forward, navigated the curb, and picked up speed as it got back onto MacDill and its siren began to wail again. I watched the lights disappear down the street as Chris Reed turned back to me.

"What happened?" he asked.

I shook my head and looked down to the ground, trying to understand it myself. "I heard him make a noise. The

Russian guy heard it, too." I paused and looked back at Charlie's body. "It all happened so fast."

I reached into my back pocket, grabbed my phone, and tried to call Morgan back. The line rang several times, then went to voicemail. I asked him to call me back, unsilenced it, and dropped it back in place.

Chris followed me over to Charlie's body. I still couldn't believe what had happened. I stared at the bag over his face and narrowed my eyes when I saw what appeared to be movement. I took a step closer and saw it move again. *He's breathing*, I thought. I knelt down next to Charlie. With two hands, I grabbed the hood and gently lifted it up over his face and stared at it. "Oh my God," I whispered as I pulled it the whole way off and Chris drew his weapon. We were staring at the face of another man. *It wasn't Charlie.*

In that moment, I realized we had been played by Dimitri Ivanov.

The terrorist stared blankly at the sky. Then he blinked and his eyes moved, confirming that he was alive. "Who are you?" I asked the man in a low voice as I reached for my weapon, but there was no response. The man turned his eyes back to the sky. "Please," I said. "Tell me where Dimitri is and I'll get you help."

Slowly, his eyes drifted to his left until they met with mine. He took a deep breath and opened his mouth. "Go to hell," he whispered with a thick Russian accent. He coughed, and a moment later, there was a gurgling sound. I watched a mass of crimson blood pour from his mouth. It ran down the side of his face. He coughed again. The man was dying and I was running out of time to get information out of him.

"This was Dimitri's plan, wasn't it?" I asked and paused a

beat before I continued, trying to read the man. "And I bet you told him it was a bad idea. He's young. Inexperienced. Doesn't follow the normal rules of engagement. I bet you told him that even if I *did* have his father, even if I turned him over to you, there was no way I'd just let you walk away from all of this." I leaned in closer. "You knew better, didn't you?"

I was using training I'd received years ago as a SEAL to read the guy. I could tell that I was getting to him. The man curled his lips in disgust, sucked in a deep breath, and coughed again. He breathed some more and said, "My allegiance isn't to Dimitri. It's to his father, Nikolai." He paused and added, "And I would do anything to get him back." He coughed again, and another gush of blood spewed from his mouth.

"Nikolai Ivanov is dead," I said and watched the man's reaction to the news. "That's why he's not here."

His eyes darted over to Chris Reed, then flicked back to me. "You're lying."

"He died a month ago in an underground prison. That's why I don't have him." Chris stepped around the guy and kept his weapon trained on him as I tried to get the man to talk. "I'll get you help. Just tell me—"

Before I could finish asking my question, the man's face went slack. I put two fingers against his neck. "Damn it," I whispered as I came off my knees, sat on the ground, and stuffed my weapon in the small of my back. I grabbed the back of my head and slid my fingers down my neck as I stared out across the field, thought about everything that had just happened, and wondered how I was going to get to Dimitri Ivanov.

I tried calling Jami as Reed started to pace, but she didn't answer.

"Where do we go from here?" he asked.

I shook my head. “I don’t know.” I thought about it some more and stood. I stuffed my hand in my pocket, felt my fingers brush by the ring, and pulled out a small folded piece of paper and handed it to Chris.

“What’s this?”

“The address we got at Meg Taylor’s apartment.”

Chris took it from me.

“Can you go check on Jami?”

Chris stared at me. “You shouldn’t have let her go off on her own,” he said. “She could be in trouble.”

I saw an ambulance approach. Its siren was off and directly behind it were two Metro Police cruisers. I watched the three vehicles turn into the base. Over my shoulder, I saw a military police vehicle approach from the south. “I’m sure she’s fine,” I finally replied as I turned back to look at the ambulance. “I couldn’t have stopped her, anyway.” I nodded at the vehicles. “I’ll handle these guys. Call me when you get there.”

Reed nodded. “I’ll check things out,” he said as I crouched down and checked the pockets of the two men on the ground while I still could, and I found a set of car keys on the guy who had shot Mark Reynolds.

“What about Landry?” Chris asked. “Why would he lie about Ivanov? Why would he set you up like that?”

I held up the car keys. “That’s what I’m going to have to find out,” I said and dropped them in my pocket.

Chris stretched out his hand and we shook. He took a look at the address and cocked his head to one side. “Seems familiar,” he said and looked up at me. “Not too far from here,” he added and jogged to his SUV.

I watched as he approached his vehicle and one of the police cars pulled up next to him. Chris walked around to the driver’s side window and spoke with the officer for several seconds before pointing at me. The cop nodded, pulled his vehicle forward, and parked as Chris climbed inside his SUV and left the base.

The other patrol car parked behind the first cop, and I watched as the officers got out and headed in my direction while the military police vehicle jumped the curb and pulled onto the grass. He stopped ten yards from me, stepped out of his vehicle, and waved the ambulance in until they got close to the bodies. The officer motioned for them to stop, turned to look at the men on the ground, and headed right for me.

"Bureau guy told me what we're dealing with over here," the military police officer said. "We got word that the FBI needed the use of our heliport and needed the main gate to be cleared, but we didn't expect all this," he said, looking at the lifeless bodies on the ground. "Afraid I'll need to get a statement from you, Mr..."

"Jordan," I said as I looked across the field. The sky was getting brighter as the sun started to break free from below the horizon. "Blake Jordan," I added and reached for my credentials and showed them to him.

The officer looked it over, nodded, and moved over to the bodies and started to examine them. I grabbed my wrists and looked down at them. I saw how raw and red they were from when the Russians had me tied to the ropes at the abandoned building. As I massaged them, I couldn't stop thinking about that building. It gnawed at me and wouldn't let me go. "I need to make a call," I said, and the man nodded his approval.

47

I WALKED THROUGH THE FIELD, HEADED TOWARD THE PARKED vehicle that the terrorists had driven. I reached for my cell phone and thought through the events of the past twenty-four hours, trying to put the pieces together and make sense of it all. I felt hungry and weak and realized that I hadn't had anything to eat since yesterday's breakfast meeting with the president. I thought briefly about the two dead men who had roughed up Sammy. Then my mind drifted back to the abandoned building near the Naval Observatory.

That was where my mind stayed for several minutes as I remembered Jami saying that it looked like it had been abandoned for thirty years. I thought back to when the man driving the Town Car had brought me into the building. The lawn had been perfectly manicured. The outside looked immaculate. But inside, the home was stripped of everything. Jami's words went off in my ear like a warning. *Abandoned thirty years.*

Jami was right. There was something about that building that didn't make sense to me, and I had to figure out what it was. I dialed Morgan again and brought the phone to my ear as I turned back to see the other officers gathered by the bodies, and watched as a crime scene vehicle pulled in behind the other cars.

"This is Lennox," he answered.

"Morgan, it's Blake."

"I watched the whole thing, mate," said Morgan as I looked up, remembering the drone overhead.

"I need your help," I said, lowering my gaze. "That building where I was being held—what was that?"

"What do you mean?" he asked after a long pause.

I shook my head and looked down. "I don't know. The lawn was taken care of, but on the inside—it was like the building hadn't been used in decades." I thought some more. "Something's not right, Morgan. It's a good neighborhood. It shouldn't have been abandoned. It doesn't make sense, and I need to know why."

"Okay. I'll look into it, mate, and I'll get back to you."

"No," I said. "I need you to look into it right now for me."

Morgan sighed. "Blake, we have a bit of a situation over here that I'm dealing with, and I really need to bring you up to speed on it, actually. Lynne May has been gone for several hours, and I asked Simon to—"

"Morgan, please," I said, interrupting him. "This is important. I need to know more about that building."

He sighed again. "Hang on," he said, and I heard the sound of the analyst typing on his keyboard as I turned back to the officers behind me and noticed that they were all looking in my direction, and one of them was pointing at me. "Okay," Morgan finally said. "The building was at thirty-four ten Garfield Street."

The officer I'd been speaking with lifted his hand and pulled four fingers toward him several times, letting me know that he needed me back to talk with him. I held a finger in the air. He shook his head and again motioned for me to return as Morgan continued.

"Looks like the building's owned by the Iranian government, Blake. It's been unoccupied since—" I heard more typing "—nineteen seventy-nine."

"I don't understand," I said.

There was more typing. "Looks like that's right around when the United States severed ties with Iran."

"Okay," I said. I thought some more about it and asked, "Morgan, are there any others like it nearby?"

"Abandoned residences?"

"Vacant buildings in Washington still owned by the Iranian government."

"Checking," he said.

I looked back and saw the officer I'd been speaking with leave the others and step through the grass, headed straight for me. "You almost done? Need you back," the man yelled as he got close to me.

"Almost," I replied. "Gonna grab a bottle of water from my car and I'll be right there. Want one?"

The officer stared at me and shook his head. "No, but finish the call and let's get this over with, okay?"

I nodded. The cop turned, lowered his gaze, and shook his head as he walked back to join the others. "Come on, Morgan," I said as I headed in the opposite direction, toward the Russian's vehicle.

"Got it," said Lennox. "I see two more locations. The first is at twenty-nine fifty-four Upton Street."

"How big is it?"

"Not very. Looks like it was the residence of the Iranian minister of cultural affairs back in the day."

"What was Garfield used for?" I asked.

Morgan checked briefly. "Iranian military attaché."

I thought about it some more. "Okay, what's the third address?"

"It's the former Iranian embassy, Blake. Close proximity to the other two locations I just mentioned."

I slowed my approach to the vehicle, feeling adrenaline surge through my body. "How big is it, Morgan?"

"Pulling it up in Maps now," he said with a brief pause. "It looks huge, Blake, an old two-story mansion."

"Where?"

"Half a mile south of the Garfield address. Three thousand five Massachusetts Avenue."

"Move the drone and let me know if you see any activity outside. I'll call you when I'm close, okay?"

"Blake, wait. I need to tell you about Bill Landry."

I stopped when I got to the vehicle and listened as Morgan continued.

"Simon let me know that Lynne May has been gone for a couple of hours now. Landry told him that she was resting in a privacy room, but when I asked Simon to go get her, she was gone. I was able to access the Hoover Building's security cameras, but can't find the archive. It may have been deleted. Simon alerted security, but they're adamant that May hasn't left the building. I don't know what to do."

"Morgan, Bill Landry lied to me. He wanted this to go down the way it did here at Bolling. He wanted me dead," I said. "Landry's involved somehow. So forget the archive and go find Landry." I climbed into the car, shoved the key into the ignition, and turned to see the officer across the field, still watching me. "I'll call you back. Move that drone, Morgan," I said as I turned the key, put it in drive, and stepped on the gas.

48

JAMI BROUGHT HER HAND DOWN HARD ON THE STEERING wheel, angry with herself for letting Bill Landry get away, as she slowly drove her SUV back to the address she had found at Meg Taylor's apartment. While on the road, she had wanted to call Morgan to help track his vehicle, but realized that her phone was missing and remembered that she had set it on the kitchen counter while she was talking with Taylor.

She drove the SUV to the end of the street, turned around in the cul-de-sac, and parked the vehicle facing the exit to the neighborhood, just as she had done when she first arrived. Only this time, she pulled the SUV all the way to the front of Landry's house so she could go inside, grab her phone, and get out quick.

The street looked different now. The sky was brighter, the streetlights were off, and the eerie orange glow that it had cast on the house was now gone. Jami sat inside her vehicle, looking out the passenger window at the beautiful home. She grabbed her weapon, stepped out of the car, and approached the front door.

Jami got to the front door, where she and Meg Taylor had had their conversation earlier. She grabbed the handle, depressed the lock with her thumb, and pushed the door open. She heard two beeps from the alarm system, indicating that an entry door had been opened. To her relief, the alarm did not sound.

Closing the door behind her, Jami held her weapon out in front of her, aimed it toward the ground, and moved through the foyer, which was now brighter with light coming in through the glass door. She stepped closer to the kitchen and lowered her weapon when she saw her phone.

Grabbing it, she saw that she had several missed calls. She shoved the phone into a pocket, put two hands back on the weapon, and looked for a light switch. She found it, flipped it on, and searched the kitchen.

A roll of silver duct tape was on the kitchen counter close to the door that led to the garage. A nearby drawer was ajar, and Jami stepped closer to it, pulled it all the way open, and checked inside before pushing it shut. She glanced across a few scattered papers on the counter, knowing that she needed to get out of there, but looking for anything that might tell her where Landry might have taken Meg Taylor.

When Jami heard a car engine rumble and felt the house vibrate as it had earlier, her blood ran cold.

She moved to the opposite side of the kitchen, crouched, and aimed her weapon toward the door leading to the garage and waited. The engine was killed, and Jami realized that something was different. She had expected to hear the mechanical sound of the garage door opening. Her eyes grew wide as she realized that her vehicle was parked directly outside the home—not near the end of the cul-de-sac, like before.

As Jami stood, she heard a knock at the door and spun around the kitchen, aiming her weapon toward the front door. She could see a figure on the other side of the glass. It was a man, and it looked like he had a weapon in his hand as well. Jami ducked behind a wall and watched as the door was slowly cracked open. Two beeps from the security system sounded somewhere close by. A toe pushed the door all the way open.

"Drop it!" yelled Jami from behind the wall, aiming her weapon toward the figure in the doorway.

"Jami, it's me," said Chris Reed.

She lowered her weapon, stepped out from behind the wall, and stuffed the Glock into the small of her back. She met Chris in the foyer and pushed the door closed behind him. "What are you doing here?"

"Blake sent me," he replied, holding up the small yellow note with the address on it that she remembered taking from Meg Taylor's apartment. Chris lowered his hand and took a look around. "I know this place."

She narrowed her eyes. "You do?"

"Bureau Christmas party. Made an appearance and left." He looked around. "It's Bill Landry's house."

Jami nodded. "He was here. I was with Meg Taylor, trying to get her to tell me who was feeding her information, and Landry showed up. She said I had to go, but it was too late, he was already stepping into the kitchen." Jami paused. "I recognized his voice. I heard a struggle. He dragged her to the car and left."

"It's all making sense now," said Chris.

Jami furrowed her brow, not understanding what he meant.

"Bolling," he explained. "We went out there and waited on the chopper that Landry said was coming." Chris shook his head slowly. "It never came, Jami. Nikolai Ivanov is dead. Bill Landry set us up."

Reed shared the details of the exchange, what went down with the terrorist in the hood that they had made out to look like Charlie Redding, and that Mark Reynolds had been shot and was taken to the hospital.

Jami gasped and cupped a hand over her mouth as she stared at Chris. "Is he okay?" she whispered.

"Don't know yet," said Chris as he reached for his phone. "But I need to find out." He noticed an incoming call and answered it. "Morgan?" he said, switching the call to speakerphone. "I have Jami here with me."

Morgan brought Jami and Chris up to speed with Lynne May's disappearance and how he and Simon had been trying to locate her using the Hoover Building's security footage. Jami told Morgan about what had happened at Bill Landry's home. Morgan had more to share. "Guys, I think Blake may have found Ivanov."

Jami and Chris exchanged a look. "How?" asked Jami.

Morgan explained the connection between the abandoned house on Garfield and the former embassy. He said that Blake had left Bolling and was headed to the embassy and would arrive there in a few seconds.

"He's going alone?" asked Jami, but Morgan didn't reply. He didn't need to.

"I think he could use your help, love," said Morgan. "That's why I'm calling. I can try to come up with an excuse to stall him until you get over there, but you're going to have to leave now. Can't stop him for long."

"How far out are we?" asked Jami.

There was typing in the background. "Based on that northwest DC address that you gave me earlier, it's exactly three miles south of you. You could get there in five minutes. I can't delay him longer than that."

She pushed open the front door and stepped outside as Chris followed. She turned back to look at him.

"You should go to the Hoover Building and meet up with Simon. Help him find Lynne May," said Chris.

Jami furrowed her brow and realized that Chris knew what she knew—that the Russians wanted her, too. She understood that Blake must have shared that information with Chris and Mark after they had split up. Chris was right, they needed to find Lynne May. They also needed to figure out where Landry was and understand why he had taken Meg Taylor. She bit her lip and stared at Chris, shaking her head. "No, we'll both go."

"Guys," interrupted Morgan, "he just arrived. If you're going to go, you need to go now."

"Maybe he doesn't want our help. If he wanted us there, then he would have called us," said Chris.

Jami frowned. "No, he wouldn't," she said and shook her head knowingly. "Morgan, send us the address."

49

MORGAN USED THE DRONE TO HELP ME LOSE THE COPS. I stopped the vehicle on Thirtieth Street, just short of a fork in the road at Benton Place that jutted out to the left. Through the windshield, to my right, I had a clear shot of the embassy. I saw a large green dome at the left of the building and asked Morgan what it was. He told me that it had been known as the Persian Room during the embassy's heyday.

Two large windows at the back of the building faced me, right behind the green dome, which appeared to be located in an east wing of the main building. There were three tall, vertical windows in the back of the building with what looked like a large uncovered courtyard underneath. Surrounding trees blocked the west wing from my view. I saw a white concrete wall that surrounded the perimeter of the property.

"Morgan, this is taking too long. What's the status of that drone?"

"Just give me another minute or so, mate," he replied as I continued to stare out the vehicle's windshield.

An occasional car rushed by me on the left, headed for Massachusetts Avenue, which Morgan said was lined by more embassies. He said that this was the best location for an approach into the building where I believed Dimitri Ivanov might be operating from. Another car approached, and I turned to my left to watch it through the driver's side mirror. As it passed, I noticed two blacked-out vehicles right behind it.

I looked up and, through the rearview mirror, watched the SUVs slow down and park directly behind me. "Morgan, what's going on?" I asked as I reached for my Glock and kept my eyes fixed on the vehicles until I saw that it was Jami who had parked behind me. That was when I understood what Morgan was doing.

Opening the door, I climbed out of the vehicle as Jami and Chris did the same, and I walked toward them.

"Are you crazy?" asked Jami. I stopped in front of her while Chris took another few steps closer to join us. "Blake, you're not going in there alone." She crossed her arms and tilted her head.

"I'm *not* alone," I replied and moved the phone away from my ear and held it out in front of me.

"That's not what I meant," said Jami.

I looked them over and nodded. "I know," I said and forced a smile. "You're right. I could use your help."

Jami told me about the address that she and Chris had gone to, and said it belonged to Bill Landry. She told me about meeting Meg Taylor when she got there, and said that she and Landry were romantically involved. We understood that Bill Landry was her informant. He was taking advantage of Taylor being new in town. I decided that she had found out about me on her own and Landry had filled in the details. Then Jami said that Landry had shown up and taken Taylor away by force, but I couldn't understand why.

The three of us walked to the sidewalk and huddled together next to Jami's vehicle. I put the call on speakerphone and held the phone out in front of us. "Okay, Morgan," I said, "tell me what you've got."

"Just moved the drone north of the embassy. All clear. Didn't see any movement in the courtyard, either. Now I'm south of the building and still not seeing anything. No Tangos visible on the perimeter, Blake."

"You got schematics?" asked Chris.

"No, and I'm not even sure what it looks like inside. The building's still owned by Iran, not many pictures."

"Morgan, we need to know what we're dealing with," I said.

"Here's what I can see from overhead," he said. "There are three ways in. The first is through the courtyard at the north side where you're positioned right now. Another up a ramp that'll take you to the second floor from the west wing of the building. The last way in is from the south, through the front door."

"It's a big building," I said as I turned my head to glance back at the old, abandoned embassy. "Ivanov could be anywhere." I turned back to the team. "And if he's in there, he has Charlie Redding with him."

Jami turned to me. "What's the plan?"

"There are three ways in and three of us," I said as Chris motioned for us to join him at the back of his SUV. He pulled open a drawer, revealing extra ammo, and handed some to us. "We've all got to take an entrance to make sure that Ivanov doesn't get past us." I pointed down the road we were parked on. "Chris, you head south on Thirtieth Street and take the main entrance in." I looked to the small hill leading to the back of the property. "Jami and I will enter through the back. Jami, you go in through the courtyard. I'll move over to the west wing and take the ramp up to the second floor, and I'll meet you two inside."

I grabbed two extra magazines and stuffed them into the pockets of my jeans. Chris found a charge pack along with a small brick of C-4. I went to the passenger door, found my messenger bag, and returned. Chris placed the charge pack inside; then he opened a smaller drawer and handed earpieces to Jami and me. We paired them to our phones, I patched them in with Morgan, and Chris pulled down on the hatch.

"Guys," said Lennox, sounding worried.

I dropped the phone into my back pocket since I had Morgan on Bluetooth. "We're here. Go ahead."

"I've got the Predator drone north of the property, and I'm seeing movement inside the courtyard now."

"What kind of movement?" I asked.

"Trying to zoom in," he said and paused while I turned to look back at the building through the trees. "Looks like two Tangos, wearing all black. One of them has a weapon in his hand, the other guy's outside my line of sight now, but I'm assuming he's also armed. Don't think Chris can go south on Thirtieth now."

I looked and saw that he was right. They'd be able to see him from the courtyard. We needed another plan. "Okay, we'll all head in from the north and split up at the courtyard. Keep the Predator in place, Morgan."

We climbed the steep hill and stopped when we got to a large oak tree on our side of the wall. I stepped up to it and used it to hide my face as I slowly moved my head to the left until I caught a glimpse of the men that Morgan had spotted from the drone circling overhead. They had semiautomatic weapons. I dropped to my knees. With four fingers, I pointed left, and Chris moved south along the wall. Jami remained where she was as I moved north, past her, crouching as I went. I stopped and leaned my back against the wall.

"Morgan, do you still have a visual?" I whispered into my earpiece.

"Yes, but I can only see one now. Looks like he might be talking to the guy I can't see," he said.

"I need you to tell me when I have a clear shot," I said, whispering again. I turned to my right and saw Jami staring back at me. Chris was farther down from her, also looking in my direction. "Chris, I'll need you to create a distraction, okay?"

He nodded, and I faced forward, took a deep breath, and closed my eyes.

Finally, Morgan spoke. "Now," he said.

I opened my eyes, gripped my weapon, and nodded to Chris.

50

Still gripping my weapon, I watched as Chris turned to face the wall, found a rock, and tossed it close to the courtyard. As soon as I heard it hit the ground, I spun around, raised my Glock over the wall, and saw the two men looking in Reed's direction. Then they noticed me. I closed an eye and squeezed twice.

"Go," I said, knowing that Ivanov would have heard the shots and would know that something was wrong.

Chris, Jami, and I got over the wall and started to move. Chris ran south along the building, past where the large green dome was located, and disappeared from my line of sight as Jami and I moved west.

From what I could tell, the area just inside the courtyard was clear. With my left hand, I let go of my weapon and motioned toward the back entrance. Jami approached as I continued moving west across the back of the property. As I moved, I watched her approach the back door to enter through the courtyard.

As soon as she disappeared inside, I got to the west wing of the building and scaled the steep ramp that Morgan had told us about so I could enter the building from the second floor. I was breathing hard as I moved quickly and carefully climbed the ramp while scanning my surroundings. To my right, I saw three tall windows lining the outer wall, and I tried to look into the building as I passed them and approached the door at the top of the ramp. They were old and the glass was dirty, making it difficult to see inside.

"Can't get into the big room on the left," said Jami through the earpiece. "Two large doors, both locked."

"Keep moving," I said. Then two shots were fired near the front of the property as I got to the top of the ramp and I crouched by the door. My eyes grew wide and my heart was racing. "Chris, you okay?"

"Had to use my key," he answered. "Jami, I'm at the front and moving your way."

"Copy that," she said.

I studied the door. It opened from the inside. I couldn't kick it in. I stood, aimed my weapon, and fired. It took three shots to get it open. I stepped inside and was overwhelmed by the same mildew smell I had experienced hours earlier inside the building at Garfield, the smell of a building that hadn't been used by anyone in decades. I moved fast, sweeping my weapon from side to side, and stepped through the room.

Doors had been taken off their hinges and rested against the walls. Blue, seventies-era velvet tufted sofas were covered in dust, and several of them had large mirrors and lamps resting on top of them. "First room upstairs is clear," I said to the team as I continued to the next room and tried to keep myself focused.

As I stepped inside, I noticed oil paintings and old, framed photographs. They were all of the same man, either wearing a suit and tie or an olive-colored military uniform. I guessed that the man must have been the Iranian ambassador. I continued to step across the dirty floor, but nobody was in that room, either.

Large boxes were pushed up against the wall in the next room. I glanced down and saw that they were filled with old documents and what looked like Iranian passports. Stepping through, I found a huge grand ballroom, empty, with electrical wires dangling from the ceiling along with a large chandelier in the center of the room. I didn't go inside, just checked it from the door. I looked down at one of the large doors taken off its hinges. The doorknob was golden and stamped with the symbol of the Imperial State of Iran.

"Upstairs is clear. Heading down to join you," I said as I moved to the stairs and descended. On my left were tall, thin stained-glass windows with dim light shining through from outside. To my right, I saw that the metal railing was decorated with golden birds weaved in an ornamental fashion from a time long ago.

"Rest of the building is clear," said Jami as she and Chris met me at the bottom of the staircase.

To my left, a tall set of windows stretched from the floor to the ceiling, revealing another courtyard. This one was in the center of the building, which wrapped around all four sides. In the middle were remnants of what looked like an old fountain. What was once a regal decoration was now just a rusty centerpiece.

"Show me the room, Jami," I said, referring to the room with the locked doors that she had mentioned. She motioned for me to follow and led Chris and me down the hallway, and we stopped outside the door.

I looked to the left, out a large window. Past the inner courtyard, I saw the green dome on the roof. "Morgan," I said into my earpiece, "looks like we're outside the Persian

Room you told me about earlier." I paused for several seconds while I checked the door. "I need to know what we're walking into over here."

"Just a sec," said Lennox. Several seconds passed as we heard the man typing. "Okay, found an old image on the internet, Blake." There was more typing in the background. "But the image is about thirty years old. Looks like a very large room, thirty-foot ceiling. Looks like a good place for Ivanov to set up shop in."

I knelt and pulled the strap for my messenger bag over my head and I set it on the floor. I opened it up and motioned for Chris to join me. "Can you set the charge, Chris?"

He nodded as I handed it to him.

"Just need a minute or two," he said as he took it from me, went to the large doors, and got started.

"We checked the other rooms downstairs," said Jami as she turned and gestured to the other side of the building. "All of the doors were off their hinges. I don't understand why these are up and why it's locked."

She was right. It didn't make much sense to me, either. I shrugged as we watched Reed quietly at work. "Found the same thing upstairs," I said as I checked my weapon and got ready to enter the room.

"What are we going to do if Charlie's not inside?" Jami asked with a whisper, keeping her voice down.

I kept my eyes on the door. "No need to whisper," I said. "I'm sure they heard the shots I fired earlier."

"Blake, you didn't answer the question."

We exchanged a look. I shrugged again because I didn't have an answer.

Chris finished securing a strip over and around the area where the two doors locked together. He set the charge and ran over to join us. "Back up," he said, and we took a few steps backward and ducked behind a wide concrete column. The three of us knelt together. "Got it set to thirty seconds. Get ready," he added.

"I'll lead us in," I said and started to count as I closed my eyes and thought about Charlie Redding.

I thought some more about Jami's question. What would I do if Charlie wasn't inside the room? If I was wrong and Dimitri wasn't inside? I took a deep breath and tried to slow my pulse. This had to be Ivanov's location. I was sure of it. I kept counting. A few short seconds later, there was a loud bang as the explosive detonated. The sound was deafening, and I flinched as chunks of wood and concrete flew past us. I looked at Chris, then at Jami. They looked back and I nodded. I spun around the column and moved to the door.

The three of us approached, weapons drawn, and stepped through a blanket of thick white smoke. I stepped closer to the door and swung my weapon left to right and continued with the sweeping motion as I crossed the threshold and moved farther inside. My eyes moved back and forth, scanning the room as I moved past the thick haze. I kept moving until I finally saw what was waiting for us on the other side of the smoke. I slowly lowered my weapon. "Morgan," I said, trying hard not to panic, "we have a problem."

51

"What is it?" asked Lennox from my earpiece as I turned back and watched Chris and Jami step through the smoke. They lowered their weapons and joined me in the center of the large Persian Room.

"We've got two laptops, some papers," I said as I turned back and walked to a table at the end of the room. "But no sign of Charlie or Ivanov." I scanned their work space. "Looks like we just missed them, Morgan."

I stuffed my weapon into the small of my back and turned a laptop around to face me as I kept my back to the door. Chris started to check out the rest of the large room as Jami started looking at the other laptop.

The laptop I was looking at was locked. I noticed a small webcam indicator light turned on. To our surprise, Jami's was unlocked. She started to check the various applications that were up and running. "Looks like they were monitoring the news. I've got a story up about the ransomware attacks from yesterday and the explosion at DDC." Jami tucked a lock of brown hair behind an ear, stood up straight, and shrugged. "I'll have to keep digging, not seeing much else. Maybe I'm missing something."

We heard Lennox sigh. "Guys, I'm getting pinged by Simon again. He says it's urgent and he needs to call me right away. Give me a minute to switch over, love, then I'll come back on the line, and I'll help walk you through setting up a direct connect so I can get into that laptop, and we'll see what else we can find, okay?"

Jami pushed the laptop away and stepped back. I followed her gaze as she started to look up along the walls and turned around to take in the room. I glanced over to Chris Reed and saw him doing the same.

The Persian Room, as Morgan had called it, seemed to be perfectly intact. It was the only room in the entire embassy that had remained exactly as it had been, I imagined, for over thirty years. The walls and carpet were green —the same color as the dome overhead. A large red carpet covered the length of the room, from the entrance to the back wall. Three red sofas were placed at the back and sides of the room, and the upper part of the walls, halfway to the top of the ceiling, were covered with large oil paintings.

Jami went back to the laptop and started to get ready for when Morgan would come back on the line as Chris stepped closer to us and said, "I'm sorry." I guessed that he could see my disappointment. "I was hoping he'd be here."

I nodded, thinking about Charlie Redding and wondering where to go from here. Then I thought I heard a sound from inside the main building we had come from. I turned and listened.

"Sorry, guys," said Lennox through our earpieces as he came back on the line. "Simon told me that—"

"Morgan," I said, interrupting him as I reached behind my back, grabbed my weapon, and held it steady and level, "are you seeing any activity outside the embassy? I just heard something outside the room."

Jami turned back from the laptop and grabbed her weapon. I watched as Chris reached for his as well.

"Pulling the Predator around, hang on." Morgan paused for several moments. "Bloody hell."

"What is it?" I asked as my heart started to beat faster.

"I see several men entering the embassy through the courtyard in the back. They're going in fast, Blake." Morgan paused as I turned briefly to Jami and Chris. "And I see one more walking over from the building next door." We heard Morgan typing frantically. "It's the former ambassador's residence, looks like it's part of the same complex. I'm sorry, guys. I don't know how I missed it. They've been waiting next door."

I took a step closer to the door and gripped my weapon tight as Jami and Chris stood on both sides of me.

"It's a trap," said Jami from my left. "They were just trying to draw us in. Now we have nowhere to go."

We watched as a group of men approached the entrance, their guns trained on us. I counted five of them. They stood just outside the room and yelled for us to drop our weapons, but we held them steady.

"We need a way out of this," I said to Morgan over the loud voices of the men shouting from the doorway.

"There's nothing I can do," replied Lennox.

"Yes, there is, Morgan. Just think of something."

The men just outside the Persian Room continued to shout. One of them fired a shot and it came close to Jami. "Okay!" I yelled and raised my Glock into the air and held my other hand up as well. Slowly, I started to kneel and lowered my weapon, setting it on the rug in front of me, and got back to my feet.

"Kick it away," another man yelled.

I kicked it to the left side of the room and watched it slide to the wall.

"Now it's your turn," said the first man as his eyes moved between Chris and Jami on both sides of me.

I turned to Chris, then to Jami. I nodded. They lowered their weapons and kicked them away just as I had. The three of us stood defenseless as the five men entered, kept their weapons trained on us, and stopped. From behind them, I heard the sound of someone clapping outside the room. The clapping was slow and distant. The sound became louder as we watched the men step aside and create a pathway at the door.

It was Dimitri Ivanov.

The young man kept walking and passed between his men. When Dimitri was just a few feet in front of us, he stopped clapping and dropped his arms to his sides. He smiled and looked us over with smug satisfaction. "Mr. Jordan, it is great to see you again," he said as his voice filled the expanse of the room. His smile widened. "I was wondering how long it would take you to find me." Dimitri glanced at his watch. "An hour," he said with a raise of his eyebrows and surprise in his eyes. "Not bad for a washed-up special agent like yourself." Dimitri Ivanov cocked his head to one side and lost the smile. "Where is my father?"

"Don't tell him," Morgan said through my earpiece, and I realized that he could hear what was happening.

"First, tell me where you're keeping Charlie Redding."

One side of his lips curled up. He was enjoying this. "I handed him off to someone. Insurance, if you will."

I glared back at the man. "Landry."

Ivanov raised his eyebrows again and nodded. "You're starting to catch on, Mr. Jordan." Dimitri brought his hands behind his back and kept them there. "Now what Mr. Landry does with him is his business." Ivanov cocked his head to one side again. "Where is my father?" he repeated as he started to pace.

I stared back at the man, deciding what to do. I took a deep breath. Let it out. "Your father's dead."

"Very good!" Dimitri stopped pacing and clapped slowly again. "*Very* good," he repeated, with inflection.

My eyes scanned left to right as I looked over Dimitri's men. "If you knew, then what's this all about?"

Ivanov shrugged. "It's called a distraction, Jordan. A diversion. Misdirection." He smiled. "And it worked."

52

I STARED AT DIMITRI IVANOV AS HE RAN HIS FINGERS THROUGH his hair. "How long have you known?" I asked.

"About my father?" His smile faded. "I was contacted last month. I learned that my father survived the explosion in New York. They were supposed to get him out of Mount Weather." He looked away briefly. "But he was killed." He looked back at me somberly. "So I was given an opportunity to avenge his death."

"By helping Landry," I said. "So that's how your father got connected to the Bureau six months ago. Landry tried to help your father dismantle the surveillance program at the NSA substation in New York."

"Help?" said Ivanov. "He *recruited* him. Just like he recruited me to finish the job that my father started."

"What's your goal? What are you trying to do, and what's he paying you? How much is all of this worth?"

Ivanov shook his head. "It's not about money, Mr. Jordan. It's about *power*." He checked his watch again. "And soon, Landry will be in charge of the most powerful intelligence agency your country has to offer."

In my earpiece I heard Morgan clear his throat. "Are Ivanov and his men in the center of the room, mate?"

Dimitri took a step closer and also asked me a question. "Do I need to connect the dots for you, Jordan?"

"Yes," I said, answering both of them.

"Initially, we were just going to kill the girl," he said, looking at Jami. "Then I had a better idea—detonate the bomb in Agent Davis's vehicle at the DDC field office, forcing the agency to go to the Hoover Building. Combine the DDC and Bureau teams. Put them under one roof." He paused and his eyes fell back on me. "Distract you and your team—and in effect, distract your president—while Landry kept Mulvaney busy. Get him occupied so we could take him out. Then we'd kill you." He smiled. "Right about now, actually."

I narrowed my eyes and shook my head, trying to understand. "You're going to take out Mulvaney?"

"We'll take the whole thing out. Anyone inside." Dimitri laughed. "Then Landry becomes acting director."

"Listen, Blake, I have an idea," said Morgan. "I'm assuming that Ivanov and his men are at the entrance to the room. I need you guys to move to the north and south sides of the room on my mark. Do you copy?"

"How?" I asked. Morgan started to respond, but I interrupted him. "How are you taking the building out?"

Ivanov grinned. "The only way you *can* take a building out, Mr. Jordan—we'll blow the damn thing up."

"Where's the bomb?" I asked, but he shook his head, and I knew he wouldn't tell me. My mind started to race. "Who else is involved?" I asked. "Simon Harris? What about Lynne May? Is she a part of all of this?"

"Okay, guys. I need you to move right now," Morgan yelled. I turned to Jami, then Chris. "Do you copy?"

"There are many who oppose your president and will stop at nothing to bring him down," said Dimitri.

I knew what Morgan was going to do. We all did. Morgan yelled again that we needed to move. I stared at Ivanov. "You need to know that we're gonna stop Landry."

Dimitri looked confused.

"Now!" I yelled. Chris dove right. Jami and I went left. We braced for impact as the massive Predator drone breached the wall.

53

When I opened my eyes, I was on the ground next to Jami. I looked back and saw a gaping hole in the wall. Bright rays of sunlight streaked across the room and caught the dust and debris that still hung in the air. I saw the damage that the mangled, twenty-seven-foot drone had made. My eyes moved to where Ivanov and his men had been standing, but I saw nothing but rubble.

"You guys okay?" asked Morgan.

"I think so," I replied as I saw Chris get to his feet. I reached down and grabbed Jami's hand to help her up.

Jami regained her balance, bent to grab our weapons, and handed my Glock back to me. "We need to check the ambassador's residence next door."

I nodded and walked to the rubble, scanning everywhere, and confirmed that Ivanov's men were buried underneath the wreckage. I kept scanning and found Ivanov's bloody face—his eyes were tracking me from an opening in the debris as I approached.

"You can't stop us," he groaned. "Landry's too powerful now. And we're going to keep coming after you."

I lifted my weapon, aimed it between Dimitri's eyes, and shook my head. "I've heard that before."

I squeezed the trigger once and sent a round into the man's forehead. Squeezed it again to make sure. I lowered my weapon and turned to Jami and Chris as they stared back at me. "Morgan?" I said.

"I'm here, mate. Guess it worked," he replied as I stepped over more debris and got to the door to leave.

"We're going to check out the residence next door," I said. We left the Persian Room and entered the courtyard. "Morgan, you were about to tell us something when we heard Ivanov and his men approaching. What was it?" I asked as we crossed the parking lot and stood outside the former residence.

"Simon had something to tell us, but now he's showing as away on messenger. I'll try to get a hold of him so I can patch him through to talk with us. I'll be back in a few minutes," he said, and the line went silent.

Jami, Chris, and I huddled together as we checked our weapons and discussed our approach. We decided to enter the same way we had gotten into the former embassy next door—only Jami and I would take the back entrance together while Chris took the front. We'd clear each room and meet up in the middle.

We entered and cleared the residence quickly, finding nobody inside. We were coming out the back and headed to our vehicles when we heard Morgan's voice again. "Okay, guys, I've got Simon on the line now."

"Can you hear me okay?" asked Harris.

"Copy," I said as we continued to head toward our vehicles. "What do you have for us, Simon?"

"Mrs. May had me tracking Agent Davis's vehicle after she lost contact with her," he said. Jami and I exchanged a look as he continued. "After she disappeared, Mr. Landry came to see me. He gave me access to the Bureau's fleet-tracking system so I could help him track Chris Reed and monitor both vehicles."

"What happened?" I asked.

"Mr. Landry never came back. Now he's missing. I tried to talk to Director Mulvaney, but he blew me off."

We approached the wall behind the embassy and climbed over as we kept moving toward our vehicles.

"Security isn't helping much. So I've been sitting here trying to figure out how I can find Mr. Landry to try to get some answers. That's when I realized that I still have the access he provisioned me earlier."

I stopped short of the vehicles and stood still. "Access to what, Simon? The Bureau's fleet tracker?"

"Yes," he said nervously, following a long pause.

I turned to look at Chris and Jami. "Simon, what are you telling me? Are you tracking Bill Landry?"

There was another pause before he spoke again. "Yes. He's here. He's at the Hoover Building right now," he said, and I knew it wasn't nervousness that I was hearing. It was the sound of a man who was terrified.

I looked at Chris and said, "You've got a Bureau vehicle. Can you get us into the Hoover Building garage without raising any red flags?"

He nodded.

"Good. You drive, then," I said. We left the DDC vehicle behind as Jami and I climbed into Chris's SUV. "Morgan, are you still there?" I asked as Chris started the ignition.

"I'm here," replied Lennox as Chris approached Massachusetts and floored it.

"Do you have access to the live feeds from the security cameras in the building?"

"I'll have to confirm, Blake. Simon and I were just trying to access the archive to figure out where May went. I'm sure I can tap into the cameras and monitor what's going on in real time if you need me to."

"Get me eyes on Landry," I said as Reed continued pushing the car faster down Massachusetts, slowed as we approached Dupont Circle, and stepped on the gas as we continued our approach to FBI headquarters.

"Chris, any idea where Landry might be?" asked Jami from the backseat.

I turned to Reed and saw him shake his head slowly. "No. He could be anywhere."

"But we know where he's going," I said as I faced forward and thought about what Dimitri had told us. "Simon, there's reason to believe that Landry may try to harm Mulvaney. We need to make sure that—"

"I just saw him a second ago," said Harris, interrupting me.

I turned to look at Chris as I listened to the man.

"I'm standing up at my cubicle and I just saw the guy walk down from his office. He just passed me."

My mind was racing. We were still a few minutes out. "Simon," I said, "I need you to go after Mulvaney."

"Hang on," he said, and we heard Simon breathing hard as he ran down the corridor to follow the director. "Okay, I'm at the elevators. I think he went to another floor, but I have no way of knowing which one." Harris paused. "I can check the other floors and see if I can find him. Maybe he's meeting Mr. Landry."

"No," I said as I held a hand against my ear to try to block out the road noise. "Listen, Simon. Bill Landry is a very dangerous man." I looked up ahead and added, "Stay away from him." There was no response. "Why don't you head down to the garage and meet us there in two minutes." Still no response. "Simon?"

"Okay," he finally replied. "I'll go there now."

I held on tight as Chris took a sharp turn at Ninth Street and pushed the vehicle hard and fast. We sat in silence as Chris approached the Hoover Building. I thought about every interaction I had ever had with Landry over the years. I thought about the first time I had met the man in Chicago the night that Keller had been kidnapped. I thought about the operation he had kept me in the dark from in New York six months ago. I thought through every time he had tried to work against me. And now he wanted me dead.

As we approached FBI headquarters, I was focused on one thing: stopping Landry before it was too late.

54

WE STOPPED AT THE HOOVER BUILDING'S GUARDHOUSE AS AN officer stepped out and reached for Reed's credentials. The guy looked them over briefly and then tapped on the back-seat window. "Lower it for me," he said and then looked at me. I reached across Reed and gave him my Executive Office of the President ID. He nodded, recognizing me from prior visits with Chris and Mark. "What about you?" he asked Jami.

"Agent Davis," she said. "I'm part of the DDC team visiting from across the street. I should be on the list."

He took her ID, went into the guardhouse, and emerged a minute later. "Thank you," he said and waved us through. Chris waited for the barrier arm to lift up, pulled into the Bureau's employee garage, and parked. The three of us stepped out and jogged to the elevator, where I saw Simon Harris waiting for us.

"Never saw Director Mulvaney," he said with concern in his voice. "He might be back in his office now."

"Chris, why don't you and Simon go check," I said and turned to Jami. "We'll search for Landry's vehicle." I put my hand to my ear. "Morgan, are you still with us?" There was no response. I reached into my back pocket and grabbed my cell and saw that the call was dropped. "We lost the signal," I said, turning to Chris.

"We'll look for Mulvaney, and I'll call Morgan from upstairs, see if he's seen anything from the cameras."

I looked around and noticed that there weren't any cameras inside the underground parking garage where we stood. "It'll have to be from inside the building. I'm not seeing any surveillance down here, Chris."

Reed took a quick look around, agreed with me, and pushed a button on the wall to call an elevator. The doors opened and he stepped inside, followed by Simon. "We'll be back in a few minutes, Blake."

A thought crossed my mind and I held the elevator door open. "Does Landry have his own parking spot?"

Chris thought about it and nodded. "Far corner," he said, pointing to his right. "All the way at the end."

I let the elevator doors close and turned to Jami. "Ready?" I asked, and she nodded that she was. I reached for my weapon and we jogged to the far corner of the garage. When we got there, I looked up and saw a fire extinguisher, a pickax behind glass, and a small red pull station underneath it to trigger the fire alarm. There were two reserved parking spaces—one for the director and the other for the deputy director. Both were occupied. I walked up to the space marked deputy director and felt the hood.

"Engine's warm," I said. This had to be Landry's vehicle. I stepped to the back, knocked on the trunk, and listened carefully, but didn't hear anything. "Need to get this open," I said as I pulled on the locked trunk. Looking past Jami, I saw the pickax and walked up to it. I used the butt of my gun to break the glass and placed my weapon in the small of my back as I reached inside and grabbed the ax with two hands.

"You think Taylor's in there?" asked Jami.

I shrugged. "These guys all work the same. Hope I'm wrong," I said and got ready to work on the trunk, but had a better idea and stepped to the driver's side window. I brought my arm back and swung hard. The blade pierced the window. The glass cracked like a spiderweb and the ax got stuck inside the glass. I pulled it out and swung again. The glass shattered. I got the door open and reached inside to pop the trunk.

I went to the back and looked inside. "It's empty," I said as I pushed it closed and leaned on the back of the car with two hands. I looked up at Jami. Her eyes grew wide as she looked past me and reached for her weapon. A gun fired from behind, causing me to flinch. I watched Jami fall to the floor. "No!" I yelled.

55

I TURNED BACK AND SAW BILL LANDRY STANDING BEHIND ME, smiling. I started to go to Jami as Landry fired at the floor next to me. I raised my hands and kept my eyes on Jami, looking for any sign of movement.

"Turn around, Jordan," said Landry from behind me, firing again. "Go ahead. Nice and easy. That's it," he said in a low voice as I turned to face him, and I realized that he could see my weapon stuffed into the back of my jeans. "The gun," he continued, "on the ground, real slow like. Then kick it over to me."

"You killed her, you son of a bitch," I said, my heart beating faster and harder than it ever had in my life.

"The gun," he repeated. "Do it now."

I did as the man asked. I slowly reached for my weapon, lowered it to the ground, and kicked it to him. I watched it slide across the concrete. Looking at Jami over my shoulder, I heard Landry kick my gun farther away. I turned back and watched him shrug. "She's gone, Jordan." Landry stepped closer. "I've waited a long time for this," he said as he brought his weapon to his face. He admired it briefly, turning it from one side to the other, thinking. While he wasn't paying attention, I took a small step to my right. I wanted to be able to see Jami and get Landry's back to the elevator doors for when Chris Reed returned.

"I know what you're doing, Landry," I said and glared at the man. "I know how people like you work."

Landry smirked.

"You saw an opportunity and you took it. You want power," I said and shook my head. "You think you can just get rid of Mulvaney and assume control of the entire FBI? It's never gonna work."

"Really?" He laughed, stopped admiring his gun, and used it to point at Jami. "Plan's working good so far."

I took another small step, slowly, trying not to show my hand and what I was doing. Landry started to pace back and forth. "I know about your plan, Landry," I said, trying to distract the man so he wouldn't realize what I was trying to do. "Dimitri told me all about it. Right before I put a bullet in his forehead."

Landry raised his eyebrows, then shrugged again. "Dimitri Ivanov was just a puppet. Someone I needed to help distract you and your president for a little while, that's all." He smiled. "All you did was take care of a loose end I would have had to deal with." He lifted his weapon in the air and moved it around in a circle, using it to point at the ceiling. "Everything that happens here today will be blamed on him, anyway."

"How do you plan on doing that?"

Landry smiled again and shook his head, amused by the question. "Easy, Jordan. I'll tell the truth. I'll launch an investigation. Findings will show that terrorist Dimitri Ivanov traveled from Russia to Cuba, boarded the *Viktor Leonov*, and exited the ship as it made its way up the US coastline. Got picked up by Russian men living in the United States who had connections to his terrorist father. His motivation? The guy wanted to avenge his father's death." He paused to think as I took another step to my right. "His men got a bomb into the DDC field office." He laughed to himself. "Some fine agents, such as yourself, found Ivanov and his men and took them out—but not before they found a way to get another bomb inside the FBI's Hoover Building." He paused and stared at me. "The agents died in the blast as I stepped out to pick up breakfast for the hardworking DDC and Bureau teams. By chance, I wasn't here when it all happened." Landry grinned. "Mulvaney's killed and I take over the world's most powerful law enforcement agency. I rebuild the Bureau with like-minded people." His smile faded. "I take back my country. Like I said. Easy."

I took another step as Landry looked across the garage to make sure nobody was coming. I looked past Jami and noticed something I hadn't seen before—a hidden security camera up in the corner. I nodded to it. "Not sure it's that easy. The Bureau's got eyes on you. My guess is your speech will be exhibit A."

Landry slowly shook his head. "You know what the problem is with you, Jordan?" he asked sarcastically. "Everything is so damn black and white with you. There is no gray. There's good and then there's evil. Right and wrong. Heroes and villains." He paused a beat. "Don't you think I would have thought about the cameras? Don't you think I would have covered all of my bases if I returned to the building minutes before the whole place is blown to nothing? Before I killed a DDC agent?" He glanced to his right at Jami's body before he laughed again. "Security doesn't monitor the garage. The footage goes straight to a hard drive that's stored upstairs. What do you think happens to that hard drive when the building no longer exists?"

I narrowed my eyes. Something he said bothered me. "Why *did* you return to the building, Landry?"

Landry shook his head. "Loose ends, Jordan. Come on, you're smarter than that." He paused. "Meg Taylor and Charlie Redding—I believe you may know the man?" He laughed to himself before continuing. "They'll be so close to the blast, they'll never find their bodies. Two missing persons. Nobody will care."

I paused for several seconds and glanced at Jami. Her eyes opened as she looked at me, then to Landry. My heart started to beat even faster as I saw her hand move closer to the weapon next to her. Landry started to look at her, so I asked another question to distract him. "The bomb—where is it?" I asked.

He turned back. "You'll find out soon enough."

"You leaked my file to Meg Taylor, didn't you?" No answer. "Why haven't you killed me yet?" I asked.

Landry looked at his watch, and as he did, I saw his demeanor change immediately. A concerned look fell over the man as he gripped the weapon with two hands and straightened his arms, more determined now.

"You're right—I should get on with it," he said as he started to squeeze the trigger while I turned my head and closed my eyes. A shot was fired and I jerked again, unsure for a moment if it had come from Landry or from Jami. I looked back and saw Landry flinch and take two steps backward. Jami had missed.

I dove to my right, in between two cars, as Landry fired several rounds in my direction before firing back at Jami. I got behind one of the cars and saw Jami duck behind Landry's vehicle and fire two rounds at him. I started looking for my weapon and found it underneath the car I was hiding behind. Looking up, I saw Landry approach Jami. He fired at her again as I dropped to the floor and reached for my weapon.

The pain from my hurt arm was excruciating. I stopped and went for it with my left. My fingers touched the butt of my weapon. I heard more shots fired, but wasn't sure who they had come from. I stretched my arm and, with my fingers, turned my Glock so that I could grab it. I gripped it with two hands and stood.

"Are you okay?" I asked Jami as I stepped out. Landry was gone, and I saw his weapon was on the floor.

Jami got to her feet, kept a hand on her weapon, and unzipped a thin jacket to reveal the Kevlar vest I had given her hours earlier. I nodded and looked over to the security camera and noticed something else. Directly underneath, near the corner, was a closed door leading to a stairwell. "I'm going after him, Jami."

"And I'm going with you," she said as I picked up Landry's gun and confirmed it was out of ammunition.

"No," I said. "Chris will be back any minute now. I need you to stay here and tell him what Landry said. That bomb's about to go off and we still have to figure out how to get everyone out of the building, Jami."

She turned away from me, walked to the pull station, and yanked it, and the fire alarm went off. "Done," she yelled over the alarm. "That'll get everyone out and get security to check the cameras. I'm going with you."

I nodded and moved to the door as Jami followed. I leveled my weapon, opened the door, and went inside.

56

Once inside the stairwell, I swung my weapon from side to side, scanning the interior before I climbed the steps. We moved carefully, unsure about where Landry had gone. I aimed my weapon above me as we got to the second floor and stopped outside the door. I pulled the handle, but it wouldn't budge. "I think there's only one more floor," I yelled over the loud alarm as it echoed inside the narrow stairwell.

We kept moving up the stairs and approached the third floor. As soon as we rounded the corner, I saw that the door was cracked open. I imagined Landry carelessly rushing through, not stopping long enough to make sure that the door had closed completely. Jami nodded that she was ready as I pulled it open fast. As we stepped through, I held my weapon out and scanned left and right as the alarm suddenly turned off.

"What happened?" asked Jami as the last pulse from the alarm echoed throughout the large space that I noticed was completely filled with special operations vehicles used by the Bureau's various tactical teams.

"Maybe they think it's a false alarm," I said quietly, still taking in what I was seeing. "We need to split up."

I heard a noise, but couldn't tell where it had come from. Keeping my right hand on my gun, I used four fingers to point to the left of us, and Jami moved in that direction as I gripped my Glock with two hands and moved to my right. Staying on the periphery of the vehicles, I watched as Jami did the same until I couldn't see her anymore. I kept moving between the rows of vehicles, desperately searching for Landry.

I was caught off guard and struck from behind. An arm reached around my neck and squeezed it tight. I struggled to break free, but couldn't get loose. My vision started to fade as I tried not to black out. I brought my weapon up and Landry went for it. He placed his finger over mine and squeezed the trigger.

He kept firing until all of the bullets were spent. I dropped the gun, reached behind me, and grabbed his neck. I crouched and used my body weight to slam him to the ground. We struggled and I found myself on top of him. Grabbing his throat with my left hand, I started punching him as I heard Jami running toward me. Landry's face was bloody. "Where is it?" I yelled, but he wouldn't talk. "Where's the bomb?"

Jami had her weapon trained on him. I brought my fist up and held it there. I was breathing hard and realized that what I was doing wasn't working. I tried to catch my breath as Landry sneered at me, and I knew he wasn't going to talk. I looked up and noticed something that might work better. I stood, walked up to the wall, and used my elbow to break the glass. I pulled out the ax like the one downstairs, gripping it tight.

I went back to Landry. "Last chance," I said in a low

voice. He glared at me as he saw what I was holding. "Tell me where the bomb is or I promise you—" I gripped the ax tighter "—I'm gonna make this hurt."

Somewhere behind me, I heard the sound of men running toward us. The expression on Landry's face turned from terror to relief. "They're coming, Jordan," he said as I watched his chest heave up and down. "They'll be here any second now." Landry looked at Jami, then back at me. "You're out of time, Jordan."

I raised the ax above my head, determined. "Tell me where the bomb is now, you son of a bitch! Tell me!"

Landry remained on the floor and raised his hands. "You're not going to kill the deputy director of the FBI in cold blood, Jordan," he said as the men got closer. "I know who you are. You wouldn't do that."

I gripped the ax even tighter and blinked several times, feeling my heart beating hard and fast in my chest.

"Stand down, both of you!" a voice yelled to Jami and me from behind. "Drop the weapons right now!"

Jami raised a hand and bent slowly to set her gun down on the floor. I tossed the ax and raised my hands.

57

Landry lifted a hand and pointed at Jami, then me. "Arrest them," he said to the two officers as Jami and I remained standing with our hands raised. I waited for the men to cuff us, but they stayed still and wouldn't move. I turned to look at them and saw FBI Director Peter Mulvaney walking toward us. Chris and Simon were walking with him. "What are you waiting for?" barked Landry. "I said arrest them!"

The officers didn't say a word. Mulvaney stopped next to them, and they turned to look for direction from him. Mulvaney nodded to one of the officers. He went to Landry and helped him to his feet, spun him around and brought an arm behind his back, followed by the other.

"What the hell are you doing?" asked Landry as the handcuffs were fastened tight. He was forced to sit back down and glared up at Mulvaney.

Jami and I lowered our hands and got out of the director's way as Mulvaney stepped toward Landry. "I heard everything, Bill," said Mulvaney. He turned to his left to look at Chris Reed and Simon Harris. "They found me upstairs and told me about the bomb. Didn't believe them. Then a man named Lennox out of Chicago called Agent Reed here."

Landry didn't respond.

Mulvaney nodded to himself. "Said he was watching a feed from one of the building's cameras. Asked him to send it to my screen for me to see." Mulvaney stepped closer. "Where is it, Bill?" he asked, but Landry remained silent. "Where's the bomb?"

"He's not gonna tell you," I said.

"Then we'll detain him here until he does," said Mulvaney.

Landry stared back with panic in his eyes.

"We're running out of time," I said and stared down at Landry as he sat on the cold concrete. I studied the man and tried to think through the last several minutes and what he had told me. "You said you came back here to tie up some loose ends." I turned to Jami briefly. "I know you brought Meg Taylor with you, because Jami was inside your house talking with her minutes before you got there," I said. Landry shifted his eyes to Jami as I continued. "You already told me that you had her here with Charlie Redding. And I bet wherever you're keeping them is where we'll find Lynne May, too," I added and looked over to Simon.

"Bill, I suggest you tell us what we need to know," said Mulvaney. "Or you will be prosecuted to the—"

"He's not gonna talk," I said, interrupting the Bureau director. "I'm telling you, it's not gonna work with this guy. Damn it," I said, frustrated. I placed my hands on the back of my head as Landry smiled at me.

Then I stopped—a thought occurred to me—I turned back, and my eyes scanned the level we were on. I stepped back to Landry. "Why *did* you run to this floor, Landry?" I asked, and he looked away. "Second floor would have been easier. But you came up one more level." I paused. "Why the third floor?"

I turned to Jami, and she nodded. I looked back across the countless rows of vehicles. "It's here, isn't it?"

Landry's smile slowly faded as I continued to scan everywhere, taking in what I was seeing in front of me.

Row after row of Bureau vehicles. Countless black SUVs spanned the first several rows, followed by tactical vehicles so far back, I couldn't see where they ended. The entire level was full of Bureau vehicles.

"What are you thinking?" asked Mulvaney.

I turned to Reed. "Chris," I said and paused for a moment as I tried to put the pieces together in my head. "Landry admitted that he's responsible for everything." I paused again, turned back to the countless vehicles located on the third floor, and turned back to Chris. "We were supposed to meet at DDC yesterday. But an anonymous tip came in about a home with explosives inside. Landry asked you to investigate." I looked down and stared at Landry. "Nobody called in that tip. Did they, Bill?"

He remained silent.

"No, they didn't," I said, answering my own question. "You had Ivanov's people plant those explosives in that house, didn't you?"

Landry didn't respond.

"I went there. Watched ATF and Bureau agents carry out those bricks of C-4. They loaded that Bureau truck." Suddenly, I understood what was going on. I turned to Director Mulvaney. "The Explosives Unit—how many of those trucks do you have, and where are they?"

Peter Mulvaney looked across the sea of vehicles parked in front of us. "We only have two," he replied. "The one that picked up those explosives waited here while we contacted officials at TEDAC. Left a few hours ago." Mulvaney gestured toward a thick load-bearing column. "The other truck's parked over there."

I walked past Landry and picked up the ax I had thrown aside, thinking I might need it. I gripped it tight as I stood in front of Landry. The man's eyes moved up and down, watching me carefully and trying to figure out what I was going to do with it. I held his gaze; then I turned back to Mulvaney. "Take me to that truck."

Mulvaney looked at the officers and pointed at Landry. "Keep him here for me," he ordered and turned.

We walked quickly with Jami, Chris, and Simon following close behind. We passed several rows of black SUVs before we turned and cut through the middle of the garage. Mulvaney pointed and I looked past two rows of unmarked sedans and saw the larger vehicles parked. One was marked "Washington Field Office Evidence Response Team." I saw another large vehicle next to it marked "Federal Bureau of Investigation Mobile Command Center." Next to that one was a truck just like the one outside that east DC home.

I ran to the truck. The director caught up to me as I noticed a lock on the back, securing the roll-up door. "That shouldn't be locked," said Mulvaney as Jami, Chris, and Simon approached and stood back, watching me. I turned to Mulvaney. His eyes moved from the lock back to me, and he nodded his approval.

My heart was racing. I lifted the ax and brought it down hard, chipping away at the lock. I did it again.

The second attempt cut right through the metal, and the broken lock fell onto the concrete. I tossed the ax aside and breathed hard as I lifted the roll-up door. Mulvaney stepped closer to look inside the dark truck.

Jami gasped behind me as we saw Charlie Redding, Lynne May, and another woman sitting on the bed with their backs against the truck's wall. Their wrists were bound behind them, and duct tape covered their mouths. I stood motionless as I stared at the three of them. "Hurry," I said. "Get out of the truck, quick."

I helped the woman out. She looked at me like she recognized me, and I knew it had to be Meg Taylor. Mulvaney helped Lynne May climb down as I reached inside and helped Charlie get down from the truck.

Chris used a knife to cut the zip ties off as they peeled off the duct tape. Charlie and I held a long embrace.

Peter Mulvaney put his hands on May's shoulders. "Are you okay, Lynne?"

She nodded quickly.

"I knew something was wrong," she replied. "I overheard a conversation. He told someone to go to his house and said he'd be there soon. I walked into his office, and Landry said he was talking to his daughter."

I looked over to Meg Taylor. She was standing next to Charlie, arms crossed, looking at me with remorse.

"I knew that any man who had a daughter would have a picture somewhere in his office."

Jami explained that there were explosives inside the truck. Meg looked back and asked where.

"In the boxes," I said as I walked to the back of the vehicle and looked inside. The boxes were stacked high and packed tight, except for the left side of the bed where Lynne, Charlie, and Meg had been sitting. I climbed inside and looked around to understand what we were dealing with. Chris climbed in behind me.

At the far end, I noticed a faint red glow reflecting off one of the boxes. I stepped closer to it and moved one of the boxes carefully to get to it. Chris looked over my shoulder as I worked. The red glow brightened as I moved the last box. "We've got a problem," I said, remembering the load-bearing column next to us. "There's a timer, Chris. We've got five minutes until this detonates and brings the entire building down."

58

I GOT OUT OF CHRIS'S WAY SO HE COULD TAKE A LOOK AT the triggering mechanism for me. Since he had more experience with explosives, I needed him to tell me what our options were. He shined a flashlight over the box, followed the leads and wires down to another device, and moved the light back to the countdown timer.

"I think I can deactivate it, but there isn't much time. I need Morgan to look something up for me."

"Okay," I said and reached for my phone. I dialed the number for Morgan Lennox, but the call didn't go through. "Chris, there's no signal in here," I said as Reed turned to me briefly, then continued to touch the wires, moving them carefully as he looked over the box they were connected to. He shook his head and let go.

"I'm not sure about this one," he said and scratched the back of his head in frustration. "Could be this one right here," he added and shined the light on one of the wires. "Or it could be this other one. I'm not sure."

"And if you're wrong?" I asked.

Chris turned to me briefly, then looked back at the box, deciding not to answer.

The timer ticked past the four-minute mark. I heard Mulvaney say that he was going to alert security and have them evacuate the building. "There's not enough time," I said as I set a timer on my watch to match the clock on the bomb. I climbed out of the vehicle and looked back, seeing Reed struggling with the device.

"Then what do you suggest?" asked the director as I ran my hand across my face, thinking about it.

I stared at the truck and broke into a cold sweat. I turned back to Mulvaney. "The keys. Where are they?"

Mulvaney narrowed his eyes for a beat until he understood why I asked. "In the cab. Under the visor."

"Chris, come on out for me," I said.

Reed stepped to the back, climbed out, and I reached up and grabbed the top of the roll-up door and pulled it shut. I snapped the latch in place and looked at my watch.

"Blake, what are you doing?" asked Jami, but I ignored her, ran to the front of the truck, and climbed in.

I pulled down on the sun visor, and a key fell into my lap. I grabbed it, shoved it into the ignition, and turned it. The truck came to life and I put it into gear as the passenger door opened and Jami climbed inside.

"Jami, you're not gonna stop me," I said.

"I don't want to stop you, Blake. I want to help you." Her chest was heaving up and down, breathing hard.

I nodded. Jami slammed her door closed and I removed my foot from the brake and eased out of the spot.

"Left," she said, pointing across my chest, and I turned the wheel. Once I straightened out, I gunned it.

I pushed it hard, then slowed at the end of the row and turned the wheel to the right, passing Landry and the two officers with him. The man glared at me as we passed him. I tapped the brakes as we descended one level, then picked up speed as we passed the general employee parking on our way to the first level.

We got to the first floor and I stepped on the accelerator again. We raced toward the exit, but the barrier arm remained lowered. "Hang on," I said as we broke through it. I hit the brakes as we came up out of the building and pulled the truck onto Tenth. Jami yelled for me to turn left and head south. A few seconds later, she yelled for me to turn left onto Pennsylvania. I checked my watch. "We've got one minute."

"Right at the next block!" she yelled as we passed Ninth, ignoring my comment.

"Seventh?"

"Yes! Right here!" she yelled. I hit the brakes and yanked the wheel to the right and we almost overturned.

The light at Constitution turned red and the cars in front of us came to a stop. I pulled the truck to the left into incoming traffic and navigated around vehicles waiting to turn onto Seventh. Drivers blew their horns as I weaved around the cars and crossed the intersection. I picked up more speed and approached Madison.

"Blake, slow down—you're gonna kill us both," she yelled, and I gave her a look. The light at Madison changed to red and I got through the intersection. "Right," she said, tapping on the passenger-side window.

I pulled the wheel hard and saw that Jami had navigated us to the National Mall. It was empty and we had plenty of room before the Fourteenth Street cutover. *Smart girl.* "Fifteen seconds," I said as I straightened the wheel. I held it steady with my right hand and grabbed the door handle with my left and pulled it hard. The door opened. I looked over at Jami and saw her do the same before she turned back and looked at me.

"Tuck and roll?" she asked, out of breath, and I nodded urgently.

"Watch your shoulder when you hit," I said and turned to look at the path ahead of us one last time. "Go!"

Jami pushed the door all the way open and rolled out. Once I saw that she was out, I pushed mine open, hit the grass hard, and rolled left. I rolled several times and finally came to a stop. My head was spinning. I looked back and saw Jami twenty feet behind me. I got to my feet fast and ran over to her. I fell on the ground next to her and put my arm over her, tucking her head into my chest, and looked back at the truck.

The truck exploded with an intense orange flash. I closed my eyes and turned my face and held onto Jami. Looking back again, I saw the vehicle on fire. Traffic on Madison and Jefferson came to a standstill. Drivers stepped out of their vehicles to look at the burning truck with flames reaching high into the sky. The few joggers and tourists out that morning had been far enough away not to be harmed by the blast, as far as I could tell. I scanned the area, looking for anyone that might have been hurt, but didn't see anyone.

"Are you okay?" I asked Jami as she lifted her head and looked behind us. We were both breathing hard.

She nodded and lowered her head and held onto me tight and wouldn't let go. "You did it," she whispered.

I looked back again at the bright flames. Dark, black smoke billowed into the sky. "No. *We* did it."

Jami and I sat up, but kept holding onto each other as we sat on the grass. A siren wailed in the distance, and I stood, reached for her hands, and helped her up. She put her arms around me. I pulled her in close and held her tight. For a moment, time stood still. I tucked her head under my chin and closed my eyes.

We heard more sirens behind us. Several unmarked vehicles pulled in from Seventh and approached where we were standing. A few passed us and I watched them get close to the burning vehicle. Past the charred truck, a fire engine turned in from Fourteenth. Firefighters got to work to control the flames. Car doors were being opened all around us. I watched a Metro PD vehicle pull up, and a man stepped out. "Hands in the air!" he yelled, but Jami and I ignored him. I wasn't going to let go. And neither was she.

"Back off," a familiar voice said. I turned and saw Lynne May. "DDC," she said. "They're coming with me."

59

We arrived at the covert spot used by the Bureau and DDC at Reagan National thirty minutes later. Chris Reed drove us with Lynne May in the passenger seat as Jami and I rode in the back of the vehicle. We parked and waited for Emma Ross to arrive. Through my window, I could see the Gulfstream G550.

Its stairs were down and led to the forward entry door. The hum from the engines could be heard from inside the SUV as the pilot kept them idling. I looked to my right. Jami held her hand out. I grabbed it and held it tight as Lynne May turned from the passenger seat. "Are you sure you want to do this?" she asked.

I nodded and turned to my left. Out the back window, I saw a vehicle approaching. "I have to."

May raised the volume on the radio. Voices were discussing the explosion at the Mall. "Fast news cycle," she said. "They've already moved on from you and Keller's black ops team—they'll catch wind of Landry within a few hours." She paused, and I felt her looking at me. "You don't have to do this, Jordan."

I shook my head. "There'll be an investigation. They'll tie it all together and they'll go after the president." The vehicle parked next to us. The driver got out and stepped around, and I watched him open the passenger door and help Keller's chief of staff step out. I turned to face May. "They'll use this as leverage to force him to resign." I shook my head again. "I'm not gonna let myself be the reason for that, Lynne."

"They'll look for the body," she said as I grabbed my messenger bag and lifted the strap over my head.

Chris turned to May. "That's why you and Mulvaney need to make sure that they don't," he said to her.

May's eyes were still on Chris when I squeezed Jami's hand and said, "We don't know if Landry was working with anyone else."

May turned back to me.

"You have to find out. See how far this goes."

May nodded.

"I have to go," I said and let go of Jami's hand. I pulled on the door and stepped onto the tarmac.

Emma Ross was standing between both parked vehicles, waiting for me to exit. She looked me over with her arms crossed as Chris, Jami, and Lynne got out. I looked down and saw that Ross was holding a cell phone. She turned briefly to the Gulfstream as the pilot descended the stairs, noticed Emma, and nodded.

Jami approached from my left and stood next to me as Chris and Lynne May waited by the front of the SUV. Emma handed the phone to me. "The president wants to talk to you."

I looked at the phone, then looked back at Ross.

"You're doing the right thing, Blake," she said and nodded to the phone.

I took it, held it up to my ear, and turned to look at the Gulfstream. "Mr. President," I said and waited.

There was a long sigh on the other end of the line. "Blake," he began, "Emma told me about the new plan."

I kept my eyes on the Gulfstream, waiting for him to continue.

"We just thought you should disappear for a while, but this takes things to another level." He paused again. "Are you sure you want to do this, son?"

I turned to Jami, then looked away. "Mr. President, if I don't, you and I both know what will happen. The media will come after you. You know how they operate. Once they smell blood, they're never going to stop. You asked me to create a black ops team for you, sir. And I didn't always follow the rules of engagement."

"By way of presidential finding, I had every damn right to—"

"Trust me, sir," I said, interrupting my friend. "They'll bring me in front of a senate hearing committee for all of my actions over the last eighteen months. They'll look at everything. They'll say I did your dirty work for you." I shook my head. "I'll never let them do that to you. Our country needs you, Mr. President."

"And our country needs *you*." Keller paused for several seconds to compose himself. "Where will you go?"

"Emma and I both agree that it's better if you don't know that, sir."

Jami stepped closer and put an arm around me. I wrapped my arm around her shoulder and looked into her eyes, seeing what I was giving up.

Keller sighed again. "Then as of this moment, Blake Jordan is dead." He paused. "Ben would have been proud of you. I'm proud of you. Please do one thing for me. Tell me where we can find you if we need you."

I breathed. "Mr. President, it's been an honor," I said, pulled the phone away, and handed it to Emma.

Jami let go as Ross disconnected the line and put a hand on my back to escort me toward the waiting plane. "You'll land in about seven hours," she said. "I'll have someone meet you with new identification."

Jami, Chris, and Lynne followed behind and stopped ten yards short of the aircraft. I held onto the strap of my messenger bag and turned and shook Chris's hand. "Go see Mark," I said, and he said that he would. I pulled him in for an embrace and held it for several seconds. "Thanks for not giving up on me."

I stepped back and Lynne May approached with an outstretched hand. "Thank you, Blake," she said.

I nodded as she held onto my hand for several seconds, then finally let go. I turned to Jami. She wrapped her arms around my neck and pulled me in. I closed my eyes and, in that moment, thought about the last six months without her. She let go and I looked into her eyes. I couldn't imagine never seeing her again.

"You need to go," said Ross.

Jami and I kissed and embraced again before she finally let me go. I stepped backward, repositioned my messenger bag on my good shoulder, turned and went to the Gulfstream.

I climbed the stairs and sat down. Looking out the porthole, I saw Jami standing alone. The pilot started to lift the stairs. "Wait," I said and moved to the front of the jet. I jogged down the stairs and went to Jami. I stopped when I got to her and looked into her eyes. "Come with me," I said. "I can't leave without you, Jami. I walked away from you once. Biggest mistake of my life. I can't do it again."

She didn't speak.

"Please."

Jami stared at me. I was breathing hard. Then she smiled and nodded. Slowly at first, then determinedly.

I noticed Lynne standing next to us. She nodded. "Okay. We lost two agents in that truck bomb."

We said goodbye, walked to the Gulfstream, went up the stairs and settled in. The pilot lifted the stairs and entered the cockpit. The sound from the idling engines grew louder. A minute later, we were taxiing onto the runway and made a turn onto a straightaway, and the pilot told us to get ready for takeoff.

Jami put a hand on my arm as we raced down the runway. "Give me the ring," she said to me softly.

My heart beat fast. I turned to her. "How do you know about that?"

She smiled. "Charlie," she whispered and touched my arm again gently.

I dug into my pocket and found the ring I had carried with me every day since that night in New York. I took her hand and slipped it on her finger. She smiled and gripped my hand tight as the pilot pushed it faster.

We kissed. Then we leaned back in our chairs, my hand in hers, as the jet lifted off the ground. I closed my eyes and listened to the engines scream as we continued to climb higher into the early morning sky. Jami took her right hand, brought it to my arm, and squeezed it tight. We held each other close, neither of us saying a word. I loved Jami more than anything and I didn't want to be anywhere else in that moment. Sunlight fell on my face. I opened my eyes, looked out the window, and got one last view of the homeland.

60

ONE WEEK LATER

James Keller emerged from the second floor of the Executive Residence, headed for the dining room so Chef could bring him his breakfast. It was the same routine he followed every morning, only it was much earlier today. The president passed his private study and turned a corner, where he stopped, surprised to see his chief of staff. "Emma?" He looked at his watch. "It's five o'clock in the morning. What are you doing here at this ungodly hour?" He paused. "Don't tell me *you're* having trouble sleeping now."

She shook her head slowly. "No, just had to drop something off. I didn't think it could wait until later."

Keller furrowed his brow and finally nodded, deciding not to ask her about it. Emma handed him a newspaper. He took it and held it out. "Blake was right," he said, showing his chief of staff the headline.

Ross smiled knowingly. "I thought you'd enjoy seeing

that," she said, keeping her eyes on the president. "They've made Jordan out to be the hero that he is. Sacrificing his own life to save the people in that building. And now we'll have a long, drawn-out trial with Bill Landry. Looks like Blake's plan worked."

Keller nodded again and took on a more somber tone as he folded the paper, held onto one end, and tapped the other end into an open palm. His gaze dropped to the floor as he asked, "Any update on Agent Reynolds?"

Emma smiled. "He's getting there."

Keller shook his head and looked away. "When can I go visit him?"

"Give him another couple of days."

Keller smiled and started to continue to the dining room when Ross called to him.

"Mr. President," she said, and Keller turned around, "I left something for you at the table."

Keller furrowed his brow again. "Thank you, Emma," he said as she shot her boss a warm, gentle smile.

The president entered, pulled out a chair, and sat down. On the table, he found a thin package, crumpled and creased. He picked it up and started to inspect it when he heard two knocks at the door behind him.

"Your breakfast, sir," said Chef Gregory, balancing a tray with one hand as he entered the room. The man slid the plate in front of the president and set down a steaming mug of black coffee. "Anything else, sir?"

Keller shook his head. "Not right now, Chef."

"Then I will be back in a few minutes," he said and showed himself to the door.

The president pushed the plate aside and placed the package in front of him. Fumbling for his glasses, he looked it over, ran his fingers across it, and found the postmark. "London," he whispered to himself as he stared at the postmark for several seconds before he reached inside the already opened package that had been cut on one side. Keller grabbed hold of something thin inside and pulled it out of the package gently.

He pushed the package aside and carefully turned right-side up a copy of *To Kill a Mockingbird*. Looking up over his glasses at the empty chair across from him, he remembered a conversation from a week earlier. He stared at it and thought about the story he had told about Margaret, feeling himself start to get choked up.

Looking back down to the book, Keller opened the cover page and found an inscription written inside. "Making it count. —Blake and Jami," it read. Keller smiled to himself and closed the book. He held onto it tight and stared at it for a long time as he thought about his late wife and Blake and the decision he had made.

There were two knocks at the door and Keller became present again. "Sir? Everything good?" asked Chef.

Keller remained still and, after a brief pause, finally spoke. "As good as it can be, Chef," he answered softly.

HALF A WORLD AWAY, I STOOD ON THE DARK SIDE OF A window, two fingers lifting the blinds so I could look out onto a busy London street as Jami slept soundly on the bed next to me. I couldn't stop thinking about that night in New York when I walked away from her. She had pleaded with me not to. Yelled it out to me, her voice cutting through the cold night air. But I had kept on walking, never turned back, never told her the truth—that I loved her more than anything and I was walking away from her to try to keep her safe.

I had told her that I felt empty. I had lost my wife and my father, the people in my life that I cared about the most, all because of my actions and my job. I loved Jami and thought the best way to keep her safe was to walk out of her life and leave her behind. I rejected her love because of a broken past that haunted me.

But I never could have kept her safe by keeping my distance. Instead, I made her pay for a mistake she had never made. I was the one that made the mistake all those months ago, choosing my job over the girl.

Jami stirred and I turned from the window to look at her. I walked to the edge of the bed and sat down next to her. She opened her eyes, smiled, and closed them as she nestled her head against the soft pillow.

I looked away and thought about past mistakes. How they're meant to guide you, not define you. How every morning is a chance to start over, a chance to change and be somebody different if you choose to be.

What I finally had to learn was that I had to leave my past in the past so that it wouldn't destroy my future. I could only live for what today had to offer and not for what yesterday had taken away from me. That the only way I could heal a broken past wasn't by dwelling there, but by living fully in the present.

Jami stirred again. I looked down and saw the ring on her finger. I stared at it and thought again about second chances and how sometimes life gives you one because maybe the first time, you weren't ready.

I closed my eyes and lowered my head as I thought long and hard about the old life I had left behind.

I was finally ready.

Ready to let go of my past so that it would let go of me.

Ready to embrace life, understanding that today, I could decide who I was and what I believed in.

And I was ready to live life with an open heart, no matter where it would take us, so I could finally make it count.

Because you only live once.

And the truth is, if you do it right, once is enough.

I hope you enjoyed book 4 in the Blake Jordan series. Go to kenfite.com/the-homeland to start book 5.

The man responsible for a deadly mass shooting is going to strike again. Can Blake Jordan stop him?

After faking his own death and fleeing the country to protect the president, Blake Jordan is determined to forget his past. But his past hasn't forgotten about him.

When someone he cares about falls victim to the deadliest mass shooting in American history, Blake returns to the homeland. But when he arrives, he learns that the man responsible did not act alone.

If he wants to stop the killer from striking again, Blake must reveal he's still alive to get help from the government he's been hiding from. But a man from Blake's past holds the answers... and it all leads back to what happened fifteen years ago. THE HOMELAND is a spellbinding, fast-paced thriller you'll be reading late into the night.

HERE'S WHAT READERS ARE SAYING...

★★★★★ "Outstanding read, I couldn't put it down."
★★★★★ "The story line is gripping. What a ride!"
★★★★★ "A book and series not to be missed!"
★★★★★ "Another edge of your seat thriller."
★★★★★ "...keeps you guessing to the end."
★★★★★ "Takes you on one wild ride after another!"
★★★★★ "If you like twists, you'll love this book."
★★★★★ "Go along for the thrill ride."
★★★★★ "...wait for a twist at the end."
★★★★★ "Another great book in the series."

READY FOR A GREAT STORY? START READING NOW:

kenfite.com/the-homeland

WANT THE NEXT BLAKE JORDAN STORY FOR $1 ON RELEASE DAY?*

*KINDLE EDITION ONLY

I'm currently writing the next book in the Blake Jordan series with a release planned soon. New subscribers get the Kindle version for $1 on release day.

Join my newsletter to reserve your copy and I'll let you know when it's ready to download to your Kindle.

kenfite.com/books

THE BLAKE JORDAN SERIES

IN ORDER

The Senator
Credible Threat
In Plain Sight
Rules of Engagement
The Homeland
The Shield
Thin Blue Line
Person of Interest
Abuse of Power

Made in the USA
Monee, IL
22 August 2023

41452638R00184